W9-CZZ-001

Altmann's Tongue

STORIES AND A NOVELLA

by BRIAN EVENSON

INTRODUCTION TO THE BISON BOOKS EDITION BY
Alphonso Lingis

With a new afterword by the author

UNIVERSITY OF NEBRASKA PRESS
LINCOLN AND LONDON

Altmann's Tongue © 1994 by Brian Evenson
"Two Brothers" © 1997 by Brian Evenson
Introduction and afterword © 2002 by the University of Nebraska Press
All rights reserved
Manufactured in the United States of America

First Bison Books printing: 2002

Some stories in this volume previously appeared, sometimes in slightly
different form, in the following publications:
Airfish: Your Flight to the World's Rim: "Altmann's Tongue"
Blood & Aphorisms: "Bodies of Light," "Eye," "Hole," "Shift-Work"
Contagion: "Two Brothers"
The Dominion Review: "Two Brothers"
Magic Realism: "The Evanescence of Marion le Goff," "Job Eats Them Raw,
with the Dogs"
Nomad: "The Evanescence of Marion le Goff"
O. Henry Award: Prize Stories, 1998: "Two Brothers"
The Quarterly: "Altmann's Tongue," "The Blank," "A Conversation with
Brenner," "The Father, Unblinking," "Hey, Luciano!," "Killing Cats," "Mix,
Mex, Somebody," "New Killers," "Stung," "Usurpation," "What Boly Seed"
A Theatre of Blood: "After Omaha"
Young Blood: "Hébé Kills Jarry"

ISBN 0-8032-6744-4 (pbk.: alk. paper)

This edition of Altmann's Tongue *is for Joanna.*

"The Sanza Affair" is for my mother.

... more and more incisive, precise, eschewing seduction in favor of cruelty ...

—*Julia Kristeva*

Contents

The Eye on the Killer

Alphonso Lingis

One day I received, without any note, a copy of this book in the mail. The poisoned gift of a seer I was to finally meet years later, in a place called Stillwater. With a distracted and fateful movement I tore open the wrapping, looked inside, sank into a chair, and for hours found myself alone with the whimsical and depraved, farcical and vicious people released from these pages. I would never have thought words could still have such power. But I do not want to perversely draw the reader's attention to the astonishing prowess of Brian Evenson's language.

The reader will alight on back roads in the American West. You will drive the interstates. You will stop in a suburban back yard where a boy has a hive of bees. You will find yourself among Germans with shadowy political pasts. Here seems to be central Europe, country and time unclear. The linked stories "The Blank," "A Slow Death," and "Extermination" locate you in a nameless land, in the future. The eye of the reader then is on wings. Along with vultures, crows, birds of prey, bats, exterminating angels. When you touch ground there are silverfish, lice, fleas, ants, spiders, flies, bees. You gape bug-eyed at people outside of the communities we form through our practices, institutions, and common language. Suddenly you see them committing unforgivable acts.

These are stories, narratives—not feats of linguistic virtuosity, not games played with language. The sentences you read leave you agape: what next? Like the violent events they narrate, the stories are quickly over. You are left dazed and groping. You cannot just sway hypertonic in vicarious thrills, nor decompress in catharsis. You are not able to weave over the breach other kinds of language—literary references, psychological exegeses, mythic generalizations.

There is a heady energy in these narratives, where protagonists and victims alike are bereft of fear, worry, deliberation, or scruple. There is an uncivilized hilarity in this book. It is not that you find yourself tickled by witty metaphors and wry turns of phrase. It's that the more brutal the deed the more it betrays a farcical side. You will not be able to recall or recount "Hébé Kills Jarry" without harsh, liberating laughter.

The reviewer may let his mind wander and cite a dozen of the most radical writers of the past century within whose company to place Brian Evenson. But within the book, the only text alluded to is the Book of Job. "Job Eats Them Raw, with the Dogs" is a merry tale, but the humor is not in blasphemous parody of the Biblical Book of Job. The comedy lies in starting with an individual reduced, according to the plot of the Book of Job, to the last limit of affliction, who is, incredibly, still alive, still moves about and talks—without tongue or lungs—about his predicament. Riddles for you: how call a dog without being able to whistle, how make out with a woman who has no limbs? The story brings the reader to the limits where the extremities of absurdity and torment break out into peals of laughter.

Eighteen of the twenty-six stories of this book are stories of killing people. Another is about killing cats. The dogs that show up get killed. The readers' eyes are kept on the killer, not the victim whose life is often not evoked at all, already passed away. But when the harm that the victim had done to the killer is not even invoked, then the killing does not aim at annihilating a specific wrong and wrongdoer. The victim is generic. Could be us. The killing then is something unlimited.

But isn't any act of killing an absolute act, out of proportion to any wrong the killer may have suffered? For the wrong someone had inflicted on you, in having deprived you of goods or even of body parts, was a relative harm—you still have your life. Only if he had murdered your kin, your spouse or child, can the wrong done you seem absolute. Then "an eye for an eye, a tooth for a tooth" can seem proportionate, and rational. But of course far from righting the balance, it doubles the absurdity.

The stories see and tell the point of view of the killer. Where the victim is not done away with at once, he becomes one with the killer. In the linked stories "The Blank," "A Slow Death," and "Extermination," a fortress allegedly in a state of siege is sealed, but the besiegers are its own inhabitants. The killers will be killed; their deaths are not retributions for, but repetitions of the killings they perpetrated. The birds that strip their flesh begin tearing one another apart. In "The Evanescence of Marion le Goff" the victim wants to be annihilated, assists the killers. "Killing Cats" tells how an outsider with no interest in the violence becomes not an accomplice to the killers but the sole killer himself.

The story "Usurpation" is one of the most intense, in fixing the setting and the consciousness of the narrator; the strangeness of that consciousness invades the reader and will stick in the mind. The consciousness of the one involved in the business of killing others does not now become ethical, does not produce objections to killing, when he turns into a victim. In "Hébé Kills Jarry" two men, socialites, have been friends for years; now the one must torture and kill the other under orders from some-where. In the usual scene, the killer, in power, would be cool, ironic, civil, but the victim seething and histrionic. Here the vic-tim is polite, helpful, grateful for small gestures, for the killer giving him a pillow. The victim had ordered a blond escort to accompany him to the theater; he thinks to leave her for his killer to enjoy. Just as the order to kill is nowise motivated by the real relationship between them, it does not affect their relationship now: they continue to interact as friends.

In "The Boly Stories" the distance between one's relations with strangers—where consideration of gain rules—and one's relations with kin—where the most fundamental morality and religion rule—only serves to make the clearer their equivalent violence. As a result retribution and punishment for crime appear preposterous.

When this book first appeared, some readers denounced it as a wallowing in degradation—and the author lost his teaching position at Brigham Young University. It is true that ethical considerations never occur to the killers nor to their victims, and religious motivation occurs in but one story, that of a religion that kills, an infanticide religion. Yet it is evident that a very acute moral sensitivity delineates each story, and alone could circumscribe crimes without naturalist justifications or psychological explanations. For moral consciousness does not consist merely in judgment of praise and condemnation; it must emerge from an exact recording of the obscure forces and depths from which beneficent but also absurd and vicious acts emerge.

The stories exhibit murder, as it is in itself, in isolation. The killing is not shown to be the response to the socio-economic situation or to a series of wrongs perpetrated on the killer, nor is it told as the consequence of a series of convictions or resentments on the part of the killer. The killer is not opened up to show a mind working in strange and intricate ways to produce the intent to kill, nor a mind working ingeniously to escape after his crime: the killer is most often stupid. The killing is not seen to be issued from a higher strength or audacity, it is not made incandescent with tension, risk, and suspense, it is not glamorous. Killing is killing a body but also a mind, an intelligence, an intelligibility. Killing kills its own intelligibility.

In particular here killing is nowhere motivated by lust—Thanatos is utterly separated from Eros. This is why these stories seem not to belong to our psychoanalytic century, why they seem to come from medieval Japan or the land of the Mayas. (Often the names of characters have a pre-Columbian sound.)

Of course some of the killings are motivated—that of son killing his father in "Stung" and of father killing his daughter in "The Munich Window." But the stories do not yield psychological insight. As a result the visible act of killing stands forth in stark relief. The killings appear to have a material, rather than psychological, inevitability. No killing actually occurs in "Usurpation," but you reach the end of the story with the sense that a killing is now so inevitable that the author need not put down what happens in words.

Psychological explanation does appear in the book, in the person of a psychiatrist in "The Munich Window." The psychiatrist has indeed discovered the truth, and the motives—but she proves completely unable to divine anything of the mind of the narrator now. She has, from the trauma in the daughter, divined the crimes the daughter had suffered and the crime she had witnessed. The psychiatrist is fixated on the scientific schema of cause and effects and the conviction that a murder has consequences in the life of its witness and that of its perpetrator. But what she utterly fails to realize is that there will be no difference between the cause and the effect: the effect is a repetition of the cause.

The vision of killing in this book will be resisted: we readily object to Evenson's isolating the act from any socio-political context, stripping away all psychological motivation. But have not these generated delusive explanations, which have only served to cover over the strangeness of this act—how different the act of killing is from productive and purposive actions?

There is an utter disproportion between the fact of death, of killing, and anything that has been said about it, to understand or justify or explain it, anything that could be said about it. Yet acts of killing generate language, stories, and language generates acts of killing. Acts of killing generate language, even if the language does not and cannot provide explanation. In "New Killers," Kline "wrote what they did on a pad of paper, so as to remember all." Acts of killing also produce silence, stupefy.

In the opening story of this book, "The Father, Unblinking," a corpse provokes silence. But the silence of the father will provoke interpretation. Because he asserts he has not seen their child but will not go look for her, the mother's state of mind cannot stop generating hypotheses, multiplying interpretations that will never be brought to an end in the evidence of fact.

The last story, extended to novella length, is about a corpse exhaustively observed, outside and in, which generates a veritable delirium of language. The detective and also each party involved interprets differently every item of evidence, each of these interpretations generates a further interpretation by each party and by the detective; the reader second-guesses the detective. The suspicion begins that the detective, or his superior—or both—are not seeking to track down the truth but instead to cover up the original crime, or their own crimes. The proliferation of interpretations without settlement generates paranoia and may well have generated the original crime or may generate now a subsequent crime.

The title story "Altmann's Tongue" finds the silence in the corpse itself. The killer is self-composed and settled with the untroubled calm that lies in the corpse of Altmann, one of those people who, when you have sent a bullet through the skull, you know you have done the right thing. A certain Horst urges the killer to eat Altmann's tongue, so that language will come—wisdom, the language of birds. The narrator kills Horst too.

The killer is also the narrator. He does speak, and the bird he becomes is a bird of prey. Is language itself then murderous? Does not language itself produce brutality, cruelty, killing? Is the killing in the very words of this book—instead of being outside of them, merely reported on in them?

Brian Evenson's language is trenchant, brief, minimalist. There is no hesitation, no approximation; the word used is always the right word. The extreme precision of language isolates, cuts away the bed and the comfort of allusions and ambiguities. Is not the language, in "A Slow Death" and "Stung"—the language of the protagonists but also the language of the narrative—more unequivocal and unflinching than the murderous will and force could be? And is it not language that opens up the great variety of ways to kill—shootings, bludgeonings, pushing from windows, plunging into vats of acid, stuffing the throat with ping pong balls, with bees.

How the killings by gunfire or bludgeoning in this book contrast with the slow death by starvation! There is the most graphic account of the extremities the starved go to so as to sustain themselves—searching their bodies for vermin, eating the blood-soaked mud from where their comrades have been shot.

The unrestrained probings of the mind lead inevitably into fierce explorations of the body. Knowledge, we know, is acquired through penetrating, taking apart, putting back together. A narrator tells of cutting open stitches, pulling open the wounds, sewing up lips, eyelids. A narrator tells of nailing his own hand to a table. Job takes his bones apart, cleans them, inserts them back in place. Job is nothing but bones, but he is alive. Life is in the bones. So is killing. Job seeks God, but also seeks an axe—the Redline axe with which he kills the lumberjack. Having killed him, he eats his flesh. Only one way to know: is this the only way to get flesh on his bones?

The last of the shorter stories is entitled "Eye"; it is the most graphic story, the most grisly. The dialogue is comic: "You want to know what your problem is? Your problem is the company you keep." This story keeps company with the opening scene in Luis Buñuel and Salvador Dalí's film *Andalousian Dog*, George Bataille's "Story of the Eye," and Jerzy Kosinski's *The Painted Bird*. In that series this story is the most perverse and also the most illuminating.

The setting is a bed, where a man has taken a woman for sex. Voluptuous impulses rarely figure in these stories. But eyes are intrinsically seductive. There is an invitation to carnal pleasure in the ray emanating from the eyes. Our gaze is drawn to eyes, human eyes, but also the eyes of cats, eagles, octopuses, dragonflies; eyes are always beautiful. They are also the most vulnerable part of a body.

And eyes are the cruelest parts of our bodies. Eyes feast on blows, wounds, spilt blood. We cannot keep our eyes from accident victims sprawled on highways. Each evening we feast our eyes on television spectacles of bodies flailed with fists, blasted with bullets, braised with acid, melted down by bombs. Our other senses shrink back from cruelty: we do not enjoy listening to the coughing and moans of sick people and stop our noses from the smell of burnt or putrefying flesh.

We are afraid of eyes, of the power, the cruelty, in eyes. We fear the vindictiveness of the eye of conscience. We do not stick our forks into the eyes of the cattle, sheep, and pigs, whose bodies we eat without uneasiness.

In "Eye," "Hébé Kills Jarry," and "The Sanza Affair," the eyes are attacked. In this book, where generally the killer strikes with a gunshot, an axe, or smashes the skull with a tire iron, killing instantly, it is only eyes that are tortured. It is not a matter of "an eye for an eye"; the violence done to eyes is not a retribution for what they have done. It is a cruelty done to eyes just for their nature of being cruel organs. And these cruelties are the most abhorrent scenes in this book. They repel all understanding and provoke visceral spasms of repugnance. In "The Sanza Affair," where every detail of the murder scene is subjected to every possible interpretation, there is no move at all to offer an explanation for the coins pressed against the eyes of the two victims.

How is it that we shrink back in visceral horror from violence done to the eyes, those most cruel parts of our bodies? I do not know. But there is in us a powerful taboo that protects the eyes, even the eyes of killers.

And this seems to me to illuminate the relationship of the reader to these stories. Ordinary literature of crime elicits the latent distrusts and fears of the ordinary reader, so as to make the killer loom before the reader as potentially threatening to him. In these stories the eye of the reader is on the killer. But there is no visceral and instinctual complicity nor is there an identification in pleasure. The killer remains an object; there is a distance maintained. This distance is not the distance of an observing eye, which views a scene synoptically, with a vision that because it puts together evaluates and judges. Here the focus is too narrow and too surface: the killer, and his act, are bought out in isolation from any context, any past that might motivate or future that might justify his act. Killing is not observed as a psychological process unleashing movements and effects; the eye watches the material act of lifting the shotgun and the reaction in the flesh of the killed. "He fumbled for the trigger, fired. The bullet kicked up a spray of sand, scattered yellow grains over Ivar's quivering flesh. Bosephus watched the body tense, the blood rushing out of the nose, the mouth."

What protects the killer, from any condemnation on the part of the reader's eye, is the taboo that protects the eye from cruelty—protects the cruel eye of the killer, and the eye of the reader fixed on him.

And this perhaps makes us understand why, although in the ordinary crime story, identification with the killer depends on sympathy with him on other levels—he is depicted as sharing much with us—here, where there is no such empathy, our eye can remain fascinated with killers whose acts we would never be able to commit.

Altmann's Tongue

The Father, Unblinking

He had that day found his daughter dead from what must have been the fever, her swollen eyes stretching her lids open. The day had been a bright day, without clouds. He had found his daughter facedown in the sun-thick mosquito-spattered mud, by the back corner, where the dark paint had started taking air underneath and was flaking off the house now and falling apart at a touch like burnt turkey skin. He squatted over her and turned her up, and she came free with a sucking, the air coming out of her in a sigh, blowing bubbles of mud on her lips. He smeared away the mud from around her mouth. He worked at bending the body straight until the muck on her face dried ashy, then cracked.

He slapped mosquitos dead on her. He picked her up, folded her best he could, and carried her across the yard. He ducked under the window, hurried past the worn back stoop with the door at the top of it. He kicked hens and chicks out of the way, booting loose turbid clouds of pinfeathers. Hooking the barn door with his boot, he hop-skipped back until it was open wide enough to let his foot free and for him to shoulder himself and his girl in. It was quiet inside, and dark except for the shafts of light from the roof traps, four long pillars of bright dust descending to the scatterings of hay below.

He went to the far wall and ran his eyes over the hooks and what hung there: shears, axe, hatchet, hacksaw, handsaw, hand-rake, horse-rake, pitchfork, hoe. He stood staring, running his eyes over them again from the beginning. He looked over each shoulder in turn, turned in a slow circle in the half-dark of the barn, and walked jaggedly around the barn, kicking apart the damp clumps of hay that coated his boots in a yellow mold.

Moving hay in loads across the uneven dirt with his boots, he dragged some together in a pile at the far wall and put her atop the pile. He brushed the dirt off the dress, pulled the socks up past the calves again, loosened the buckles of the blunt-ended shoes. He scooped up an armload of hay and dumped it on top of her.

He scraped the soles of his boots on the edge of the stoop. He stamped a few times, pulled the screen open, went in.

She was cutting venison into thin strips. "Your shoes good?" she said.

"Yes," he said. "Boots," he said.

"Better be," she said, and turned in a squint toward him, red hands and all.

He held on to the end of the counter and lifted first one foot, then the other.

"Pass," she said, and went back to cutting.

"Seen my spade?" he said. "The long-handled job?"

"What for?" she said. "What do I want with it?" she said.

"You seen it or not?" he said.

"You lent it out to Quade," she said. "Your mind's a blunt one today."

"I reckon it is not," he said. "Quade, is it?"

"Heard me, or did you?" she said.

He saw her shoulder blades shiver beneath the dress with each blow. He did not say a thing.

"You seen your little lullaby?" she said as he pushed open the screen.

He stopped.

"I haent seen her," he said.

"You tell her get her butt in here, you see her," she said.

"I haent seen her," he said. He pushed out onto the stoop, letting the screen clap to. "You know where I'm off," he said, loud.

"I know where," she called.

He went into the barn, to the far wall, and took down the hoe. Uncovering the girl's face, he looked at her, then covered her quickly over again. He went out with the hoe in his hands. Drawing the doors shut, he jammed the handle of the hoe through where the rings lined. Grunting, he shook the doors, pulled on their handles.

He set off down the path, walking on the mounded sides instead of down in the ruts. The day was a bright day. Without clouds. The mud in the low spots was drying up, going white and hard. He walked the sunlit half-mile downslope to Quade's fence. There were ants aswarm, darkening the knotty rails. Jumping up, he grabbed the old oak limb. He swung a time or two and then heel-smashed the gate, shaking off hordes of ants, leaving the gate ashiver. He took a few more swings to make his body really go, and then flung himself over to the other side.

"Hey, Quade," he said, from the door.

Quade looked up from the box he was nailing, his half-gaunt face red and stringy, lumpy as the flesh of an old rabbit slaughtered too late.

"Bet I know what you are after," said Quade.

"Bet you do," the man said.

Quade spat nails into the box, dropped his hammer on the dirt. He rubbed the sweat off his neck, undid his bags to let them slide off his waist down to the floor. He went to a corner which sprouted handles. Messing about for a bit, he pulled forth an axe from the angry snarl.

"That mine?" said the man.

"Isn't it?" said Quade.

"Hell," said the man, spitting. "I come for the spade."

Quade squinted, looked at the axe. "Well, whose the hell is this?" he said.

The man shrugged.

Quade went back to the snarl, fished around, poked his way through it, drew out tool after tool, leaning them in a row. His hands hanging loose, he stood staring at the row of handles stacked stiff against the mold-blistered wall.

"Well, I'll be damned if I know where it got to," he said.

"Got to have it today," said the man.

"What you need it for?" said Quade.

"Digging," said the man.

"Digging what?" said Quade.

"Just digging," said the man.

Quade shook his head and went out. The man scavenged loose a quarter sheet of plywood from underfoot, threw it on top of the box, and eased his full weight down upon it. The wood had been ripped ragged on one end, leaving a furry edge. Bending down, he picked up the hammer, hefted it, let it fall onto the dirt. He stared at his big, empty hands. On the inside of one of his thumbs was a shiny gray smear.

Quade came back in, shovel in hand. He stopped moving at the sight of the man.

"Can't say it is good luck to be sitting on that," said Quade, "even with the plywood between."

"It don't matter, Quade," said the man. "It really don't."

Quade shrugged. The man took his time to stand up and reach for the shovel.

"How's the wife?" said Quade.

"Good," said the man, taking.

"The girl," said Quade.

"Sick," said the man.

"You take care of those two," said Quade.

"You got it," said the man, walking out the door.

Opening the latch with his shovel blade, he let the ant-ridden gate swing his way. He went through, on the other side turning the shovel scoop-down and reaching back over the gate with it, dragging it back, pulling the gate closed. He smashed a couple of hundred ants, listening to the shovel ring dull against the scrubby bark-flaked pine. He swung the shovel up over his shoulder and made his way, through the heat, home.

From the path, he heard his wife calling out. He rounded the bend to see the house in front of him, the woman standing in front of it, hands cupped around her face.

"You seen her?" she called, this time to him.

"I haent seen," he said.

"Where in hell?" she said.

He shrugged.

"What of that hoe there?" she said, pointing.

"I put it there," he said.

"What about it?" she said.

He shrugged. He walked over to the barn doors and pulled the hoe handle out of the rings, leaving a long streak of rust on it. He stepped inside and pulled the door shut. Hanging the hoe back where it went, he paced out the floor and started to dig, heaping the dirt against the wall. He pulled out shovelfuls, feeling the pressure in his back deepen the farther down he had to go.

Banging the shovel clean on the side of the hole, he hung it in its proper place. He sprinkled the bottom of the hole with hay, dropping in handfuls. He dug through the hay, pulled out the body, jaundiced now with grain dust. He kneeled, lowered it in, dragged with the shovel blade the dirt back in over it, stamped the grave down, kicked the rest of the dirt around the barn until it was no longer visible.

He put the shovel away. He left the barn.

The woman was standing on the stoop, looking out in the low, clear sun.

"What you been doing?" she said.

"Nothing," he said.

"Thinking?" she said.

He drew time out long, to figure her. "Thinking," he said.

"About what?" she said.

"About nothing," he said.

"You know what I been thinking about?" she said.

"I can guess," he said.

"You think we give the sheriff a call?" she said.

"No," he said.

"You seen her?" she said.

"No," he said.

"You going to look for her?" she said.

He did not answer. He looked at what the sun was doing through the aspens. He looked at the way the stoop had grown worn underfoot, and at the difference in how the sun shone off the rough spots.

"Will you look for her?" she said.

"I will not," he said.

"Look at me to tell me," she said.

He turned to face her, turned all the way around, feeling his boots drag hard over the rough patches until he was facing straight at her. He opened his eyes all the way open and stared her in both her eyes. He looked at her in the eyes and looked at her, and looked at her, without blinking, until it was she who blinked and turned away.

Killing Cats

They wanted to kill their cats, but the problem was the problem of transportation. They invited me to dinner to beg me to drive them and their cats out to the edge of town so that they, the cat killers, could kill their cats. There was no need for me to participate in the slaughter, they said, beyond driving, nor any need for me to watch them kill their cats. Probably it was better someone stayed in the car and kept the motor running, they said. They did not know what laws existed about people and their cats, about what people could inflict, legally speaking, on their own cats. Nevertheless, they assumed there were laws and statutes and ordinances, books and books of legalities concerning felines and their acceptable modes of death, they said. Laws and statutes and ordinances which, they informed me, they were prepared to break.

I did not much care to try my hand at cat killing, but all I would have to do was to drive. I did not have to kill the cats. So I told them, yes, I would drive them, yes, as a token of friendship—if they would pay for gas. They said all right, they would pay, and introduced their cats to me. The mother Checkers, the female kitten Oreo, the male kitten Champ. They apologized for the banal names—although knowing what I knew about these cats I was hardly in a position to

establish rapport. I would have preferred not to have known
their names. Better that they be for me just "the cats." I was
only the driver: all I knew, if questioned, was the road there
and the road back from there, nothing about what occurred
at the place itself. But the people insisted on telling me names,
and once they told me they insisted on apologizing, telling
me the cats' names were not names the people personally
would have chosen, but had been, they unfortunately insisted on telling me, the names their children had chosen.

The man went to the hall closet and rummaged out a gun
and wads of stiff, filthy rags. He rubbed the gun down with
the rags. He polished the gun up and, after sighting down the
barrel at me, handed me the weapon.

"Think it can do the trick?" he said.

I held the gun a moment, for form's sake, before returning
the gun to the man. I said, yes, it probably would.

The man pointed the gun at the dining room table, telling
me how sometimes, when he saw the cats climb up there to
lick the plates, he wanted to "blow their furry bodies right
off the table." He had wanted to "blast the cats away" for
quite some time, he said, Checkers most of all, he said, but
Oreo and Champ were no exception. Tonight was the night,
he indicated. He pointed the gun and made a sound so I
would know what he meant.

I watched the woman wander on tiptoe down the hall, peek-
ing through doorways. She came back into the kitchen,
started picking up cats.

"Sound as angels," she said. "Let's be on our way."

"Slugs, honey?" the man said.

"Honestly, dear, I haven't the least," said the woman.

The man returned to the hall closet. He opened the closet,
kneeled down before it, thrust his hands in. He threw things

out. He threw out metric wrenches and mason jars full of canned peaches, ski poles and winter coats and tangled scarves, Monopoly money and airplane glue and a milk-crusted glass. He surfaced with a fist-sized plastic box.

"Kids get to them?" the man said, holding the open box upside down, shaking it.

"Am I paid to watch them?" the woman said. "Honestly!"

Saved, I was thinking.

Not the cats—myself. I cared what happened to the cats only insofar as its happening affected me. Not that I have anything against cats, but people pay good money for their pets. They have a right to do what they want, as long as they leave me out of it.

"Perhaps the hardware store?" said the woman, looking at her watch. "Or Carl might."

"Charles? Jenkins, you mean? Old Chuck Jenkins?" the man said.

The man looked at the cats, spat into the shag rug.

"Cats like these are not worth the waste of lead," he said. "These three are dumpers."

The man demanded to know what I thought of the idea, the idea of dumpers, it being my car, me to be the one to get the ticket if things went awry. As long as he paid for gas and did the dumping himself, I told him, I was with him.

They sat in the back seat, stroking the cats, their faces fading in and out with the passing street lamps. The wife suggested it might be a nice gesture to give each cat a good solid crack with the pistol first, the butt end of it, for certainty's sake. It would be the kindest thing, she thought.

I told them please to wait until we were on the highway. There was no point in being premature.

There were three, they said to me, three cats, counting kittens as cats. They said they could not help noticing that there were three cats and three of us too, when they counted me.

I said, no, no need to include me, that was okay, not at all, but thank you, thank you, I really appreciate the offer, thank you for asking.

The cats screeched like power saws when they hit the pavement. I watched the man and the woman in my mirror, dropping cats. I kept watching afterward, watching them look out the rear window.

"Whoops," the man said. "Oh, no."

"What?" I said.

"Nothing," said the man.

"Awful," said the woman.

"Such a mess," said the man.

"Should have given them the smash," said the woman, hefting the pistol.

The man leaned forward, put his hand on my shoulder. He put his mouth close to my ear. I felt his warm breath.

"Drive back and finish them, buddy," said the man.

"It's the merciful thing," said the woman.

"Turn this rig around," the man said.

In the rearview mirror I watched what I could see of his face next to mine. He remained motionless, not speaking, the street lights flashing into and out of the car.

I kept driving.

"Be a friend to me in this," he said. He took the empty pistol from his wife and held the snout against my neck. "Aim for their skulls."

Altmann's Tongue

After I had killed Altmann, I stood near Altmann's corpse watching the steam of the mud rising around it, obscuring what had once been Altmann. Horst was whispering to me, "You must eat his tongue. If you eat his tongue, it will make you wise," Horst was whispering. "If you eat his tongue, it will make you speak the language of birds!" I knocked Horst down and pointed the rifle, and then, as if by accident, squeezed the trigger. One moment I was listening to Horst's voice, his eyes brilliant—"the language of birds"—and the next I had killed him. I stared at the corpse next to Altmann's corpse. It had been right to kill Altmann, I thought. Given the choice to kill or not to kill Altmann, I had chosen the former and had, in fact, made the correct choice. We go through life at every moment making choices. There are people, Altmann among them, who, when you have sent a bullet through their skull, you know you have done the right thing. It is people like Altmann who make the rest of it worthwhile, I thought, while people like Horst, when killed, confuse life further. The world is populated by Altmanns and Horsts, the former of which one should riddle with bullets on the first possible occasion, the latter of which one should perhaps kill, perhaps not: Who can say? I felt remarkably calm. I prided myself that moment on my self-composure, taking a minute to sit down next to the two corpses, Altmann and Horst, and to feel the calm to its greatest extent. This calm, I supposed, was not the result of killing Horst but, as one might expect, of killing Altmann. There are two types of people, I thought—type Horst and type Altmann. All people are either Horst or Altmann. I am the sole exception. I repeated the phrase *sole exception*, alternating it with *unique exception*, trying to decide which was the better, unable to decide. I flew blackly about, smelling my foul feathers and flesh. I stuttered, spattered a path through the branches of trees, sprung fluttering into blank sky.

The Munich Window
A Persecution

I

STATION

The face of my daughter, my eldest—the daughter who later that day threw herself a second time from the open window of her Munich apartment, this time to her death—was not unknown to me, though I had not seen her face for eighteen years. After the untimely death of her mother—who had also died by throwing herself from a window (this being a window in Dresden) in what police and reporters had maliciously referred to as suspicious circumstances—I had found it expedient to leave Germany for warmer, more hospitable climes. I had left my eldest and only living daughter with our neighbors for what I promised would be no more than thirty minutes, but which had in truth been eighteen years. And which, had she not killed herself, would have been eighteen more. Leaving her eighteen years ago, I assured myself that I had not so much abandoned a daughter (although certainly I had done that as well) as done that which I had logically and methodically determined to be the absolutely ideal solution for her—and of course for myself, in consideration of my circumstances. Circumstances which, to say the least, were troubled, absolutely unsuitable for children. I left my daughter with a family bearing the name of Grunders, who quickly proved themselves not unworthy of the task I had assigned them in the care my daughter, all the more impressive in that these Grunders had accomplished this task without any monetary compensation for their pains during the full eighteen years. Despite, however, what must initially appear a neglect of my daughter, I can assure you that, during my self-imposed exile from Germany, not a day passed in which I did not glance at my daughter's picture. It is the only photograph of any type which I possess, a photograph which, for the greater part of the last eighteen years, has been pinned to the wall above my desk. I had succeeded, through daily study, in engraving the image mercilessly upon the walls of my skull. Or so I believed. For, despite my careful study, I failed to recognize my daughter's face at the Munich station. Perhaps the photograph I possessed was atypical. Possibly my daughter's physiognomy had undergone a revolution over the last eighteen years. Perhaps the photograph above my desk was not a photograph of my daughter at all, but a childhood picture of my wife—for my daughter had resembled my wife, my wife as a child, *alter idem* to a troubling degree. When my daughter made herself known to me at the Munich station, however, she resembled my wife not in the slightest, nor did she bear any resemblance to me. Rather, she was the spitting image of the Grunders woman who, along with the Grunders man, had taken her in. I immediately discerned that my daughter possessed the most irritating habits of the Grunders family— mannerisms which, due to my eighteen years without contact with Grunders, I believed to have completely expunged from memory, but which immediately leaped to the fore of my consciousness upon seeing my daughter. I realized, the instant I saw her, that my daughter had adopted not only the name of Grunders (a repulsive name at best), but also these people's most despicable etiquette. The rubbing-the-nose habit, the clearing-the-throat habit, the coughing-up-the-phlegm habit, the curling-the-middle-finger habit, the slouching-shuffling-gait habit, even the cracking-the-neck habit: she had marked all these tics for her own. When my daughter introduced herself to me, I thought at first, bombarded suddenly with her nervous Grundersisms— bombarded above all by the slouching-shuffling-gait habit as, slouching, she shuffled toward me—I thought at first that the creature awkwardly introducing itself to me could not possibly be my daughter. Rather, I assumed she was a Grunders sent to the Munich station to chauffeur me to the place where my daughter was recovering from her leap from the window, her first leap, the non-fatal one. My daughter had to grip my arm, had to repeat her name several times before I paid her the slightest heed. While she addressed me, I wondered if this Grunders person thought herself jocular for passing herself off as my daughter, when, as any fool could see, she was anything but my daughter. However, against all logic, it turned out that she was my daughter and, being my daughter, was only in exteriority of the Grunders breed. For although my daughter, judged by her appearance *ex ungue leonis*, as it were, resembled the Grunders to an uncanny degree—had even made the mistake of exchanging her mother's face and figure for the face and figure of a Grunders (and thereby sustained a substantial loss)—she had, even before I arrived, revealed that interiorly she was her mother's child. My daughter had proved herself to be the suicidal type, as was my dead wife, by making her (first) attempt to kill herself. Through this act she had proved herself not only the suicidal type, but also, as was my dead wife, the vicious type. Both of the window leaps, the mother's and the daughter's, had been intended to soil my character. Both the suicide of the mother and the suicide attempt of the daughter had been performed without the slightest degree of *disinterestedness*— the most necessary component of the aesthetically successful suicide. My daughter had hurled herself from the window (the first time, not the second) out of pure viciousness, in an attempt to force me to submit to her will, to force me to visit her in Munich. She assumed, after that excessive display, I would have no choice. Of course, *entre nous*, a mere suicide attempt is not enough to provoke a man of my caliber. A mere suicide attempt is a quotidian occurrence for a man of my caliber, worthy of no notice whatsoever—particularly when it is strictly manipulative, as hers undoubtedly was. I was not to be provoked by such sophomoric tricks, I wrote to her. I wrote to her that she did great dishonor to her mother by merely pretending to kill herself, instead of actually killing herself. I encouraged her to take the task of killing herself as seriously as her mother had. Indeed, a mere suicide attempt was not enough to bring me to Munich. I only began to consider that a journey to Munich might be justified when she wrote to inform me (definitively proving herself the vicious type) that there were certain matters having to bear on my personal character, matters which she must discuss with me *immediately*, in person, in Munich. Otherwise, she would, she indicated, be compelled to take *legal action* and make arrangements for my *extradition* from my adopted country. These were *matters of the greatest import*, she claimed, although she remained elusive about the content of these so-called important matters. No doubt these matters were the spawn of lies, lies which the Grunders and the press, with only an imperfect knowledge of my true family circumstances, had instilled within her. However, I purchased a ticket and came to Munich and, once I found myself standing in the Munich station confronted by my daughter, I could not help but sense the Grunders in her. I could not help but notice that she chose to utilize the slouching-shuffling-gait habit as she approached me, nor could I ignore her use of the clearing-the-throat habit as she prepared to speak. Although both her middle fingers were invisible once she had embraced me, I had no doubt that she practiced, even while we embraced, the petit bourgeois curling-the-middle-finger habit. The assault on my senses of all these habits made me desire to push my eldest daughter, now renamed Grunders (another indication of her viciousness), under the train, a desire which grew as my daughter now did her best to exchange the light embrace I had initiated for a full, tight embrace of the kind unsuitable for public display, inappropriate for all but a married couple. It was instantly clear that my wife, by taking my other daughter, the younger daughter, the dead one, with her when she killed herself, had saved my younger daughter from the terrible prospect of becoming Grunders. This humane sentiment certainly had not been my wife's primary motivation for her jump, nor even an afterthought, though it had been one of the few happy results. In our nine years of marriage, I had never known my wife to be motivated by anything except a general viciousness toward everything around her coupled with a specific persecutory viciousness toward myself, who, of all people, was the least deserving of such treatment. I divined that my daughter was a woman of the same stripe. I had long ago let my arms fall in embarrassment, but my daughter continued to embrace me, kept her arms locked around my ribs, refused to let go despite the fact that the patience of etiquette had long since been exhausted. I stood helpless in her embrace, observing crowds shuffle past, attempting in this painful interim to determine why, despite perpetual dedication to the photograph of my daughter, I had failed to recognize her. Equally important, how had the girl, who must have been young when she last saw me, seven or eight or six (I have her age written down somewhere, surely), and who had no photograph to aid in recalling me to memory, how had my daughter managed to identify me? Perhaps I was wrong to believe she had no photographs of me, there being some likelihood that, in my hasty departure eighteen years ago, when I had incinerated all important documents and possessions, including my photographs—first and foremost my photographs—I had passed over one or two critical photographs. The family Grunders might have found these photographs, I imagine, and had passed them on to my daughter, and she had pinned them to her wall, subjecting them to serious daily study. Or perhaps the Grunders themselves had, without my knowledge, taken pictures of me themselves, pictures which had fallen by default into my daughter's hands upon her coming of age. It was perhaps even more likely that my daughter had practiced her indefatigable viciousness in order to extort a picture from my business associates—I should say ex–business associates—my ex–associates from the period before my wife threw herself from the window, an act certainly calculated well in advance, but which, out of her own viciousness, she arranged to take place under circumstances which seemed sudden and, as police and reporters had indicated, suspicious. After fleeing Dresden, I had made the mistake of writing to my business associates (leaving no forwarding address, of course, crossing national borders to mail the letters so that the postmarks might be a misdirection) to request that they shred all my correspondence and, I wrote, all photographs as well. This request must have had an effect opposite of what was intended, insuring not only that they refused to shred my correspondence but that they went to the extreme of examining my correspondence in its minutest particulars. It was equally possible, considering how indefatigable my daughter had been in her pursuit of me, that she had obtained more recent photographs, photographs which had been taken without my permission, through the exceptionally infuriating investigator who had located me or through one of his equally repulsive minions. Even engrossed in my exploration of such serious issues, I could not help but feel exceedingly embarrassed in the station by my daughter's public embrace, particularly since I noticed now that a young woman leaning against the wall was staring at us, and that, no matter how sharply I returned her gaze, the woman refused to avert her eyes. Quite the reverse: this woman had the audacity to smile at us, to actually smile, so that, confronted by her gaze and smile, I was forced not only to refuse to return my daughter's embrace, but finally to take hold of my daughter's arms and pry them off of me. I took my daughter by the hand and shook her hand warmly, introducing myself properly and without affectation. Was it true, I asked her, that she had exchanged the surname I had proudly given her for the quite frankly repulsive name of Grunders? She said she had, whereupon I congratulated her on her lack of taste. I indicated that there was some confusion in my mind about whether she considered myself or Grunders her father. I could not help noticing that the other woman was still staring at us, the woman who, I now noticed, was sporting brightly colored petit bourgeois clothing—moreover, this woman was practicing a variation of the curling-the-middle-finger habit, a variation even more irritating than its original Grunders manifestation. I took my daughter by the arm, propelling her down the quay, demanding she explain immediately how she had recognized me. Perhaps from some weakness in her rational faculties—weakness which had no doubt been cultivated into full bloom by her transplantation into Grunders manure—she was absolutely unable to explain. "Instinct," she told me, whereupon I uttered the word "bosh." Instinct, I informed her, had been the type of nonsequitur which had composed her (late) mother's equivalent of the rosary. So-called instinct had proved her mother's downfall, and it was, by all appearances, proving my daughter's downfall as well. I told my daughter that her mother had thrown herself out the window as a result of *instinct*, although the actual fall from the window—which had been suicide, not murder, I said, make no mistake, the only murder being that of my youngest daughter, killed when her mother chose to take that daughter out the window with her—the fall from the window had, though triggered by "instinct," been reasoned out *aequo animo* beforehand. I informed my daughter that I had no doubt that her own leap out of the window had been a result of *instinct* conjoined with the same cold viciousness, corollary to which viciousness had been her demand that I make this futile and perilous journey to Munich, in order to satisfy her whims. I was close enough to her face now to see, beneath her heavy *maquillage*, the webwork of scars that the window glass had left on her face and neck. Glancing behind us, I saw, pursuing us down the quay, the woman who had so brazenly observed us earlier. Already? I wondered, though I saw neither badge nor camera. Redoubling my steps, dragging my daughter forward, I shouted at my daughter the words "legal action?" and demanded an immediate explanation. I could hear the woman's footsteps close behind. "Matters of the greatest import?" I shouted at my daughter, "Child abuse? My mother's murder?" and demanded she explain without further delay, and without slowing her pace. I sped up, threw a glance backward, saw the woman quicken her pace as well. "Ludicrous! Ludicrous!" I couldn't help expostulating. It was evident, I told my daughter, that my daughter's leap—a leap which, had she been a woman of respectable character, in all rights would have killed her— had merely succeeded in leading her into the wildest and most unfounded imaginings. I swerved, heard the woman's footsteps behind us stutter, mimic my course. I would, I told my daughter, deign to spend thirty minutes convincing her that her accusations were faulty, at the expiration of which time I would board the express train again and return home, where, I informed her, I proposed that she should not disturb me further. We were running down the quay, the woman matching our pace. I let the woman close on us, then stopped abruptly and flung myself backward, jerking my daughter back with me, sending the other woman off her feet to leave her sprawled on the floor, her hand cupping her mouth. I straightened my clothing, stepped over her body. I attempted the walk back up the quay, but found my daughter had dug in her heels. I released my daughter and watched her actually fall to her knees before the other woman, actually reach her hands out to the other woman, through whose fingers blood had begun to drip. I demanded my daughter stand and deliver an immediate explanation.

"Psychiatrist!" she sobbed out.

"You poor, stupid creature," I said. "Not in the least!" I pointed to the woman's mouth. "A dentist! A dentist!"

II

CAFÉ

I informed my daughter, as she helped her psychiatrist friend to her feet, that I had brought only the single valise to Munich, that I had every intention of departing upon the next train. In the meantime, I would allow her a few minutes which she could use, if she used them wisely, to explain succinctly and to my satisfaction the threatening letter she had mailed. *Immediate legal action, matters of the greatest import, child abuse, my mother's murder:* Were these phrases proper to employ with one's father? She had, I told her, a few minutes to present her case in the station café, where she would purchase for herself a *Coca Blanc* and for myself a glass of Perrier—since I had never fallen into the vice of drinking alcoholic beverages, though she, having been raised by Grunders, surely drank gallons of the cheapest lager. My daughter's psychiatrist friend had removed from her pocket a wad of crumpled, undoubtedly soiled, paper tissues which she pressed against her lips and gums in a futile attempt to halt the bleeding. Watching her, I felt obliged to inform my daughter that I was not, in all honesty, interested in being shadowed by such a person. Her psychiatrist friend was, I told my daughter, as the psychiatrist woman pressed bloody tissues against broken teeth, obviously a tapeworm, or perhaps a ringworm. A dabbler in sir-reverence, no doubt. I advised my daughter to sever the connection between herself and the psychiatrist woman without further delay, by all means within her power, and to do so while her psychiatrist friend's mouth remained *hors de service* and incapable of spewing its venom. Imagine my surprise when, purely for viciousness' sake, my daughter refused to dismiss her psychiatrist friend, having the gall to insist that her psychiatrist friend was what she called a "nice person," making perfectly clear to me how far she was under the psychiatrist woman's spell. She even attempted to introduce me formally to this psychiatrist woman who, I had no doubt, was not in the least a "nice person" but was a disgusting and vulgarly unbearable person, was even more of the Grunders type than my daughter was—a person who participated for money, in the most ugly sort of mountebankery—viz. that of, upon promise of a cure, stripping people of their personalities, as doubtless she was doing even now to my daughter. I would not, under any circumstances, I said, sit at the same table with this psychiatrist woman. In all this, motivated as I was by principles of reason, I was blameless. What I finally did allow, against my better judgement, was for the psychiatrist woman to sit at a table near us, where, forbidden to take notes on the matter my daughter and I discussed, she could remain, as long as she promised not to penetrate our conversation with "insights," particularly insights of the psychological kind. Psychological insight, I confided to my daughter, was synonymous with psychological nonsense. I pushed the psychiatrist woman, who had not succeeded in arresting the bleeding of her mouth, toward a table two tables distant from the table I had chosen for my daughter and myself, a table at which I sat in such a manner that I could see at all times this psychiatrist woman and, above her and beyond her, the station clock. Once seated, I told her, told my eldest daughter, to begin speaking without further delay, removing at that same moment from my breast pocket the train schedule, examining it with the greatest avidity. The next train, I saw, the train which would take me from Munich, was departing in slightly less than twelve minutes. I folded the schedule neatly again, telling my daughter to have done with niceties and gibberish, and to come to the point in the next ten minutes, for in eleven minutes she would see the last of me, and in twelve she would see me not at all. Waiting for my daughter to speak, I made the mistake of glancing at the psychiatrist woman. Holding up one hand to my daughter to keep her from speaking, I was compelled to command the psychiatrist woman to stop staring at us unless she desired to be personally escorted from the Munich station. I leaned closer to my daughter and asked her, confidentially, if she actually employed this woman, a woman who was now in the process of stuffing an entire tissue up her left nostril in an attempt to stop the bleeding of her nose which, perhaps from sympathy, had joined the bleeding of her mouth, creating a veritable symphony of bleeding. I informed the psychiatrist woman that the most effective method of stopping this type of bleeding was first to heat the end of a spoon, second to thrust the spoon handle up the nostril. I graciously offered her my utensils and the use of the candle on our table to perform this delicate operation, all of which implements she declined. I whispered to my daughter that surely it was impossible for my daughter to have hired such a woman. I told the psychiatrist woman that, as regarded her mouth, the proper thing to do was to see a dentist, which I encouraged her to do without further delay, without minding us, as we would proceed without her aid. I informed my daughter that she had approximately seven minutes to enlighten me as to what events the accusations mentioned in her letter alluded. At the least, I could not help but say, holding up a finger to stop my daughter for just a moment more, the psychiatrist woman should volunteer the gratuity for having imposed herself upon us—although her volunteering the gratuity would have done absolutely nothing to repair the miserable impression she had made through cramming whole boxes of paper tissue into a single nostril. Waiting for my daughter to speak, waiting while my daughter did not speak, I sipped at my drink. How refreshing! I told my daughter, holding up a finger, to be in a country in which drinks made their appearance unencumbered by ice cubes, a country where one did not even have to ask for one's drink to be served without ice—where one's drink was *each and every time* served without ice. The drink itself, of course, was no good, I said, no good at all, but the fact that the drink had no ice, *automatically* had no ice, *eo ipso* made the drink verge on the bearable. Germany, taken as a whole, is absolutely unbearable, I said; however, Germany's relationship to its ice is a relationship of sublimity—Frankfurt, I informed my daughter (who certainly could not help being interested in such matters), is the unfortunate exception, as is West Berlin. I settled back a moment to allow my daughter to absorb these simple facts, and then elucidated. When one goes to Frankfurt or to West Berlin one never knows, because of the American soldiers in the first case, and American soldiers and American tourists in the second case, one never knows whether one will or will not be served ice. In the same Frankfurt restaurant, in the same West Berlin restaurant, on the same day of the week, served by the same waiter, I informed my daughter, one might in the morning be served a beverage with ice, in the evening be served a beverage without ice. *Appalling!* I yelled. *Appalling!* One must spend one's time in Frankfurt, in West Berlin, in mortal dread of whether one's drink will be served with ice or without ice. East Berlin, however, I said, finishing my drink, is an altogether different story. One is never served ice in East Germany—but how long will it last, how long? "One must rebuild the Berlin Wall for the sake of ice," I declared, pounding my fist on the table to punctuate my statement. I put my empty glass on the table, asking my daughter why she had dragged me to Munich and now refused to discuss those matters which, she had insisted, were crucial. "Matters of greatest import," I reminded her. "Child abuse!" I shouted, "My mother's murder! Immediate legal action! My mother's murder! Child abuse! Matters of the greatest import! Child abuse! Immediate legal action!" I said. I was all ears, *arrectis auribus*, I told her, checking once again, the station clock. Why didn't she speak? I wanted to know. She had exactly two minutes, I told her; she would have to be succinct and extremely precise, but it could be done, she was my daughter. My daughter looked away from me, looked over her shoulder at her psychiatrist friend. The latter clutched her hand into a fist and pressed it against her breast, contorting her face into what was supposed to be an expression of solidarity, I assume, but which, with one wad of tissue crammed up her nose and another wad hanging out from under her top lip, made her look as if she were a hospital case. My daughter, who had far too much Grunders in her, apparently found this nauseating gesture reassuring, for immediately thereafter she turned toward me, though refusing to meet my gaze, and informed me that she knew I had slaughtered her mother. My daughter said she knew that I had pushed her mother out the window of our Dresden apartment; that, with the help of her psychiatrist friend, she had been able to "reconstruct the original scene" as it had "actually happened" eighteen years ago, along, she said, with some other scenes which illustrated how I had treated her as a child, what (she said) I had done to "abuse her trust" as a child. After many months of therapy, she claimed to have reconstructed the murder of her mother, and was prepared to repeat this elaborate joint fabrication of a non–existent original scene to me had I not stood and told her that her time had expired. I informed her that she could not have possibly seen me murder her mother, since she had been in the closet at the time. She had been unable to see anything, let alone her mother's murder. Her mother had not been murdered by me, I told her, although circumstances had been contrived by her to throw suspicion onto me. Her mother was a victim of self-murder, having thrown herself out the window of her own free will and choice—my daughter herself had recently been the victim of attempted (failed) self-murder. Her so-called psychiatrist friend had created false memories in order to keep extracting a fee from my daughter, I said. I was not impressed, I said, by the viciousness of her psychiatrist friend, nor was I impressed by the viciousness of my own daughter, nor had I anything else to say to either of them. Having proved her "matters of the greatest import" to be no more than mere trivialities, I would waste no more time at the café, nor at the Munich train station, nor, for that matter, anywhere in Munich. Shaking my daughter's hand vigorously and thanking her for a delightful visit, I picked up my valise, walking hurriedly back to the quay to catch my train.

III

THE HAMBURG TRAIN

I soon found a compartment which, although filthy was less filthy than the other compartments, and had the additional qualification of being empty of other passengers. I took out my handkerchief and unfolded it, using one side of it to brush clean the seat upon which I placed my bag. I took off my coat, folding it neatly, placing it on a seat two seats from the bag. On the seat between bag and coat, I carefully spread the handkerchief, soiled side down, and sat down myself. No sooner had I insured my comfort than I heard an odd repeated tapping on the window, devoid of any percussionary sense. Glancing over, I was not surprised to see the ruined mouth of the psychiatrist woman, whose index finger was engaged in erratically striking the glass. She began to wave madly. I refused to acknowledge her existence, whereupon she actually began beating on the window glass with both palms, as if to break the glass. I stood, pulled the shade down between us, sat down again on the handkerchief. I stretched my legs out in front of me, eyes closed, waited until, with a jerk, the train began to move. I stood to open the blinds, found the quay deserted, my Grunders daughter and her psychiatrist friend gone. I had sat down and just closed my eyes when the compartment door burst open and I found myself confronted by both my daughter's psychiatrist friend and my daughter herself, who entered the compartment without asking my leave, one removing my coat and the other removing my bag from where I had placed them on the cleaned seats, moving them to filthy seats, so that, doubtless, I would later have to burn both items. After having managed these two great assaults upon etiquette, they mounted a third, sitting in the very seats they had cleared of my possessions, and whining at me from both sides. I stood, excused myself, gathered my things without further speech, moved to another compartment. They, proving themselves again to be of the *Grunders* type, the *persecuting* type, the *tormenting* type, followed me, sat down next to me. I asked my daughter if she was in fact crazy, following me onto a train as she had, ignoring all the responsibilities awaiting her in Munich, responsibilities which, I told her, she could not afford to ignore. *Entre nous*, I said this though I had no doubt that her responsibilities were responsibilities of the Grunders variety, the most lifeless of banalities: taking the trash to the curb, for instance, or scrubbing the sidewalk. I informed the psychiatrist woman that it was irresponsible for her to leave her patients alone in Munich without help, while she, for the sake of a vacation, encouraged my daughter to pursue a futile course of action. I exhorted them both to regain their sense of social responsibility instantly and to disembark at the next station. In the meantime, I suggested, they should, if they had any sense of propriety, find themselves another compartment, where they would be able to converse between themselves, on the subject of their choice, without disturbing others. My daughter took this as her cue to claim that she and I still had matters to discuss. "Matters?" I said. I was not in the least interested in matters, I said, or in listening to the matters stemming from the original scene which the psychiatrist woman had created in my daughter's mind. Indeed, if she were a true daughter of mine, rather than a Grunders half-breed, she would never have allowed anybody, least of all a psychiatrist woman, to convince her of anything. "No, no, no," I said, cutting her off. "Leave this compartment immediately; it is useless, useless." But my daughter displayed an unexpected tenacity which, though wrongly directed, revealed beneath her roughshod Grunders exterior remnants of her true heritage. Had this tenacity chosen right objects for itself, had it been directed at someone apart from me, I would have found it both admirable and endearing. In the present circumstance, however, it could not but be exasperating to the extreme, so much so that I told my daughter that if she said another word I would hurl both her and her psychiatrist friend out of the window of the compartment. "Ah-hah!" said the psychiatrist woman, stabbing her stubby little finger at me in such a manner that I immediately gathered my possessions and left the compartment. Although I walked at the most brisk pace imaginable, the two women dogged my heels. I kept on down the hall, suddenly stopping, throwing my body backward against them until they collapsed, falling to the floor of the narrow passageway. I climbed off of them, breaking the psychiatrist woman's nose while regaining my feet—sheer accident—and continued down the corridor, locking myself into the lavatory. No sooner had I shut myself in than fists began to pound on the lavatory door, to which I had no response but to contemplate myself in the metal mirror. I was not displeased with what I saw of myself, particularly in contrast with my surroundings, for I must admit I have never been in a more filthy and cramped lavatory. The psychiatrist woman had pressed her face against the door, and was speaking loudly about *child abuse*, using the words "child pornography," and even the words "sexual harassment." It was clear to me, however, that it wasn't the child being abused but the parent, myself, who, by his daughter's insistence and extravagance, had been forced to take refuge in the most odoriferous stinkhouse, the literal asshole of the train. I stood as still as I could, trying not to touch anything, gaining strength from my reflection, until my daughter and her psychiatrist friend fell silent outside the door. From time to time there still came knocks and feeble protests, until even these died as well. I would, I thought, remain in the lavatory until the end of the line if need be, from there making a rapid dash from the train lavatory to the lavatory of the airplane. I was planning my epic journey from lavatory to lavatory when the door sprang open, revealing a dwarfish, pock-faced conductor sporting a blue pillbox hat. The man slipped a heavy ring of keys back into his pocket, informing me that the "crappers" were for all alike, and that they served for "shitting," and that they were not to be used as a hiding place. I informed the diminutive yokel that I had entered the facilities with every intention of employing them for their proper use but, being confronted with their filthy condition, found myself incapable of moving my bowels. He looked into the bathroom, scratched his scalp, shrugged. He looked at the ladies to either side of him, rubbed his chin, shrugged. Extracting from an inner pocket an unwieldy device which, I divined, was employable for the perforation of paper, he demanded of me my ticket. I promptly removed my ticket from my own inner pocket, presented him with it. He looked it over, nodded his head, perforated it, handed it back, tipped his hat, and prepared to depart. I asked him about the ladies, about the tickets of the *ladies*, as I chose at that moment to refer to them. The conductor scratched his head, turned to the women, held out his hand. The psychiatrist woman and my daughter looked first at each other, then at the conductor, whereupon he requested their tickets verbally. The psychiatrist woman pretended not to hear. "What is the price of the ticket?" asked my daughter, reaching into her purse. "No tickets?" the conductor queried. I suggested that the conductor have these two women—women clearly travelling illegally and women who, I felt compelled to add, had had no intention of ever buying tickets—expelled from the train at the nearest station. Or better yet, I said, he might hurl them from the train *without further ado*. I would, I indicated, be more than happy to aid and abet him in either operation because of my great respect for his profession. My daughter was waving a somewhat meager handful of bills which began to attract the conductor's gaze. I discouraged the conductor from accepting the bribe—if he did, I told him, he would be *morally ruined*. He shrugged. Not only *morally ruined*, I said, but *professionally ruined*, for his lapse would be described by me to his superiors *in the least favorable light*. The conductor stood quite still, hearing my words, giving no sign that he understood. When his mind had gathered that I was finished, he removed from another inner pocket a flat metal case, which he unfolded. From it he pulled a set of blank tickets and a list of fares. DM 27,50 for the first stop, DM 275,20 for the last, he showed my daughter. She counted her money, asking where she might travel for DM 25. Knowing the answer to be nowhere, I volunteered this information, whereupon the psychiatrist woman informed the conductor that since they were with me I would pay the difference to make up their fare. The only fare I would pay for either of these women, I declared, was the fare due to Charon, the boatman. The conductor rubbed his chin, told me this was a train, not a boat, while the psychiatrist woman screamed out the responsibilities of a father, the duties of a parent. I told her I did not believe that I was her father, but surely she was not mine. The conductor remained rapt before this exchange, his pen poised ready over the blank ticket which he had spread on his metal case. I informed the conductor that never in my life would I, under any circumstances, purchase tickets for these women, and demanded that he eject them *instanter* from the train. He had the nerve to tell me that until the next stop he could do nothing to remove them from the train. Pocketing his metal case, tipping his hat, he left us to our own devices. I immediately locked myself in the lavatory. I listened to the pounding. I stared into the lidless metal toilet bowl. Through the hole of the bowl I could see the movement of the tracks, feel the air gush up. I closed my eyes, averted my head, waited until the pounding stopped. I slid the lock out and opened the door a crack, saw, leaning against the far wall, the psychiatrist woman. Her arms were crossed, and she was staring down the hallway, her face twitching, her nose all crammed with cotton, blackening near the eyes. I swung the door wide, politely asked her to inform me where I might find my daughter, whereupon she loaded me with verbal epithets, thereafter attempting to endow me with her psychiatric textbook-case notions of what it supposedly means to be an ideal father. I asked her politely to refrain from speaking of fatherhood and matters patriarchal, matters about which she knew entirely nothing. She had taken from her pocket a set of photographs which she waved at me, yelling, "Nothing about? Nothing about?" finally managing to hold the photographs still long enough for me to see that the photographs were the remainder of a series of *situations* involving my daughter and myself, photographs which I believed I had long ago destroyed, save for the photograph hanging over my desk. There was nothing improper about the photographs, though they could be considered in the wrong light because of my daughter's clothing and my daughter's poses, poses which she herself had chosen, but which were likely to be interpreted as my choice in a court of law. "Kiddie porn" was, I believe, the curious and inelegant term the psychiatrist woman had developed to define the series of photographs, showing once again her paucity of intelligent phraseology. I struck her in the mouth, wresting the photographs from her hands, tearing them to shreds, upon which she took great pride in informing me that these photographs were by no means the originals, that the originals were safe in my daughter's hands, hidden carefully away. I grabbed the psychiatrist woman by the neck, pulling her toward me, crammed her into the tiny bathroom, forcing her to straddle the toilet bowl while I crammed myself in and locked the door. When, a few minutes later, I squeezed out, alone, my daughter was there, outside the door, holding the psychiatrist woman's purse on one shoulder, her own purse on the other. Grabbing my daughter by the arm, I propelled her down the corridor, away from the lavatory, down to the end of the car, out of that car, into the next car. I told her, in all sincerity, that her psychiatrist friend had been a fair-weather friend, who, at the least hint of profit, had deserted my daughter. I had bought off the psychiatrist woman (it was wrong to call her "the psychiatrist friend" now, I informed my daughter), I said, quite inexpensively. Walking my daughter down to the end of the train, I asked her not to waste another thought on her psychiatrist friend. "Foremost, psychiatry," I maximed. "Lattermost, friendship of the contingent variety." I entreated her to drive all thought of the psychiatrist woman from her mind with the utmost ruthlessness, to make the woman dead to her, as good as dead to her. I placed my fingers to my daughter's lips, quelling her protests. I told my daughter I intended to compensate her in every way possible for the loss of the psychiatrist woman. I myself would return with her to Munich, to her apartment, where I would discuss with her everything that troubled her. I would stay with her as long as she wanted. I was there for her, I said, and would be there for her until the day she died. Wrapping my arms completely around her, I embraced her warmly.

IV

THE MUNICH APARTMENT

I could not help but notice that the Munich apartment of my daughter bore considerable resemblance to the Dresden apartment of my wife, of myself and my wife. Both possessed, among other charms, three sets of full-length French windows, easily accessible to a woman desiring to commit suicide. My wife, I informed my daughter the instant we entered the apartment, had jumped through the middle set. My wife had had a great love of symmetry, despite the fact that her mind was unbalanced. My suspicion was, I informed my daughter, that my wife had such a great love of symmetry precisely since she was internally imbalanced. Her suicide had been an attempt to attain a balance. It had also been, I informed my daughter, a malicious attempt to steal my symmetry, an attempt which I had of course escaped, without damage. "Which window did you throw yourself through?" I asked my daughter out of politeness, although I was sure of the answer, the answer not being the middle, which she herself confirmed. I strongly encouraged her, in future, to throw herself through the middle set of French windows. The results would be more aesthetically pleasing and would make for better photographs, I told her, as witnessed by the widely publicized photographs of her mother. "Works of art," I said, stabbing my index finger into the air. My daughter poured herself a drink, threatening to pour me a drink as well, but I would not allow it. I took a seat on the ottoman, refusing first whiskey, then chardonnay, then alcoholic drinks of all kinds, then finally bottled water. She poured herself a drink, put the bottle on the parquet, a herringbone cut, oak, freshly waxed, similar in every respect to the parquet of the Dresden apartment. She dragged her chair close to the ottoman. She offered to take my gloves. I refused

to part with them, saying finally, upon being further importuned, that my fingers were cold. She offered to take my
coat and valise, which I allowed, noting carefully where she
placed them in the closet. I informed her that the Dresden
apartment had had a similar closet, perhaps an identical closet,
in the same location. It was this closet, I assumed, in which
she claimed to have been shut at the time of her mother's
unfortunate accident. Was it that closet? I wanted to know. Was
she perhaps thinking of another closet in the Dresden apartment, one of the other three closets? I stood, walked to the
closet, opened it. I noted aloud that the closet had no lock
on the door. Commonly closets do not have locks on their
doors: What made her think that the Dresden closet had been
the exception to the rule, that in that apartment she could
have been locked in the closet? She looked confused. I confided in her that psychiatry creates its own data to fit its
assumptions, that her analyst—did she mind if I called the
psychiatrist woman her analyst?—had predetermined what
my daughter's symptoms would indicate, and had molded
her memories into prearranged patterns. I told my daughter
that I was prepared to accompany her to Dresden, prepared
to prove that there were no locks on the closet doors in the
Dresden apartment. She was pressing her palms to her skull,
refusing to respond, a gesture which belonged not to her but
to her mother. It warmed my soul to know that her mother
was not completely dead after all. I wanted to embrace her,
my dead wife, my daughter. Instead I opened the closet and
looked inside. "The inside of this closet," I decreed, "is absolutely identical to the inside of the closet of the Dresden
apartment." I proceeded to cram myself into the closet, once
in, asking her to shut the door on me, which, after much
persuasion, she did. I demonstrated how easy it was to burst
out of the closet, that it was just a matter of leaning slightly
against the door—a task which even the most feeble of children could accomplish. She, I didn't need to remind her, had
been, like her mother, a particularly well-developed child.

She sat on the chair, sipping her whiskey, not speaking. I
made my way to the ottoman, sat down, crossed my legs.
"Now that we have resolved the closet dilemma," I said,
cracking my gloved knuckles. Did she have "proof" of her
other vague accusations, material which we might examine
together, photographs perhaps? She did not respond, except
to place her empty glass on the floor. I informed her that
placing on the floor a glass which contains or has contained
liquid, *even for a moment*, would leave a ring of moisture on
the floor—a ring of moisture liable to warp the floor!—and
demanded she take the glass off the floor and carry it into
the kitchen without further delay. She did not move. I
cracked my knuckles. I repeated, whereupon she responded,
"Why did you do it?" I informed her the "it" she had used
had no known antecedent, and could not refer to anything
outside of the narrow confines of her mind. The sentence, as
it stood, had no sense. Had she never been taught grammar?
I wanted to know. "It what?" I said. "It? It?" Hastily, I
scrambled to my feet and took her glass to the kitchen myself. The liquid that had condensed on the exterior pene-
trated through the ventilation holes in the fingers of my
gloves. In the other room, my daughter was saying something, which I ignored. "Marvelous kitchen!" I shouted.
"First rate!" Opening the cupboard, I discovered that my
daughter had kept her mother's dishes, the black glazed
dishes her mother had received when she married me. I took
the dishes out one by one, examining the scratches and chips
on their dark surfaces, trying to determine which chips were
new and which, eighteen years prior, I had made myself.
Feeling my daughter standing behind me, I replaced the
plates one by one, closed the cupboard, returned to the ottoman. I sat wondering what else of my wife's was in the
kitchen, what else I might find in the apartment to threaten
what I had erected from my wife's death. Objects of the
highest danger, objects I would have to approach with the
most terminal ruthlessness and with the greatest efficiency—

dishes, ancient water-spotted glasses, a fork with a bent tine, a flour sifter with two rusted screens, a set of knives with oxidized blades, the uneven and badly carpentered corner of the third drawer down, the slow leak of the icebox, a cracked windowpane held in place with Scotch tape, the spot on the wooden handle of a spoon polished and worn smooth by my wife's thumb, my wife's long smooth fingers flicking ash from a cigarette, her fingers tracing my jaw, her hair shook down out of the pins and over my face, the feel of her body moving beneath my open palms. Across from me, straddling a chair, was my daughter, the very picture of her mother. "You are very lovely," I said. "Quite lovely." She brushed her hair out of her eyes, hooked it awkwardly behind her ear. Grunders, I realized, despite all. Saved by a mannerism. I felt rationality returning. I informed her I was aware that she had certain photographs in her possession, photographs which troubled her, and that, if they were the photographs I believed them to be, I could easily explain why she was dressed as she was, and what precisely she and I were doing, and how an unjustified unpleasant effect could be construed. I told her that, as soon as she brought out the pictures, I would explain all matters to her satisfaction—surely she was not afraid to show me the pictures, I said, when she failed to get the pictures; surely she didn't think I would do anything to the photographs. If I did destroy them, which I certainly would not do, I said, doubtless she had copies elsewhere. With her psychiatrist friend perhaps? Only with her psychiatrist friend or were there other copies? I wanted to know. I told her that I didn't imagine that she would have the nerve to show such photographs to anyone else because of the harm which (considering the possibility of their misinterpretation) such a revelation might do her own reputation, not to mention my own. Had she provided copies of the photographs to anyone but her psychiatrist? I wanted to know. Not that it would matter, I explained, but being in some of the photographs myself I had a right to know. "Does anyone else, besides your psychiatrist, have the photographs?" I demanded to know. I requested she retrieve the photographs, and, when she hesitated, kindly led her from room to room, asking repeatedly, "Are they in this room? Are they in this room?" When this failed to elicit a response, I began pulling drawers open, showing her the insides of them, my eyebrows raised quizzically. Perhaps she wanted to call her psychiatrist friend, I suggested; perhaps it would be wise to call her psychiatrist friend and ask her advice. I was, I claimed, not adverse to such an idea. I picked up the telephone and brought it as close to her as the cord would allow. She stood, dialed her psychiatrist's number. No response. I mimed surprise. I looked at my watch, told her I hadn't time to wait until her psychiatrist friend was home since I had a train to catch. It was either time to resolve everything or for us to part forever. After being confronted with similar rational reasoning, she brought me the photographs, though she did not allow me to see where they had been hidden, but she brought the photographs to me, refusing to look at me as I examined them. I looked at each photograph carefully. I requested of her a magnifying glass and a good flashlight. I informed her that, provided with the proper equipment, I could show her how the print had been tampered with. What she thought was she, in an obscene posture with myself, was in fact not she and I together at all, but two pictures superimposed by a malicious soul. Holding the flashlight close to the photograph, I looked through the magnifying glass, forcing her to look through it as well, telling her there was the slightest of lines where the photograph of her had been grafted onto the photograph of myself. The line outlining the shoulders, could she see that line? I told her it was easier to see in negative, that if you tilted the negative in the right way you could immediately see how the graft had been touched over. Did she possess the negatives for these pictures? I wanted to know. Would she get the negatives for me? She left the living room, went into the bedroom, returned with the negatives, held them a moment, handed them to me. I immediately stood, shook her hand, thanked her for obliging me in this small particular. I counted the negatives, pocketed both photographs and negatives, buttoned my coat tightly shut. I told her that the matter of the photographs had become a matter of the utmost annoyance to me, a matter which I was not interested in pursuing. If she could not see the graft on the photograph, she would doubtless fail to see the graft on the negative. I had no more patience left, I said. She would have to take my word for it, end of discussion. There was one matter, however, I told her, still unresolved, that matter being the death of her mother, and I was willing to spend a few more moments, *at the risk of missing my train*! putting my daughter to rest on that issue. Everything she had heard heretofore on the subject of her mother's death, I said, was a lie, but I had the truth, the truth being that I had not killed the woman— she had jumped of her own accord, partly out of maliciousness, partly for being the suicidal type. I was the only one who could know for certain, I was the only one who had been there, except her mother, who was dead and who, in any case, dead or alive, was an *unstable and unreliable witness.* As for my daughter's memories, a scene examined through a keyhole is distorted, and was, in this instance, even more profoundly distorted by the imagination of the six-year-old observer, by eighteen years of Grunders thickheadedness, by the dubious fabrications of a psychiatrist. Luckily, I was here to correct everything, to put everything in the context in which it belonged.

I asked her to open the windows, the French windows, all three of the French windows. She refused. Did she or did she not, I asked incredulously, desire the truth? The time to strike the anvil was *the present—or never.* After a number of similar comments, movements toward and away from the door, and similar rational argument, she roused her stolid brain enough to open the middle set of windows. "Wrong!"

I cried. "Wrong! Wrong! Wrong! Wrong!" I told her to close those windows immediately, to open the two other sets of windows first, to open the middle windows last. She closed the middle windows, opened the right-hand windows somewhat listlessly. "No!" I said, "No! Put some life into it!" I announced that she was her mother's child, no doubt about it; I had been witness to her birth, and it was time to start acting like who she was, conscious of her heritage, of her mother's influence. She began to weep, whereupon I informed her that overindulgence in alcohol had obviously ruined her ability to know when a display of emotion was acceptable. I yanked open the windows for her in a proper fashion, commanding her to stand closer to the middle windows. I took a pillow from the ottoman and threw it at her, telling her she should hold it, that it was our baby. I demanded she move closer to the window, and, when she failed to do so, took several steps toward her, fists clenched. "Don't!" she begged. I lifted my open hands, held them, fingers splayed to either side of my nose, wiggled them. "Am I touching you?" I said. "Have I touched you? Have I laid a finger on you? Have I given you a push? Have I given you a shove? Have I given you the slightest nudge?" Her only answer was to try to move past me, to move away from the middle windows. I moved in front of her, kept moving in front of her. "You are touching *me*, now," I said. "That's different, entirely different, a world of difference; you are running into me now, and I quite justly feel threatened." After she had exhausted herself sufficiently, I told her to get up and to pick her baby up. Couldn't she see that her baby was lying on the floor? Had she no shame? Was that any way to treat her baby, leaving it lying on the floor? I got close to her and yelled, "Have I pushed you? Have I pushed you?" The correct answer was no, I was not touching her, no, but she gave no response. I repeated the question until I had the response I desired. Pulling her to her feet, I encouraged her to stand on the windowsill.

I told her, as she stood in the window frame, that the photographs were genuine, utterly genuine. Not only had she committed the obscenities depicted but had enjoyed doing them, she had asked to do them, had begged me to do them with her. All this playacting with her had gotten my blood boiling, I told her; I was eager to continue our relations where they had been left off, years before. I was willing to do whatever she would beg of me, I was willing to make an effort, willing to try my best; no one could accuse me of not trying.

She stood on the sill of the Munich window, holding the pillow, hesitating. Blameless and seething love, I spread my arms wide. "Come to Papa!" I cried, sliding toward her. "Come, embrace me!"

I am blameless. *Alis volabat propriis.* She jumped entirely of her own volition. Just like her mother.

The Blank

THORNE

In mid-April, Thorne sealed himself into his room and refused to come out. *I will not*, he wrote on a half-sheet of
yellow paper which he slid under the door, *repeat Lazarus'
mistake and exit the tomb. All is the tomb.* The handwriting,
Cero noticed, was nicely rounded: Cero could not help but
point out how handsome Thorne's script was. Masma Saliere
wondered if it were not best to "break down the door and
drag Thorne out of his so-called tomb in order to talk some
sense into the idiot." But others thought Thorne made perfect sense and that he should be left alone. Someone remembered that Bosephus had an axe, that he could break the door
down; and, although they were in disagreement over Bosephus's level of sanity, in the end they made the mistake of
taking the note to him.

Bosephus was on the east wall, sitting in his chair, the
sun beating down on him. His shotgun was across his knees,
loaded, the safety off. He seemed to be staring at Preter Bedlam, who stood next to him on the outer wall, Preter staring
through field glasses out at the waste, perhaps at the hill in
the waste. They drew lots to decide who would give Bosephus the note. Roger Cuerpo lost. Roger Cuerpo climbed
the wall and brought the note to Bosephus as the others in
the courtyard watched. Cuerpo held the note out to him.

"What is it?" said Bosephus, looking all the time at Preter.

"A note from Thorne," said Cuerpo.

"Read it," said Bosephus.

"I already have," said Cuerpo.

"Read it to me," Bosephus said.

"Thorne has locked himself in his room," said Cuerpo.

"What do you think he sees?" Bosephus said, pointing to Preter Bedlam.

Roger Cuerpo looked up from the note.

"I have asked him what he is watching," Bosephus said. "He will not tell me. Perhaps he does not know."

"Should I read the note?" said Cuerpo.

Bosephus said nothing.

"It says," Cuerpo said, *"I will not repeat Lazarus' mistake and exit the tomb. All is the tomb."*

"All is a tomb," said Bosephus.

"The note indicates as much," said Cuerpo.

"It is a suicide note," said Preter Bedlam, putting down his field glasses, looking over at the two of them.

"Yes," said Bosephus, "and a death warrant."

"A death warrant," said Cuerpo. "In what sense?"

"In a universal sense," said Bosephus. "Tell that to the rest of them."

Each day there was a message found beneath Thorne's door. Bosephus would collect and read it, sometimes relaying its content to the others. Most were instructions about how to run the fortress in Thorne's absence. All were vague, in need of decipherment and interpretation. Bosephus would stare at a note for long periods before finally assigning a meaning to it. But once he had chosen a meaning, he had no doubt that the meaning was the correct meaning. Doubt, he thought, is a great deadener. One must have no doubts.

Masma Saliere, however, had her doubts. But, as Cero pointed out, she had been critical of Scrapine Bosephus ever since she had heard the other guards, laughing, call him the baby killer.

"You have personal reasons to hate Bosephus," Cero informed her.

"No," said Masma, shaking her head. "I am the only one who is not blind. What makes you think that the notes are from Thorne at all? Thorne is dead. Bosephus is the one who is writing them, writing them at night, collecting them by day. There is a yellow pad of paper in his desk, second drawer from the bottom, the same yellow paper used for the notes. Take a look for yourself."

"But the script of the notes, the smooth flowing lines," said Cero, "it recalls Thorne."

"Script means nothing," Masma said. "Bosephus has strangled Thorne and now he is slowly stifling us all."

In early May, Bosephus announced the siege. He chose to seal the fortress off from the outside once and for all, ostensibly on the orders of Thorne.

"The siege," Bosephus said, "has begun. It is time to dig in and wait for supplies to run out. Or to wait for the enemy to breach the gate. Or to wait for rescue."

The others crouched on and about the walls, listening to Bosephus speak from his chair. They looked out over the ramparts, looked for the enemy, but saw nothing save the waste. Where was the enemy?

"*Siege,*" Bosephus said, reading for them Thorne's note. "*Needleman,*" he read, "*Siege! Seal it off and wait for the air to run out. Close the tomb. Thorne.*"

Putting the note away, Bosephus declared that anyone who would care to take his chances with the enemy would be given a horse and several days' rations.

Where was the enemy?

Of the forty-three in the fortress, Thannis, Johnson, and Miss Margaret O'Grady were among the twenty-seven who accepted Bosephus's offer to leave. The horses were led out, and each person was given a leather wallet filled with biscuits and cheese. ("As if this were the seventeenth century!" cried Miss O'Grady, looking at the cracked leather of the wallets in dismay.) Bosephus sat aloof in his chair, sending Ivar the Boneless to walk among the fugitives. Ivar talked with them idly, smiled, stroked their horses, shook their hands. He asked them if they were sure they wanted to go. Would they stay just a little longer? Did they wish a few days to consider before they risked death (or worse!) at the hands of the enemy?

When the fugitives had mounted their horses, Bosephus with a gesture caused the guards to fling wide the gates.

"But be on guard for the enemy!" Bosephus warned the guards on the walls. "Take the safety off your weapons, and be ready!" he said.

The horses began to move out. Thannis on the sorrel was in the lead, the lenses of his glasses glistering fantastically in the desert sun, their circular reflections dancing out into the waste. Those who wished to consort with Thannis filed out after him. As soon as those going were gone, Bosephus ordered the gates shut. As the gates were closed, Bosephus began crying, "The enemy! The enemy!" He pointed at the party of horses led by Thannis. "Fire!" Bosephus cried. "Fire!"

There was much haste to the top of the wall to watch the mayhem. Thannis had spurred his horse and, crouching low, was trying to get out of range. His cohorts ran into each other, falling and waiting for death as the guards pulled back on triggers and bullets sprayed from shaking guns, lead weighing down the corpses lying in the waste. Those horses still alive bit at one another, reared up, slashed the air with their hooves. Miss O'Grady whirled about on a mad horse— the man in front of her slumped and dead, the horse rolling its eyes, her hand clasped to her bosom—whirling and whirling until she was thrown off to have her head staved in by her horse's hoof.

When the smoke cleared and the battle was over, there were heaps of enemy lying about. None had escaped save Thannis, who rode on, a bullet in his back perhaps, on and out into the waste.

"A glorious victory!" shouted Bosephus, feeling altogether too theatrical as he said it. "Most of the enemy dead, the remainder of them fled. And as for ourselves, we have lost not a man."

Day after day, they watched dark birds pick apart corpses. They shot the birds, and in time the black bodies of humans were covered over by the black bodies of birds. When the birds tired of being killed, they began to come at night, streaks in the darkness, when it was more difficult to shoot them. The birds cannibalized the bodies of their fellows, working away at the pile of men and dead birds.

"It is the myth of Sisyphus revisited," explained Ivar to Roger Cuerpo.

"Syphilis is no myth," said Cuerpo.

"I am not speaking of the disease," said Ivar. "I mean the ancient Greek hero Sisyphus. He pushed a stone up a hill, but always before it reached the top it rolled back down."

"Why did the Greek want to push the stone?" said Roger.

"Who said he wanted to?" said Ivar. "He had to."

"What do you mean he had to?" said Cuerpo.

"If he had to, he had to," said Ivar.

"What does that have to do with us?" said Cuerpo.

"The point," said Ivar, "the point is that the Greek was never able to accomplish the task, just as we are never able to shoot all the birds, just as the birds are unable to decrease the pile of corpses."

"Yes," said Cuerpo, "but what does all that have to do with rolling a stone up a hill?"

"Look," said Ivar, "tell me how well you know the myth of Prometheus."

GLAUSER

"What am I supposed to think?" said Cero to Glauser, who had slept through the whole thing. "What could I do to prevent it?"

They sat in Glauser's room, on blocks of stone that had fallen out of the ceiling to reveal gaps of sky. Every two minutes and ten seconds Glauser would stand and move, his hands twisting, his eyes darting about. Masonry was scattered about the room. On the bed was a chunk of stone.

Who was dropping the stones, Glauser did not know, but he was certain Thorne was behind it. The first stone had fallen, Glauser liked to think, at the instant when Thorne had twisted shut the lock on his door. Perhaps by locking his door and refusing to come out, Thorne set into process a mechanism that had caused the stones to fall. Or perhaps Thorne had commanded Bosephus to cause the stones to fall. But in any case, thought Glauser, it is Thorne who is trying to kill me.

Glauser did not know what Thorne had looked like before he had locked himself into his room, nor did Glauser know what Thorne looked like now. Glauser had never got a clear look at Thorne's face; it was always covered or in shadow. Glauser had never heard Thorne speak. Bosephus had always spoken for Thorne. If he saw Thorne now, Glauser would not know whether Thorne had changed or not.

"I thought Thorne liked Thannis," said Glauser, moving about the room.

"He did," said Cero.

"He does not like me," said Glauser.

"Nonsense," said Cero.

"No," Glauser said. "Thorne is trying to kill me."

"The stones?" said Cero. "Accidents. This is an old fortress," he said. "Things fall apart."

Glauser explained how the stone had fallen on his bed while he slept.

"Coincidence," said Cero.

Taking out his backpack, Glauser filled it with those of his possessions which had not been crushed by rocks: a stash of food, a half-carton of cigarettes, a small camp shovel, several books, his flashlight, a butane lighter, seven sets of batteries, two candles, a small hand-cranked electric generator. Thorne is cracked, he thought. He put the pack on his back. I must exploit the weaknesses of my prison, Glauser thought.

Glauser left the room, locking the door behind him, hanging a placard reading Do Not Disturb on the knob. He passed the closed rooms and the discolorations on the walls where the portraits of Thorne's ancestors had once hung.

He descended the stone staircase to the second level below ground. Here the walls were rougher, the halls less straight, less rigid, filled with half-alcoves and cubbyholes. The light of the sputtering bulb in the stairwell created an irregular strobe. The pulsations of darkness seemed to Glauser like the wings of a bat flapping back and forth a few inches from his face. What kind of bat? wondered Glauser. A fruit bat? A pug-nosed bat? A tomb bat? A ghost bat?

Glauser continued down the staircase. The stones beneath his feet were loose. Holes in the staircase caught at his feet. There was no light here. He removed a puckered candle from his backpack and lit it to guide his way, occasionally shining the light deep into the holes of the stairway to see if they contained anything.

The landing of the third level showed him one irregular hall, its walls stone-lined, its floor dirt. Glauser continued down the stairs, holding the candle near his body, trying to shield its flame. Where the steps had fallen into decay he leaped down to more stable steps. The stairway became a dirt slope. He continued down and down, passing the openings to other levels and half-levels, holding the candle before him.

When his candle was little more than a butt and the wax

was burning his hand, Glauser set it down on the slope. In bending over the candle to dig into his backpack, he cast a reeling shadow. He removed his flashlight. He left the slope and the dying candle behind, entering the dirt passage, crouching down slightly.

There are no stones here, Glauser thought. He flicked off his flashlight and turned, watching the faint glow of the candle butt from a distance. He listened to the sound of his own breathing. Holding his breath, he listened to the sound of the blood beating slower and slower in his veins. It was the sound of a clock. He breathed in and out and the ticking of the blood clock sped up. The candle butt sputtered out. Glauser lit a cigarette and, switching on the flashlight, began to explore in earnest.

BOSEPHUS

By June, the situation had changed. The temperature had risen ten degrees, making it uncomfortable to be outside. The guards still roamed the walls, but fewer now, fewer each day, as if they were slowly drying out and blowing away. Bosephus did not notice. I am the Needleman, Bosephus thought, sitting in the covered chair he had constructed on the top of the wall, staring out over the waste. He stared out at the hill. Sitting on the wall, he looked through the good lens of the field glasses at the crosses scattered on the hill. He counted the crosses slowly, moving from the bottom of the hill to the top, counting up to 199, then cursing, beginning his count again.

Each morning when he awoke Bosephus would go to Thorne's door. Beneath it, in the crack between floor and door bottom, was a slip of yellow paper either with instructions on it or blank, but always present. Bosephus wondered what would happen the day he went to get the paper and it

was not there. It depends on the heat, he thought. A hot
day, anything can happen.

Bosephus stared out at the hill. He got up from his chair
and, moving it forty paces down the wall, began to count
again. He stopped to look at his arms. The hair on them was
gray with dust. I am slowly turning to dust, he thought. He
was certain his lungs had turned gray. When I speak, Bosephus thought, no words come, only gray clouds of breath.

Bosephus coughed and shook his head. He began to count
again, moving this time from the top of the hill to the bottom. "One," he said. "Two, three." As he neared the end,
his hands shook. He could feel the dust clinging to his body,
trying to stop his count, trying to confuse him. He set the
field glasses on the edge of the wall, half hoping they would
fall and that the good lens would break. Bosephus got up
and moved his chair to the end of the wall, to the corner
where his wall, the east wall, met the north wall. In doing
so, he accidentally tore the canopy over the chair, ripping a
gash for the sunlight to bleed through. When he was seated
again, he could feel the small patch of sun on his chest, slowly
heating its way through his clothing, trying to light him on
fire. He moved his chair slightly. He was prepared to count,
but he had misplaced his field glasses. He looked up and
down the wall for them. He leaned out over the edge of the
wall, staring down at the sand below. Below, in the sand,
something was glinting. He smiled. He unbuttoned his breast
pocket. Inside were two yellow scraps of paper, tightly
folded. He sat down in the chair and unfolded one of them.
It was blank. He looked at the other one. It read, *Needleman:
Siege! Seal it off and wait for the air to run out. Close the tomb.
Thorne.* He twisted in his chair, staring down at the gate
below. It was locked, the bar drawn firmly across it. In the
far corner, smoking a cigarette, was a solitary guard. Bosephus looked at the note again. He remembered the beginning
of the siege and the first, and only, sighting of the enemy.

He remembered the way Thannis' glasses had glinted as the gates were drawn open, the sun bouncing off them. The two guns had fired quickly, the empty shells spitting in an arc back into the courtyard.

Bosephus began his count again, the gun slung across his knees. He could no longer see for darkness. "One," he said. "Two, three."

A Slow Death

PRANCING

He herded them out in the madness of midday heat, butchered the horses before their eyes. He hitched each horse to the center post, hacked off its legs with his axe. The beasts bucked and shied, limped, staggered, lay legless and mad-eyed, stumps awriggle. Their bodies roiled up slow drifts of dust while Bosephus cut through their necks, and even for a time thereafter.

Their narrow heads remained dangling from bridles, astream with flies. Guards cut up carcasses, dragged the pieces over the walls, committed them without further ceremony to the waste.

"Blame the note," said Bosephus. He removed a scrap of yellow paper from his pocket, displayed it in his bloody hands. "I would allow you to eat your fill. Blame Thorne."

Thorne was nowhere. They knocked at his door. They kicked against the bolt-studded metal. Not a word.

Bosephus sat on the east wall in his canopied chair, his gun resting across his knees. He stared out, inscrutable and unaware, motionless as the horse heads. He stared through the field glasses at the hill, counting crosses.

Ivar the Boneless and Roger Cuerpo stood guard at the

corners of the west wall, watching birds fight for horseflesh. Cuerpo removed his rifle from his shoulder, fired three rounds, brought up flurries of feathers. Ivar smoked a cigarette and stared at Cuerpo, leaving his own gun to lean against the wall.

At Thorne's door, the rest drew straws. It was Preter Bedlam who drew short and was made to venture the courtyard. He shuffled through the blood-mud, pushed his hand past the horse heads to grasp the sticky axe handle. He pulled the axe out of the circle of horse heads, flies and gore burning on his forearms.

He looked to his cohorts, lifted the axe in salute. His eyes vanished into dark holes, the roar of shots echoing off the walls, the base of his skull scattering across the courtyard.

"Instructions via Thorne," called out Bosephus. He broke the breach of his shotgun, shook out the casings.

"Nothing personal," he said, reloading.

He stood, moved his chair closer to the catwalk's edge. He adjusted the canopy. He sat down. Elbows on knees, he aimed his rifle. Preter Bedlam's corpse flinched a few inches across the courtyard.

Bosephus stood, turned his chair around to face the waste. He counted crosses.

Cero rapped thrice on the dusty wood.

"Glauser?" hissed Cero. "Glauser, it's Cero."

His cohorts took turns throwing themselves against the door. The wood around the latch splintered away, and they forced the lock. They spilled in, threaded their way through the fallen stones. The holes the stones had left falling from the ceiling spattered them with tattered light.

They chose a cylindrical stone which tightened to a tusk at one end. Four dragged the stone down the hall, into the courtyard. They pushed it up the creaking rungs of the ladder, rolled it down the walkway to Thorne's door.

The four heaved the stone up, took a few ponderous swings. The metal sang out, chimed.

Bosephus stood, stretched. He fumbled a few shells from his jacket pocket, pushed them into the shotgun. He lifted the gun, pointed it at each of the four in turn.

"Any preference to first?" said Bosephus.

He pulled the first trigger, dropping a man.

"Sorry," he said. "Second, I mean."

He ran his hand lightly along the warm barrel, watching the three remaining carriers struggle to keep the stone aloft.

"Not all decrees must be written," he said, and squeezed the second trigger.

Those who dared come at first dark drove back the murder of dry, black crows. They unhitched the horse heads by touch, dragged them by the reins back to their rooms. They cracked the long skulls against the walls, pried apart the bones to suck away the brains, stripped the hair back with fingernails to gnaw out the narrow pockets of hidden flesh. Flecked lips, cheeks, tongue.

Those who came later cut hunks from the five human corpses—picked apart and shit-sprent by birds. They warmed the meat over paper-fed fires in their rooms, choked their lukewarm fellows down.

The few last, coming just prior to dawn, caught at flies, broke bones, sucked marrow. They masticated mouthfuls of blood-soaked mud, staved off hunger another few hours.

THE UNDERGROUND KARST

Glauser sucked stones to deaden the hunger, gathering up tiny pebbles scattered through the tunnels. He licked mouthfuls of mayflies off the dirt walls, creatures all leg and wing. He lapped up whole colonies, wandered in search of more.

He found a stone chamber whose floor sloped down to form a catch basin, the water of which he shared with rats. Asleep, he felt rats scurry across his feet and legs. He killed them when he caught them, trampling their bones and flesh into a thick, dirty paste. He scooped the paste off the dirt, choked it down.

He switched on the flashlight and set it on end, mounding dirt around it to pin its beam to the ceiling. He took his possessions out of his backpack, put them back in again. He drew symbols in the dirt, rubbed them out with the heel of his boot. He dug through the clay at the edge of the chamber, turned up rocks. He clawed up fat white larvae which tasted of rancid butter. Wandering the tunnels, he scraped arrows into the walls. The bore of the flash beam grew dim, reddened. The bulb's wire faded to a pale orange, died out. He fumbled another set of batteries from his backpack, hand-cranked the generator until the bulb was strong and white. With each charge, the batteries weakened.

He slept where and when he pleased, the backpack pillowed beneath his head. He dreamt of insects worrying his eyelids, awoke to find creatures crawling within his clothing. He stripped, consuming all he could find of living things upon his scab-ridden boneheap. He dug a wolf spider out of its hole, swallowed it live. Its eight legs tapped days of indecipherable code against the lining of his stomach.

His hair fell out in patches. He wove the strands into braided crowns. He placed the crowns atop his head, knotted them fast to the remaining tufts of his scalp. He smoked his last cigarette, filter and all. He wandered farther and farther from the staircase. Tunnels ran in all senses, twisting up and down. He started coughing, could not stop.

Chambers became irregular, walls slanted inward or recessed, tunnels collapsing at a touch. Squeezing down stone chimneys, he grabbed handfuls of invisible bats. They nipped his ears in their spasmic ascents, spattered him with a bitter ammoniac guano. He felt lightheaded, his feet pressed against the sides of dark and endlessly descending shafts. He scurried down chalky side passages, dragged his fingers along wet limestone. The puddles he moved through were aswarm with vital luminescences—lethargic creatures, all eye and bone. On his knees, he lapped up water, fish, and slime. He travelled the riddled, expansive terrain of an underground karst, the ceiling so high that even a flash beam commanded by fresh batteries dared not reveal it. His footsteps echoed away into nothingness. The lava crust beneath his feet grew brittle, collapsed. He trod calf-deep imprints across this waste beneath the waste.

He forced his way into a side fissure, hairy with moss. Scraping the moss off, he found veins of pale ants flowing beneath. He licked the wall, swallowed them whole. The ants stung his tongue, the inside of his cheeks, stung him all the way down his throat. His stomach numb and churning, he vomited all up, watched the still-living ants wander blindly across the shale. He kept retching, his face dripping a milky sweat, his ragged bones shaking off his remaining flesh. He wriggled through stalactites and stalagmites, waiting for his will to fail. Cramming himself into a crack, he let water trickle onto his head, down over his closed eyes, down his cheeks. Some seeped into the side of his mouth, the rest dripping off his chin, spreading in a dark stain under his shirt. He felt the spider moving about his stomach, building webs. Pale insects wove homes from the hair of his arms, burrowed their way into the loose folds of his fleshless skin. He swallowed all that crept into his open mouth. He sucked flies into his nose and hacked them out into his mouth. He waited in the dark, slowly shutting himself down, starting with the outer extremities, working inward, putting his parts aside one by one until only the thinnest slit of him was alive. He lay wedged and upright in the dark, starved.

ON THE WALL

Once caught, Ivar struck Cuerpo in the throat and wrested the rifle from his grasp. Swinging the gun by the barrel, he struck Cuerpo just above the shoulder, broke Cuerpo's neck.

He tore the sleeve off Cuerpo's shirt, stuffed it tight into the man's mouth. He sat down on the walkway, continued to eat the horseflesh. He wolfed hunks of meat, watching Cuerpo's eyes flutter. Bosephus, Ivar saw, had remained in his chair on the opposite wall through it all, oblivious for staring out into the waste.

Ivar cut the remaining horsemeat into strips, spread it along the top of the wall. He looked again at Bosephus, saw no difference. He searched Cuerpo's pockets, took his cigarettes, matches, lucky coin.

He dragged the wide-eyed and paralyzed Cuerpo to the edge of the wall, dumped him over. He smoked a cigarette, watched the birds peck the man dead.

None of this until Ivar cut fresh meat from Cuerpo and put that out to dry as well. For a rainy day.

He had his hands full keeping the birds off the meat.

Note in hand, Bosephus fumbled a book of matches from his back pocket. He bent one out, struck it alight.

Needleman: Siege! Seal it off and wait for air to expire. Brick the tomb. Thorne.

He crumpled the note, dropped it and the match down into the courtyard. He went through his pockets, searching for the other note, for the blank. He lit a new match, scanned the surface of his chair. He lit a third match, dropped to his knees, looking under the chair. Stepping slowly the length of the wall, he lit new matches, bringing each near to the ground. He let each sizzle dead against his horned and scarred fingertips, lit new ones until the matches were gone.

He felt along the dark wall, touched the adjoined dark wall. He moved toward the faint glow of a cigarette.

"Do you have a flashlight?" he said, arriving. "Cuerpo?"

"No," said Ivar. "Ivar," he said. "No," he said.

"Lantern?" said Bosephus.

"No."

"Lighter?"

"No," Ivar said. He snapped the safety off his rifle.

"Matches?" said Bosephus. "I heard that," he said. "Please put the gun down."

"I was flicking the safety on," said Ivar. "So I could put it down safely," he said. "I am putting the gun down now," he said. He did not put the gun down.

"Matches?" said Bosephus.

"Two matches," Ivar said.

"Give," said Bosephus. "And the cigarette."

Ivar felt the matches and cigarette leave his hand, catching a shadow of Bosephus's forearm as it shot out of full darkness and vanished back into it again. He listened to Bosephus move along the wall. Lifting his rifle, he tracked the dim glow. Indeed, would have shot had he known in which hand Bosephus held the cigarette. He kept a bead on the glow until the coal ashed over.

Ivar stood, pursued Bosephus along the wall. Just past the corner, he saw a match flare up. By the time he was ready to shoot, the flame had vanished. He smashed into the corner, cursed, turned down the wall. A second match flared ahead, guttered. Ivar pushed forward a few steps. He stopped, listened. He hesitated, retreated.

"Guard?" said Bosephus.

"I am here," said Ivar.

"Did you hear footsteps?" Bosephus said.

"I heard them, yes," said Ivar.

"Did the other guard pass?" said Bosephus.

"No," said Ivar.

"Cuerpo, is it?" said Bosephus. "Not at his post?"

"I haven't seen him," said Ivar.

Bosephus stood silent in the darkness.

"How?" he said. "Ivar, might I ask how you lit your cigarette?" he said.

"I found another match," said Ivar.

"You gave me your matches," said Bosephus.

"Just a last match," said Ivar. "Loose in my shirt pocket," he said. "It must have fallen from the box."

"Do you dare deceive me?" mused Bosephus.

"No, sir," said Ivar.

Ivar stayed stretched flat against the stones in the darkness, holding the glowing cigarette as far above his body as possible. His arm ached from holding it. He made his body flat, all but the arm.

The cigarette coal shook, wavering in the darkness.

"Stop that immediately," said Bosephus.

Ivar stubbed out the cigarette.

"Why did you do that?" said Bosephus.

"You counseled me to," said Ivar.

"I counseled nothing of the kind," said Bosephus.

Ivar said nothing.

"No more matches?" said Bosephus.

"Not one," said Ivar.

"Certain?"

"Dead sure," said Ivar.

Bosephus fell silent. Ivar eased the safety off his gun. Ivar heard two slugs strike off the wall above him, felt chips of stone spat down at him. He listened to Bosephus reload.

"Dead?" said Bosephus.

Ivar said nothing.

"I can hear you breathing!" Bosephus yelled. "Are you going to answer the question posed to you by your superior?"

"I am not dead," said Ivar. "Sir," he added.

"I am sorry to hear that," said Bosephus. "Request of Cuerpo, next you see him, to kill you. Inform him this is an order, mandated from the top."

Ivar listened to Bosephus grunt, heard feet scuffle a bit on stone, heard something hit ground far below, outside the wall.

"Or you kill him, for all I care," Bosephus shouted up from below. "Somebody kill somebody, for God's sake!"

"Yes, sir!" shouted Ivar.

"You won't forget?" said Bosephus.

"No, sir," said Ivar.

"You have to swear," said Bosephus.

"I swear it," said Ivar.

"Kill somebody!" shouted Bosephus, his voice receding. "I ask the smallest of things."

Extermination

Bosephus, Nothing

The ground grew uneven. Bosephus stumbled down, sent up a geyser of birds. Wings battered his body, shot away into the dark. Struggling to his feet, he felt hardness beneath his palm. He let his fingers close on a rough cylinder oddly knobbed at both ends. He reached up, switched his headlamp on, saw bone. He spun the bone out into the waste. He switched off.

He crawled out of the bone field, switched on, swept the light right and left over the earth before him. He twisted his neck, moved the light up the wall. He tilted his head, sent the elongating oval slowly to the ramparts, moved it to shine on the canopy of the chair.

He shifted to stand below the chair. He dropped to his knees, scanned the surface of the earth.

He crawled a line out into the waste. He shone the light back and forth, turned circles, spun slowly to a stop. He crawled a line from where he stopped, found himself within a pile of dead birds, stiff wings scraping cheeks and neck. He stood, kicked them apart with his feet, raised tourbillions of feathers and dust. He stood coughing, shining the light.

· · ·

The sun was coming up, the heat swelling. He found himself on his back, his dead light shining skyward. His knees had worn through his pants, gone stiff. He stared at the raw meat of his hands.

He kicked away the birds which were settling on the bones, scattered them, fluttering and frayed, old umbrellas. He pulled himself afoot, stumbled out into the waste.

He licked his cracked lips, closed his eyes. He opened his eyes to find the hill of crosses. He corrected his course.

He climbed the hill, moved among what he now knew were cacti, touching their pale needles lightly with one hand, tracing the sign of the cross over them with the other. He wandered the hill in the hard sunlight, muttering bad Latin. He counted 199, then 200, then 201. He moved to the opposite side of the hill, lost count. He stumbled down the hillside, stopped one last time to glance back at the hilltop.

He tested his holds and began to climb, knuckling his way up the cracks. He let his fingers caress the bricks, conjuring forth handholds.

He saw Ivar a dark shape above him, leaning out over the wall, staring down.

"Lend a hand, Ivar," said Bosephus.

Ivar lifted his rifle, aimed at Bosephus. He held the barrel a few inches from the fellow's eyebrow. He squinted one eye, sighted down the barrel.

"That's an order," said Bosephus.

"Yes," said Ivar. He held the rifle steady.

"Yes, sir, to you," said Bosephus.

"Goodbye, Needlemind," said Ivar.

Bosephus sprang out from the wall, grabbed the metal barrel with both hands, dragging the rifle and Ivar off the wall. The blast in the barrel scorched his palms, the flash powder burnt his face. He landed on his feet, rolled with the shock, wrenching the rifle from Ivar's limp fingers, stumbling to standing. He fumbled for the trigger, fired.

The bullet kicked up a spray of sand, scattered yellow grains over Ivar's quivering flesh. Bosephus watched the body tense, the blood rushing out of the nose, the mouth.

He lifted Ivar's head, felt down the vertebrae of the neck. He fingered the softened cap of Ivar's skull. His fingertips came away bloody. He wiped them on his shirt. He paced around the corpse. He walked to the wall, began to climb.

Halfway up, he dropped down to the sand again. Rolling the corpse over, he searched through the pockets.

Nothing.

SUFFOCATION

Cero peered past the broken door, entered. Masma walked to the bed, sat on its edge. Cero pointed his finger, counted rocks. Masma examined her own fingers, stared at Cero's emaciated face. His finger hesitated, hesitated, dropped.

"A man with long hair and a beard divided his hair into a number of strands," Cero instructed. "He wove these strands together into a mesh which obscured his face. He sat motionless. When he was prodded, it was found that he was dead, suffocated by his own hair."

"No one suffocates on their own hair," said Masma.

"You don't know," said Cero.

He stood, left the room. She followed.

They came to the end of the dark hall, hesitated together at the outer doorway. They stared out into the blaze of the courtyard.

"I see no guards," said Cero.

Masma shrugged.

"Bosephus?" said Cero.

Masma said nothing.

Cero glanced around, walked out into the heat. He slid across the courtyard, climbed to the walkway. He balanced atop the wall, staring out into the waste. He turned to wave once, then vanished over the far edge.

Masma hesitated, standing in the doorway. She waited until she heard a faint pop, a cork leaving a bottle. Just outside the wall, birds began to gyre. From the doorway, she watched them rise and fall.

CREPUSCULE

Night, and Bosephus heard the birds below, ascreech, tearing Ivar to pieces. Outside the outer wall, the birds began to thicken, made manifold by darkness.

He heard, beneath the clacking of wings, something scrabbling along the base of the wall. He leaned out over the edge, fired his gun down into the waste. He turned, fired it into the courtyard. The shots resonated within his skull. He heard a body drop outside the wall, and thought something dropped inside as well.

"Mere birds," Bosephus hoped aloud.

He shook his fist at the night. He leaped off the wall.

He struck the dirt, rolled. He sprang to his feet, ran forward to crack his face against the dark gate. He clutched it, felt the blood run out of his nose, over the rough oak.

He reloaded the shotgun. He unlocked the gates and, grunting, drew them open. He turned, followed the wall to the door, entered the hallway, felt down past the first door to the second. He turned, fired the shotgun into the hallway behind him, saw the slug throw sparks, felt the shot surge back the length of the empty hall, through him.

He broke down the door, moved forward. His knee jarred

against the bedpost. He groped about, touched a warm leg. He followed it up to a torso, a head.

"Masma, arise!" hissed Bosephus.

He leaped and stood on the bed, straddling her. He jammed the shotgun down hard against her flesh, rammed the barrels down against her skin.

He could hear a slight wind blowing outside, just audible through the stone. Masma squirmed. He pushed the end of the shotgun down harder, ground it into her until she stopped struggling.

He waited. He listened.

He pulled the trigger, felt one hammer click down. No shot rang out. Masma started to whine. Bosephus broke open the breech, reloaded the rifle.

"A mere minute of patience, please, Masma," said Bosephus. "My deepest apologies."

He slammed the breech closed, cocked the hammers. He jammed the gun down. He pulled both triggers, heard the muffled reports. The shocks shook the bed, ran up his legs.

The body below him stiffened, shook.

He remained standing, firmly straddling her, reloading.

Daylight come, she arose and stumbled out, fingering the holes in her mouth and jaw. The ruined flesh was darkening and transforming, acquiring a metallic sheen. She mumbled her way into the courtyard, grimacing for the sunlight. Flies buzzed on her flesh, insinuated the holes in her cheeks.

She stumbled around the edge of the walls. She fell, pulled herself up, fell again. She stopped at the open gate, stared out. She struck her tongue through her cheek, tasted air and scabbed flesh.

She turned, continued walking the purgatory of walls. She fell, stayed down.

She heard the sound of wings beating together. A crow

came near her face, its head cocked to one side. She felt the claws of another bird in her back, its beak pecking at her spine. She divined the influx of birds, felt their shapes falling down darkly upon her.

Bosephus turned the chair around, stared down into the courtyard. From time to time, he stood to adjust the canopy. He smoked a cigarette. He watched the birds strip Masma clean. The birds began tearing each other apart. Bosephus stood, clapped.

He shot the birds, one after another, until the courtyard was littered with them and all ammunition gone. He turned the chair around, lifted the broken field glasses to his eyes. He stared out into the waste. He waited for nightfall.

Usurpation

I am here at the timberline, having just arrived. Ebé is not here yet. Or he has come and gone. I have looked for footprints and have found none, which might mean something. But then again, Ebé does not often leave footprints.

The timberline is much as I expected. Although it can hardly be called a line. There are gaps, and the line itself is more of a jag. But this much is true: below me are trees, above spreads bare slope.

Am I in the right place? Should I stand on the bare slope or in the trees?

It is true that I am at the timberline, but I am only at one point on said line. Perhaps Ebé is at another point miles away, hiding in the trees, anxiously fingering the object in his pocket, assuming it is in his pocket. While I, miles away, take the Ziploc bag out of my pocket, smooth it out, open it, close it, crumple it into a ball, put it away.

I am on time, assuming my watch is correct.

Looking at the place, I wonder if in fact it is the correct place. Did I not curve rather slightly as I climbed? No, it looks like the place, except that Ebé is not here. Where I am standing the ground is barren.

I could vanish in the trees!

No, this is the place.

Two questions above all others: What is the object this time, and why the timberline?

The last time the object would not fit within the plastic bag. Ebé handed it to me and then watched as I tried to cram it in. It would not go.

"No problem," said Ebé. "All he really needs is the digit."

"The ring?" I said.

"The trigger," he said. "You do the honors," he said.

I had to borrow Ebé's knife. Reduction made, it fit nicely.

But that was last time, not this time. This time there would be a different object.

I have looked behind some of the nearer trees. I look behind a tree, then leap back. It is important for me to be as visible as possible. Ebé, however, must be as invisible as possible. In this and in many other points we differ. My role is to dispose of the object. Ebé's role is to collect the object. The object's role is to be collected, and then disposed of.

Is there a method by which one can determine the object to come from the object that preceded it? If so, such a method has escaped me.

But is *object* indeed the correct word? Will this word not rather lead to confusion?

I am here at the timberline, speculating. I have looked behind several hundred trees, but have not found Ebé. I have looked up and down the slope, but have seen nobody.

It was a hard climb up. Now that I am here, I must face the fact that the climb was, perhaps, in vain.

He is not behind this tree, either. Perhaps he still struggles up the slope, burdened by the object. If the object is a) large, b) bulky, c) heavy, d) all of the above, Ebé is likely to be detained. But does the object have any of these properties?

I cannot answer any of my questions.

Another question I cannot answer is: Why the timberline?

"Ebé," I cry. "Ebé."

"E," I hear. "E."

Do I call out again? Do I hastily depart? These are some of the questions a man waiting at the timberline might ask himself. I stamp my feet, beat my arms against my body, watch the sun disappear.

There! I tell myself when the sun vanishes. Now I have done it, I think. Now I have really done it.

Or if it was not I who did it, was it Ebé?

The Abbreviated and Tragical History of
The Auschwitz Barber

When the Auschwitz Barber takes the stand, he claims he is no barber at all, that he is a Bolivian businessman named Altmann.

"You wrong me," he whines.

The Defense asks the Auschwitz Barber to lift his hands above his head and turn his palms to the jury.

"Are these," says the Defense with a flourish, "the hands of a barber?"

The observers applaud. The jury is quickly rushed out. The Auschwitz Barber is acquitted.

The newsmagazines show pictures of the Auschwitz Barber consorting with other famous barbers—the Dachau Barber, the Treblinka Barber, the Klaus Barber. In Bolivia, people get haircuts.

A Conversation
with Brenner

The edge of the counter took shape, then the end posts of the bed, little bits of order retched from the dark. He could see a lightening of the darkness. He watched the flesh build around it.

"Hello," he said, speaking slowly. "I am Ernst Jünger. Were you expecting me?"

Things continued to form themselves. The closet door, the tube leading to the sack.

"You understand my English?" said Jünger. "Do I speak clearly?"

He moved to the bed and sat down on its edge.

"You are Mr. Brenner?" he said.

Taking things from his pockets, he placed them on the bed, lining them up. He shined the penlight in the man's eyes. He nudged up one of the bandages, twisting a lock of hair out from under it. With a tiny pair of scissors, Jünger snipped the hair off, placing it in a plastic bag.

"See how they fold up?" Jünger said. "They are very small," he said.

He snipped off one of Brenner's fingernails.

He looked through the closet.

"What do you think of foreigners?" said Jünger. "I am a

foreigner, perhaps you know. Sometimes I wonder what people think."

He went through pockets, through wallet and address book, pocketing the latter.

"No opinion?" he said. "Perhaps you think I am making conversation," he said.

Jünger pulled the blankets back. He pried Brenner's hands open. He slit the bandages around Brenner's mouth and pried the teeth apart with a metal nail file, shining the flashlight down the man's throat.

"All right, Mr. Brenner," he said, "you have had your fun."

He turned Brenner onto his side. The tube to the bag became taut. Unbuttoning Brenner's gown, Jünger pulled the fellow's buttocks apart, holding the penlight with his teeth, shining it into the anus, poking at the red pucker with an index finger. He opened the packet of gel and smeared it on the very place and probed again.

"Where is everybody, Mr. Brenner?" Jünger said.

He swept the tiny beam of his flashlight from one end of the room to the other. He sat down on the bed.

"Now, Mr. Brenner," he said, "we can be friends, can we not?"

He watched Brenner's eyes to see what they would do.

Jünger said, "You know about Kaspel? He did not want to be friends."

Jünger took the scissors out and cut away the bandages. He cut apart the stitches, tearing them apart carefully, shining the light.

Jünger went to the door, stood looking at the room number. He walked to check-in.

"There has not been a mistake?" he said.

"What?" said the attendant.

"Could you look again?" Jünger said.

"Look?" the attendant said.

"Not look?" said Jünger.

He went back to the room.

"You are Brenner?" he said.

He sat down on the bed.

"Look into your soul, Mr. Brenner," Jünger said. "Mr. Brenner?" he said.

Jünger sat on the edge of the bed. He lit a cigarette, smoking it to the filter.

He smoked another.

Then another—until it was dark.

Stung

His stepfather's body was genuflected as if disposed at prayer, a bee wriggling on it, its stinger inserted into the naked back. The boy took a pillow from the bed, slid his hands inside the pillowcase, used the pillow to push the body over. His stepfather teetered and fell, crushing the bee beneath him. The mouth of the fellow had been sewn shut with carpet thread, which had begun to tear out through the lips. The hands and feet were swollen, and the face was so puffy that the cheeks overwhelmed the eyes—two squinting slits sunk deep into flesh.

The boy used the pillow to move the arms around a little. He took his hands out of the pillow and put it on the knees and sat, hearing the knees crack when they slowly straightened beneath his weight. He sat there staring down at the body. The carpet thread had been sewn in blood-tipped cross-stitch all the way along the lips, nine stitches in all, the outer two torn all the way through so that there was an exit through which a bee, its wings plastered back against its abdomen, could, and did, squirm.

Through the glass doors he saw his mother lying on her towel, her bare back up, her head hidden beneath a bleached, floppy straw hat. He hesitated, until he saw her move.

He slid the door open.

"I'm coming out," he called. "My eyes are closed."

He walked toward her tentatively, listening to the sound the straps made in dragging up her arms to her shoulders, pulling the sheer triangles of fabric up over her breasts. Through hooded eyes, he watched her arrange herself.

"All right," she said.

He opened his eyes very wide. "I just got home," he said.

"What time is it?" she said.

He shrugged. "I stopped at a friend's," he said.

"What friend is that?" she said.

"Nobody," he said. "You wouldn't know him."

She leaned back onto the towel, crushing the rim of the hat. Eyes closed, she tipped her neck back, exposed her face to the sun.

"Benny out at the hives?" the boy said.

"Upstairs, I think," his mother said.

"Has he been out to the hives today?" he said.

"Who wants to know?" she said. "He'll probably go out with you, either way."

"If I want to go," the boy said.

"If you want to go," she said. She turned her head away. "Leave me alone awhile," she said.

He sat down on the hot concrete next to her.

"What you been up to today?" he said.

"The usual," she said.

"You seen much of Benny?" he said.

"Same old, same old," she said.

"What has he been doing?" he said.

She locked her fingers behind her head. She pulled her head up to look at him.

"What little thing did I just ask of you?" she said. She let her head fall slowly back onto the towel. "Can't a woman tan?"

.   .   .

There were bees crawling about on the body and through the carpet and up the legs of the furniture. He went into the bathroom, opened the cabinet behind the mirror, took out a glass misty from water deposits and toothpaste spit. He dumped the toothbrushes out of it.

He carried the glass back into the bedroom and began to fill it with bees. He took bees by their damp wings, lifting them up as their abdomens twitched, dropping them down into the glass. He opened the top drawer of the chest of drawers, fingered through underwear and medals and Boy Scout awards until he found a plastic bag full of rings, traces of powder in it. He dumped the rings out into the drawer, turned the bag inside out, licked the powder off of it, slipped the bag down over the top of the glass.

He shook the glass until the bees were maddened. His mother was lying on her stomach, bikini top off again. He took the plastic bag off the glass.

"Get out of my sun," his mother said, without looking up.

He took a step back, put the plastic bag back on the glass.

"Where is a rubber band?" he said.

"Try the rubber band drawer," she said.

He went into the kitchen, opened the half-drawer, untangled a rubber band from the mess. He smoothed the bag down around the glass, putting the rubber band over the bag, staring at her out the kitchen window.

He took the shears from the knife block on the counter. He removed the latex gloves from their arthritic agony behind the faucet, shook them straight, slipped them on. They were warm and moist against his skin. He felt his hands already becoming slippery in them.

He climbed the stairs to the body, saw another bee crawl-

ing on the face. The bee made its way along the bridge of
the nose and tucked itself down into the nostril, the end of
its pulsing abdomen hanging out. He reached out, pinched
his stepfather's nose shut, watching the bee's abdomen split
and ooze yellow fluid.

His gloved fingers held the shears awkwardly. He opened
the paired blades, sliding the bottom blade between his stepfather's lips, beneath the carpet thread. He cut through the
thread, sheared off some of the lip with it. The opened flesh
remained dull and bloodless.

Filling the mouth was a bolus of dead bees, squashed and
stuck together, stingers missing. He poked at the clump,
broke it apart, flicked smaller clusters of bee pieces out of
the mouth and onto the carpet. The throat was crammed
with bees as far down as he could reach, and farther.

He peeled the gloves off and left them bunched up, inside
out, on his stepfather's bare chest. He moved the stiff jaw
and pulled it wide open for the ceiling light to drive the
shadows out of the mouth. He took a good, long look.

He looked at her naked back, his eyes tracing her spine up
to the wide-brimmed hat hiding her face. He pulled the plastic bag off the jar slowly, watched the rubber band flip off
and spin out over the concrete. He leaned over his mother,
shook the bees out onto her hat, watching them slide down
along the rim.

"Whatever the hell you are doing, cut it out," his mother
said, not moving.

He watched the bees wander over the pale, matted straw,
watched each err through the vastness of that ridged ex-
panse, test wings, vanish into the sky.

"No sign of Benny," the boy said.

"Hmm," she said.

"Any ideas?" he said.

"Try the bedroom," she said.

"I didn't see him," he said. He stuffed the plastic bag into the glass, set the glass down on the concrete. "I'm going out to the hives," he said. "Coming?"

"No," she said.

"Come on, for a change," he said.

She sighed, stretched her fingers, her arms, her back. "Close your eyes," she said.

He did not close them.

He stood among the bees, spraying them with smoke. She kept her distance, leaning against the willow a few meters away, arms folded loosely over her bare stomach. He opened the hive and slid out a slat thick with honeycomb, aswarm with bees. He sprayed smoke over them until they fell off the slat, back into the hive. He felt the bees in his hair, on his hands, on his face.

"Know anything about bees?" the boy said to her.

She shrugged. She looked at him bored, looked coldly away.

He felt the sound of them all through him. He tasted the honey. He broke off a bit of honeycomb, cleaned the dead bees out of it, chewed on it.

"What about sewing?" he said.

"I've done it before," she said.

"Clothes?" he said.

She shrugged. "Among other things," she said.

He held the rest of the honeycomb out to her.

She shook her head.

"Come over here," he said. "Mother."

He watched her bare feet leisurely picking their way back down the path, away from him, without hesitation. He lined the grooves and slid the slat back in place. He sprayed himself with smoke, watched bees slow, stop, drop off.

.   .   .

She had taken the hat off, sticking it on the fence post. The wind rocked it back and forth, ruffling the brim. The sun beat down on her back. Her eyes were closed.

"Benny's dead," he said.

She didn't say anything.

"Benny's dead," he said. "I mean it."

"Don't be tiresome," she said. "Just get the lotion."

He stood there a while, but then walked over and got the lotion from where it was by the glass doors. He carried it over, dropped the bottle onto the crease of her back.

"Rub it into me," she said. "Into my back."

He kneeled down beside her, opened the bottle, squeezed some out onto his fingers, began to rub it into her skin.

"Undo my top," she said. "Rub in circles, and evenly."

He fumbled her catch loose and pulled the straps off her shoulders and down her arms. He made long circular strokes until the white swirls of lotion vanished into her back.

"Good for a beginner," she said. "Don't neglect the sides."

He rubbed down the sides of his mother's body, feeling how the swelling edges of his mother's breasts were hot and dry under his lotion-slick fingers. He finished the back, remained hanging over her.

She stretched her bare arms far out in front of her. Ever so slowly she turned over. She tilted her head back.

"Now the front," she said.

He stayed there, on his knees, feeling the strength of his mother's small hands, pulling him, pulling him in.

My Possessions

I got my things, and left. I was seeing the place for the last time, and happy I was. I did not turn around, for I knew that the pair of them were there, their pale faces staring dumbly through the glass. I walked straight ahead through the rain, the doubled paper bag of my possessions in my hands. Within were my possessions, forced side by side, one atop the other. *Completely disorganized, completely.* They will never be back in order, I thought. I worried that some of my possessions had already been broken in being forced side by side, one atop the other, into the doubled paper bag. It might have been wiser for me to have stayed in that place, for the sake of my possessions. But I could not stay there, in that place, with Paya and Trollé literally reducing me to nothing. Through their influence I had become less and less a thinking entity, more and more a brute beast. At times, it amazed me that I had not gone mad in that place, though there were days. This day being the last of them, being such a day of days that I had risen quietly to my feet, leaving the post of observation which had been thrust upon me, leaving them one atop the other in the parlor. I concentrated all my efforts on ascending the twelve stairs. I threw my possessions into the doubled paper bag kept under the bed all those years. I descended the stairs, opened the door, threw myself into the rain. The water licked my face, cleansing me, welcoming me. I am leaving forever, I thought. I whispered, Forever, forever, forever. I am *gone* forever, I thought, rephrasing. To assure myself of the truth of this, I stated it aloud several hundred times, *I am gone forever*, to the surprise of the passersby. I could not blame them for stopping, for I knew only too well the state in which I suffered, the appearance I made after having suffered all those years in that place with Paya and Trollé trying to destroy me. They could not know that now, soaked with rain, I felt my health rush back to me. It was all behind me, they did not know. There behind me, I knew, was the place, with its façade, with its firm, thick door, with its so-called French windows, the inside drapes with folds just so. The wooden slats which separated the small panes of glass would dissect their faces as they stared out the window at my back. I did not look back. I felt them staring. Paya and Trollé: two pale faces framed by thick white hair, fetished by the wooden slats, holding each other fast. They will attack each other now, I thought. I shifted the doubled paper bag in my hands. Now, thought I, they will turn upon each other, they will destroy each other, just as they planned to destroy me. They had approached me *under the guise of friendship*, though finally, almost too late, I found their friendship was destruction. They opened their arms to consume me, and to consume my possessions. They had coaxed from me my invaluable possessions one by one until now I had little enough left, barely enough left to fill a single, doubled paper bag. Had I not taken my few possessions and left, I would soon have had nothing left—of possessions, of self. The rain ran down my hair and into my face, and I moved a few steps forward, farther away from them. I hugged my doubled paper bag tightly, felt inside it the shapes of my possessions. All jumbled, *probably ruined*. I had thrown them into the sack all at once, so as not to lose my opportunity, but Paya and Trollé had not even tried to stop me. I had suffered through them all those years, had felt their eyes on me all those years, yet they did not bother to disentangle themselves from each other when I left. Possibly they did not even miss me. They had no use for me. I was all used up. It had been right for me to leave. Had I not left, they would have thrown me out. I had spent my days attempting to please those once dear, gaining nothing but abuse, and finally was to be discarded. "A rind of fruit!" I cried, "A mere eggshell!" They had allowed me to leave them on a *night pouring rain*, and had not even wished me *adieu*. The soggy bottoms of the doubled paper bag dropped out, scattering my possessions over the paving stones. "My possessions!" I cried, falling to my knees. Paya and Trollé watched through the window, laughing at my dilemma. If they watched at all. In all likelihood, they had not seen my possessions fall, had not seen me fall to my knees. They did not care whether I walked or fell. They were not watching. They were still in the parlor, still entwined, unaware that I had left the place of observation thrust upon me. I pulled my possessions together, into a heap in the street. Paya and Trollé were tearing their robes open now, I thought, their long hair loose and streaming around them. They had no need of me. A pillow placed in a chair served just as well. I arranged my possessions in two piles, one unbroken possessions, the other broken possessions. The rain came through my robe, soaking my back, chilling me. The rain ruined my papers and books. I transferred them to the pile of my broken possessions. No doubt my health would suffer from the exposure. I could still return to that place, I thought, quietly open the door, climb the stairs. I could still enter the parlor, slide into my chair, without their having missed me. I stared at the two piles before me on the ground, the one small useful pile of my possessions, the other large useless pile of my possessions. I looked through the small pile, through the large pile, pushed the piles together. All these useless possessions, so many mere things. I scattered my possessions over the cobblestones with my hands and, in rage, turned and looked. Behind me I saw that place pale and luminous, Paya and Trollé in the window, their pane-framed faces staring with the greatest intensity. I looked around me. The street was empty, save for my ruination. I groped my way to a doorframe and sat down, out of sight, out of the rain. I possessed nothing. I had nowhere to go.

After Omaha

We hung the bacon in the trees—great slabs of the stuff that we had had cut for the occasion.

We waited.

Nothing.

"Oh, my Lord!" I said, slapping my forehead. "The wires!"

"The wires!" said E.J. "The wires!"

I sent him to purchase some. I turned on the floodlights and scared the flies away. When I heard the car pull out, I went into his kitchen to look around. Meanwhile, the idiot came back with thirty-gauge wire!

Can you believe it?

And not even a receipt!

I had no choice but to wait for him to correct his mistake. Of course, I looked at the layout. Occasionally, I looked into the sky. Wouldn't you have?

All right, we wrapped the wire around the nails, stretched it taut from point to point. E.J. went around crimping and tightening while I plucked each span, listening.

The flies were all over the meat again.

E.J. ran about shooing them away. "Shoo, you flies, shoo!" he insisted, waving his tiny hands.

"That does it," I said.

"I can hardly wait!" E.J. said. "I can almost taste it!" he said, beating at air with his little hands.

We cut the lights. We stayed nearby, crouching, well out of sight.

"What's happening?" said E.J. "Is anything happening?"

In Omaha, I had been kept at a distance, behind the barricades—as were the rest.

"Soon," I said. "Soon."

Omaha. At first I had been unsure of myself. I had taken notes while the others pushed from behind, crushing me against the barricade. A uniformed man had from time to time cracked his stick over my head.

I looked at the arrangement, tableau, assemblage, what-have-you. Where is everybody? I wondered. Where was the press, for example?

E.J. said, "Well?"

"Ssshhhh!" I said. "Listen!"

We listened for motion, for the dull flapping of heavy, holy wings. We sat for hours, waiting. The only sound was the flies and the rotting of the meat.

Hey, Luciano!

That was the year my father was shot for giving bad directions. That was the year my mother's motherness began to beat its wings against her bones as it died. She wandered without purpose, yelling at dish towels, eggs, shower curtains. My father raked grass, pulled weeds, clipped back hedges, working until well after dark in the gray of the porch light. That year, I could look down from my bed and see him weeding still, his body in the tiny light casting shadows which reeled in and out of the night. When I awoke he was out there, whistling, crawling on his knees, armed with gloves and trowel. The neighbors appeared to be frightened by the changes in our lives. I spent my time fleeing from my mother, hiding from my father. I dug a place for myself behind the hedge. I watched the cars drift by, noting their make and color, sometimes tracing their license number in the dirt with my stolen weeder.

When the Cadillac pulled up, my father grabbed the rake. From my hiding place, I watched and listened, and heard him tell them from there, shouting. I heard them thank him and saw them drive away, and heard my mother in the house—her own afflicted sounds and the sounds she was inflicting on that which surrounded her. Cars put on brakes, slowed. Some stopped. A man got out and wandered in front of our yard and our neighbor's yard, demanding justice. I threw myself flat and smelled the rich, worked earth.

My father exchanged rake for hoe and hoe for spade. I threw pebbles until my pile was gone. A Cadillac pulled up. My father kind of leaned against the pole and then the pole broke apart and he twisted off. When I looked for the car, the car was gone. The spade would come clean, I predicted, but the deepest grains of the wood handle would retain the stain. The blood gathered around his head and slowly slid toward a crack in the cement.

Who would take care of the lawn now?

My father called out meekly, as if embarrassed. Nobody could see me. Nobody knew I was there. Nobody could prove anything. I scratched out the license number from the earth, effacing every link between me and this and other crimes.

Shift-Work

Second nail he drove in went in easier than the first. Third went easier still. But it was tough going into the table. Son of a bitch, thought Davies. A knot, perhaps.

Harker was going for coffee.

"Davies, care for a cup?" he yelled.

Davies threw his jacket over his hand.

"I've already had three," said Davies.

"Decaf?" said Harker. "It'll do you good."

"I'll pass," said Davies.

When Harker was gone, Davies drove in another nail. It was difficult to do it one-handed. He had to poke the nail in deep enough that it would stay vertical while he hit it. The first hit had to be right on the money or the nail would just dig a semilateral gouge and get all fouled up in the bones.

Harker was off jawing with some of the others.

"Hey, Davies!" he called. "What do you think of that?" Harker said.

"What?" Davies shouted back.

"Come on!" said Harker. "Don't play smart. We want to know your opinion, Davies."

"I completely agree!" Davies said.

"That's Davies," said Harker.

Davies got another nail started. He tore paper towels off

the roll with his teeth and used his free hand to sop up the tabletop. He dropped paper towels, soggy and dripping, under the table.

"Davies," said the boss. "What are you doing here?"

"Just finishing up," said Davies. "Don't mind me."

"You'll lock it up?" said the boss.

"Yes, sir, you can count on me, sir," said Davies.

The main lights went off. It was quiet. In the silence, Davies could think.

Davies thought.

Job Eats Them Raw,
with the Dogs
An Undoing

I

BREAKING GROUND

Bone Job clawed his way through the smooth wood of the coffin lid, wearing his finger bones to stubs. He wormed his way up through the loamy soil, pulled himself skyward by the roots of trees.

He walked the dusty cemetery road, bones clicking, shards of sack fluttering, skull fixed in a grin.

"What a glorious day to search for God!" proclaimed Job.

He examined the slight knobs of finger left above the knuckles, worried that when he met God he would be unable to shake God's hand.

HAERESIS

The sun beat down. He walked through forest and field.

"My only fault," Job revealed to the stinkbug crawling along his radius, "was that I was Job." He stopped, gave a fleshless smile, flicked the stinkbug weedward. "God's only fault was that God was God," said Job.

"What does Job declare?" Job cried aloud, in distress. "*Is* God still!"

LAMENTATION

He walked ashen paths, his bones growing gray with dust. He wiped his bones clean, but the dust of the earth continued to trouble him. It trickled between his bare joints, stopped them up. His steps went jerky. He lamented onward.

"My joints—they bind, they petrify!" he cried. "Yet shall I curse the dust which, serving God, heaps affliction upon me? What is Job, but bones? And dust, but the will of God? What is man but dust, and dust but the son of man? What is man's soul but dust, and man's body but dustbin?"

Job stopped, listened for Zophar, Bildad, and Eliphaz to babble their response from deep in their rocky plots. Nothing but insects and birds.

RIGOR MORTIS GENUFLECTUS

Job Saint-Vitused down the path, his left knee joint packed tight with dust. The leg had turned straight and stiff, unbending. He heaved it along spastically.

"*Rigor mortis genuflectus* has joined my afflictions. Lord have pity!" prayed Job.

He pitched forward into the dirt. Striking the kneecap with a fleshless fist, he managed to crack his metacarpals.

"Affliction!" cried Job.

He pounded on his patella, attempted to unscrew it. After hours without success, he agonized himself to standing. The knee, he found, had regained suppleness of its own accord.

"Salvation!" he proclaimed, and continued on in pursuit of his way.

HEART OF AFFLICTION

Striding toward him was a man wearing a red-and-black plaid shirt and suspenders. The man carried, slung over his shoulder, a double-edged Redline axe.

Job quickened his pace.

"God, I presume?" said Job, extending the ruins of a hand.

"Not quite," said the lumberjack. "But put her there."

They shook hands warmly.

"I could have sworn . . ." said Job, shaking his skull. "Uncanny resemblance."

The lumberjack shook his head. "God don't have no axe like this," he said.

"I must admit," said Job, reaching out to stroke the axe. "Without doubt, a precision instrument of fine quality."

Swinging the axe off his shoulder, beckoning for Job to follow, the lumberjack left the path. The pair walked through young aspen and birch, Job trailing behind. The lumberjack wrapped his arms around trees, moving from tree to tree until he found one he could not reach around.

"Here's an eyeful for you," said the lumberjack.

He held the axe handle between his knees, spitting into the cups of his palms. He lifted the axe and, with a single blow, cut the tree through.

"Affliction!" cried Job. "What sin have I sinned, Lord, that I too have not received an axe of this caliber? My God, my God, why hast thou forsaken me?"

"Affliction?" said the lumberjack. "You want affliction? You don't even know what affliction is!"

THE HOLY CITY, AFAR

The trees thinned out, disappeared entirely. At the base of the distant hills, they discerned a walled city, a smooth lake before it. They slept on the edge of the woods, in the early morning continuing toward the city.

"The holy city?" said Job. "Beside the cloudless sea?"

"You got it," said the lumberjack.

"The light of God upon its face? The gates thrown open wide?" said Job.

"None other," said the lumberjack. "By day, that is."

BEHOLD, THE SHARPNESS
OF THE BLADE

In a field of trampled wheat on the edge of the city, they came across a woman. Her hands were tied behind her back. A dirty, frayed rope led away from her waist to a thick stake in the ground.

"You must help me," she said, seeing them.

"She is our sister in affliction," exhorted Job. "We should render her service."

The lumberjack approached the woman, axe held high. He halved her, quartered her. He kept chopping her finer and finer, until all trace of her had vanished.

"Now that's affliction!" cried the lumberjack.

The lumberjack turned, ran back toward the trees.

Job looked at the holy city, then at the receding figure of the lumberjack, then back at the holy city. Bowing low to the gates thrown open wide, he turned from them, ran shouting his pursuit.

MUCH SUPPLICATION

"Lord, I move forward but thou art not there, and backward but I cannot perceive thy presence. I turn to my left hand and find thee not at all; I turn to my right hand and thou art absent. How long must thy servant attend before he may hold the blessed weapon of thy mercy in his hands?

Thy will be mine,
Job

P.S. Speaking more directly to the matter of the weapon of mercy, I would prefer a Redline axe. If *I* had one to give, Lord, I would give it thee forthwith."

VALE OF TEARS

Spring rains washed the dust from Job's bones. Soft tendrils of mold sprouted from his spine. Water poured through his empty spaces. Chipmunks mistook him for a tree. Birds pilfered his bones for their nests. In summer, the sun bleached him. In autumn, red leaves, paper-thin scrolls of birch bark, lodged within his ribs. In winter, his parts fled him. He curled up in a snowbank, awaited a thaw.

TRANSUBSTANTIATION

He ate rot and tree mold, shat grubs and maggots. He swabbed the insides of his ribs clean with handfuls of salt grass. Masticated mint leaves worked miracles for his breath.

STANDING ON THE EDGE

He tore stiff whips from the willows, weaving them together for shelter. With the thaw, the beavers pilfered his hut strand by strand. He awoke to find the hut gone, a beaver gnawing on the tip of his coccyx.

"Affliction!" cried Job.

The beaver scuttled back, watched from a distance, fled.

"What are bones but sticks and stones? And what God if not the master builder? And what Job if not scrap lumber? Use me roughly, Lord, to fill the gaps, but discard me not.

"And provide the axe," Job prayed. "Amen."

He wandered on the edge of the forest, scaling the trees at night to sleep skewered in their branches. He gathered grubs and fungi from under rocks. He swallowed handfuls of poisonous berries, watched them drop through his jaws, rattle off his ribs. From the edge of the forest, he saw the holy city, distant, floating in a mist. Birds built nests in his pelvic girdle. Hatchlings skittered within him, demanding food. He spent hours eating, but was never satisfied.

DESPOND

Fungi consumed his feet, crept up his legs. Termites dug into his bones, consuming the pithy marrow which the maggots had passed over. He was aswarm with insects.

He mounted a large rock and stared out at the distant city. He stood atop the rock. He stopped moving. He felt things moving through him. He watched the sun slide down into the water by the city—as much as he could see of it through the trees. He did not move a muscle, having no muscles. He did not move anything he had, not even a bone.

But, in thought, he lamented.

II
———

LOPPED

The woman who wriggled her way past was nothing but stumps. She moved inchworm-style, hunching her spine and flattening, making insignificant forward progress. Her long hair tangled around her torso, setting off her nudity, impeding her already limited mode of locomotion.

Job stirred, cracking his weary bones alive.

"Might I trouble you, Miss?" he said.

After an awkward manipulation of stumps and flailing failures, the woman rolled over onto her back.

"What is it this time?" she said.

"Excuse me, do I know you?" said Job. "Can you tell me what season this is?"

"Spring," said the woman.

"I see," said Job. "Excuse me for prying, but might I ask if your limbless condition is the result of an encounter with a gentleman in possession of a Redline axe?"

"Just what are you implying?" said the woman.

"If you prefer not to elaborate, I respect your wishes."

"I should slap you for that," said the woman.

"Pardon me for saying," said Job, "but in your case that is a literal impossibility."

"You men are all alike!" she said, sobbing dryly.

"A double-edged Redline?" Job said. "It is truly a small thing I ask of you."

"Follow your heart," said the woman.

Job fell off the rock. He pulled himself up, readjusting his scapulae, dusted off his sackcloth shards. He took a few tentative, shambling steps, stopped, looked down through his ribs.

"Heart?" he said, puzzled. "Heart?"

ATUMESCENCE

The woman, when he returned several days later, had progressed five hundred yards. He approached her.

"Mightn't I borrow *your* heart?" he ventured.

"Get away from me, creep," said the woman.

"Alas," said Job. "My flesh has withered and fallen into

decay. My heart has dissolved into powder and is scattered. What is Job but lower than dust, dust but the desiccated fibers of Job's dark heart?"

"Poetry!" shrieked the woman. "You really know how to win a girl's heart, don't you? Care to woo me?"

"Alas," said Job. "Job is all bone, but what is Job now without his bone? Take, O Lord, my floating rib, but provide in exchange my fleshy bone."

He attended a moment, staring up into the sky.

"What are you waiting for?" said the woman.

"I fear I do not find myself in possession of the proper equipment for wooing," said Job. "I will have to decline."

"It's me, isn't it?" said the woman, weeping.

INDICATION OF GRACE

He followed the woman's trail backward, turning to see the woman slowly humping away from him, toward the city. Come nightfall, taking shelter in a dry riverbed beneath a bridge, Job inventoried his bones. He began with the phalanges on his left foot, ended with phalanges on the right foot. He pulled each bone off, polished it on his rags, replaced it. He worked his way up one side of his skeleton, down the other.

As to his finger stubs, should he count each worn bone as "one" or as a fraction of the original whole? It seemed a necessity to regularize his counting technique, to establish fixed values governing varying possibilities. And what of fractured bones, bones which no longer functioned but remained in place? Job felt himself culpable for a lack of planning. Yet there was no point in arresting the count now. He continued on.

His bone count was two bones more than it had been the day before! Job was gaining bones!

He fell to his knees, singing praises to the Lord for this palpable sign of grace.

Later, he realized that what he had thought was one of his bones was the skull of a muskrat which had somehow clove to his clavicle. Which left him one bone to the good. He did not search for a second falsified bone, wisely choosing not to tempt God.

CLEAR-CUT

Job saw three stumps, three feet high, firmly rooted in the soil. Their cut trunks had been stripped of branches and foliage, and lay in piles near the road.

Examining the stumps, Job found that the cuts cut straight across, without bevel. Without the angry furred spot where the last wood snaps.

The work of a Redline.

Job leaped from stump to stump, crazed with desire.

BLOOD

Job descried a fleshy man. The man waved both arms, beckoning to Job from the road.

"Halloouuu!" the man yelled.

He had a long gray beard. Job tried to ignore him. The man's boots came crashing toward him. Job did not look up.

"Hey," the man said. "Don't you know who hails you?"

"I am pursuing the path of my salvation," said Job. "The Lord will justify no vain delays."

"Do you know what day today is?" said the man.

"In all likelihood you plan to tell me," said Job.

"Passover," said the man.

"Passover?" said Job.

"Take cover," said the man.

"Do I look as though taking cover will do me any good?" said Job, poking his hand up through his rib cage.

"Frankly, no," said the man. He looked around. "You don't happen to know of any inns nearby, do you?"

"Do I resemble a road map?" said Job, preparing to leave.

"Hold it," said the man, grabbing him. "Not so fast." He lifted the struggling Job high above his head. "We have to help each other in this cruel world," the man said.

"Rape!" accused Job.

"Nothing of the kind," said the man. "Religion."

He spun Job around and around, slammed him to the earth. He sat on Job's spine, placing his heel tight against the back of Job's skull. He pulled Job apart bone by bone. He stacked the bigger bones in a pile to his right, the smaller in a pile to his left.

"What, Lord, does such ill treatment signify?" appealed Job.

"Shut it," said the man.

He popped Job's feet off at the tarsals. The rest of the leg bones he left together, pulling the femurs from their head sockets, then cramming the legs, tarsal first, into the ground. He bent the legs at the patella so that the femurs crossed, tying the femurs together with salt grass twisted into long, knotted cords, forming of Job two posts and a lintel.

"Alas!" cried Job, waxing poetic. "What is Job but bones, and what bones if not Job? My flesh has withered, my bones are otherwise employed. What remains of Job with which Job can meet God?

"I do not blame thee, O Lord, but let the axe resolve my future affliction. What is Job but axeless, the axe but without Job? What is man without the axe but—Mmpph."

Quoth the bearded man. "What is man but grass, and Job's mouth but full of grass?"

He placed Job's skull between two piles of bones. "I am leaving to find a lamb," said the man, "so as to bespatter you with blood."

Job spat out stalks.

"I counsel you to be here when I return," said the man.

"You can depend on me," said Job.

"Swear on your mother's grave?"

"I shall swear on my own," said Job. And so did.

"I'm glad I can depend on you," said the man. He picked one of Job's hands up, shook it with his own.

"You need a lamb?" said Job. "Probably any blood–filled creature will do. A squirrel perhaps."

But the man was already gone.

THE EXTERMINATING ANGEL

"Snap to it, bones," commanded Job.

The femurs strained, breaking the salt grass holding them together. The feet burrowed down into the ground, socketed themselves to the tarsals. The head rolled to the top of the spine, the sprung ribs rippled into position.

Job pulled himself up onto his legs, snapped the balls of the femurs into his pelvis. He dusted himself off, wriggled his toes until his feet wormed up out of the earth.

"God helps those who help themselves," Job told the holes in the ground, the broken strands of grass.

He ran through the stumps.

Above him swept the darkness of exterminating wings. With them a bleating, coupled with curses. All quickly consumed.

"For what is the beard but for the shaving?" ejaculated Job dryly. "And sheep but for the shearing? And the both but for the slaughtering?"

He watched the spectacle pass. He shook the dust from his feet, walked on.

PRAYER

Job yawned and stretched, slowly sitting up. He rubbed his orbits with his bare knuckles. He stood and quickly executed three sets of twenty squat thrusts, two sets of one hundred sit-ups, three sets of twenty-five push-ups. He pressed his index finger stub into the gap between his carpal bones, counted to ten.

Prayed Job: "Sow in me, dear Lord, the seeds of tendons, the tatters of muscles. I am all yours, Lord, to wholify."

He looked into a puddle of mud, a film of water shining on the dark scum. No sprouting hair, no tendons, no muscles. No cartilage, no skin, no flesh, neither epi- nor dermis. No toenails, no fingernails, no thumbnails. No eyes, no ears, no tongue. Nothing but worn, white bone.

Job shrugged. He reached out, wiped his image into ripples.

III

THE HOUND OF HEAVEN

A mangy dust-yellow mutt pissed its way from stump to stump. Job strained to muster a whistle. Lipless and lungless, he found himself unable.

"Alas!" cried Job, rending his sackcloth. "Here, boy!"

The dog wagged its tail slightly, continued to mark its path. It slowly wended its way to him through the stumps.

Job reached out toward the dog. "Fellow traveller in this most glorious of the Lord's creations, I befriend thee."

Growling, the dog clamped onto Job's metacarpals, snapping the hand off at the wrist. The dog trotted away with the bones in its mouth, Job running after it. The dog ran ahead, then waited, its tail wagging, for Job to catch up. As Job neared, it spurted off again through the stumps, the slobbery hand bones hanging from its mouth. Job pursued. The dog ran. When Job stopped running, the dog stopped running. When Job sat, the dog sat, dropping Job's hand in the dirt. The dog sat over the hand, panting, drooling, its tongue hanging loose. It tipped its head quizzically from side to side. Job watched. The dog began to dig a hole.

"Lord, I beseech thee, extend thy beneficent hand and strike this dog! Shatter him, in thy wisdom, into motes of dust!"

The dog gnawed hard on the hand. Job winced, flailed his stump at empty air. Waving the bony end of his wrist, he leaped into the pursuit.

GRACE ABOUNDING

Around him, out of the stumps, whole trees reared up, first randomly, then in clumps. The way narrowed to a stump-scattered path. The dog slid through and around the stumps. The trees thickened, moved together. The sunlight dimmed.

The dog became three dogs, with more slinking out of the forest to join them. Three dogs grew to seven, then to legion, a thick hairy stream eddying through the narrow path of cut stumps.

Ahead, Job saw the path open into a clearing. The stream of dogs broke apart, spilling around the edges of the clearing. They clumped together on the opposite side, a dark, howling mass.

Job stared. Could it be?

He dropped to his knees, poured forth his thanks to God.

THE WAGER

"Not so fast," said a voice. A fleshy hand grabbed the ruins of Job's remaining hand at the wrist.

Job struggled to free himself. Dogs howled.

The lumberjack thrust himself between Job and the axe.

"The Lord consecrated this axe wholly for my holy use!" said Job.

"Gawd, schmod!" said the lumberjack. "It ain't God's to give." He slapped Job's skull.

"I am nowise at fault," said Job.

"Tell you what," said the lumberjack. "We'll roll for it. Bones versus the axe."

The lumberjack brushed off one of the stumps, squatted, sighted across it. He picked up the Redline, shaved the stump-top even. He grabbed Job's wrist, popped off two phalanges at the knuckle.

"You first," the lumberjack said.

"After you," said Job.

"I insist," said the lumberjack.

Job took back the finger bones, awkwardly rattled them with his remaining digits.

"Lord," Job prayed aloud, "let this be a holy roll!"

He let go. The bones fell onto the stump, tips upward.

"A balooky!" said the man. He grabbed Job's bones, shaking them in both hands. "Brace yourself!" he cried.

He lifted the bones over his head, rattled them hard, dropped them. They came down, spinning on their tips.

"Grand high lickabou!" the lumberjack cried.

But Job, having already wedged the axe handle between his radius and his ulna, now proceeded to cut the man into a thousand pieces.

"Bless thee, dear Lord, in thy infinite wisdom," said Job, redoubling his chopping.

"Foul!" the bits of lumberjack protested.

"Nothing personal," said Job. "But an axe is an axe."

The dogs rush forward to cough the bits down. Job falls down onto all fours. He crawls, and snaps, and whines, shoves the smaller dogs away. Skull streaked red, he eats bits of lumberjack alongside the dogs—raw, with the dogs.

Hébé Kills Jarry

Having sewn Jarry's eyelids shut, Hébé found himself at a loss as to how to proceed. He grabbed Jarry's shoulders, shook them. Jarry's head lolled from side to side.

"Jarry!" Hébé said. "Jarry!"

Jarry swallowed, tried to open his eyes. Hébé watched the skin of Jarry's eyelids strain against the thread.

Jarry cleared his throat. "What is it, Hébé?" Jarry said.

"Difficulties, Jarry," said Hébé.

Jarry tried to sit up. Hébé held him against the floor.

"I have a problem," Hébé whispered into his ear. "There is a serious problem."

"What is it, Hébé?" said Jarry, trying to blink. The thread on the insides of his eyelids scratched against his eyes, damaging them.

"I can't seem to recall the sequence," Hébé said.

"No written instructions?" said Jarry.

"Yes," said Hébé. "But the note is ruined."

"You didn't memorize?" said Jarry.

"I hadn't time," said Hébé.

Hébé let go of Jarry. Jarry did not move. Hébé drew his hands slowly away, keeping them open and ready. Hébé stood, examined himself in the mirror. He brushed the lint

off his tuxedo sleeves. He saw Jarry behind him, naked but
for the thread on his eyes.

"Hammer?" said Jarry. "Hatchet?"

Hébé did not say.

Jarry said, "Hébé?"

"Yes," said Hébé. "Admirable choices, both, Jarry. Would
you happen to own either?"

"Regrettably not, Hébé," said Jarry.

"What a shame," said Hébé.

Dots of blood had appeared on the flesh, at the points
where threads pierced Jarry's eyelids. Hébé removed a handkerchief from his pocket, wiped the blood away.

"Thank you," said Jarry. "Have you searched your
pockets, Hébé?"

"Yes," said Hébé. "The ruined note, some tickets, a handkerchief, a gun."

He removed the tickets from his pocket. He read what
was written on them, studied his watch.

"There it is, then. The gun," said Jarry.

"No, not that," said Hébé.

Jarry began to sit up. Hébé strode over, kicked him in the
throat. Gasping, Jarry fell back.

"I always carry a gun, Jarry," said Hébé.

He shook Jarry's shoulders, rubbed Jarry's temples. He
chafed Jarry's hands, massaged Jarry's throat.

"Don't be silly, Jarry," Hébé said. "I always carry a gun."

"Would you care for a pillow?" Hébé said.

"That would be delightful," said Jarry.

Jarry tried to open his eyes, failed. He rubbed his throat.

Hébé took a pillow from Jarry's bed, carried it out to
Jarry. He placed it beneath Jarry's head.

"There, now," Hébé said. "How do you feel now, Jarry?"

"A thousand thanks," said Jarry. "I feel like a new man."

He lifted the pillow up, daubed his eyelids on the silken case. He lay on the floor with his head elevated, turning his head to follow Hébé's footsteps.

"You might have left it at home?" said Jarry.

"I think not," said Hébé.

Hébé searched through the pile of his original clothing, discovered nothing. He threw the clothes into the fireplace, set them alight. The fabric withered, writhed, glowed, charred.

"What's that smell?" said Jarry.

"Burning clothes," said Hébé.

"Are the clothes supposed to be burning?" said Jarry.

Hébé shrugged. He stirred the fire with the poker. He turned to see Jarry awaiting an answer, blindly attentive.

"Did they say anything specific to you, Jarry?" said Hébé.

"Not a thing," said Jarry.

Jarry smiled toward where he thought Hébé was—where, in fact, Hébé was not.

"I wish we could get on with it," said Hébé.

Jarry turned his head.

"The fire perhaps?" said Jarry.

"No," said Hébé. "Not the fire."

Hébé saw the fireplace, a desk, a pillow, three chairs. A number of books on the desk were arranged in three nearly equal stacks, their bindings against the wall. Two pokers leaned against the casing of the fireplace. Hébé picked one, brandished it. He stabbed air, replaced the poker. He went to the desk, tried the drawers. They were locked.

"Did you know that this desk is locked?" said Hébé.

"Really?" said Jarry. "How odd."

Hébé poured himself a drink, went to the window. Cupping his hands around his face, he pressed his nose to the glass. Below him ran the sidewalk, the canal next to it. The water flowed swiftly past, glistening in the darkness. He followed the current down with his eyes.

Turning, he found that Jarry had fallen asleep.

He ransacked the bedroom, discovered a loaded 9-mm Browning taped to the underside of the box spring. He slid it into his pocket, atop his own gun. He opened the closet, counted the tuxedos. Four: a black Spencer, a black Fîchtelle, a lapel-less blue Luciani, an old three-buttoned maroon. He searched through the pockets, found them empty.

On the bathroom counter was a small mirror, a fire-blackened can of hair tonic, a comb whose teeth were plastered with strands of damp hair. He broke the mirror, discovered that the shards were too small to serve his purpose. He removed the tickets from his pocket, examined them. He studied his watch.

"How about knives?" said Jarry. "I own knives of all varieties. Might I propose a knife?"

Hébé observed Jarry straining his eyelids. He saw that the pillowcase was smeared with brushstrokes of blood.

"Hébé?" said Jarry. "Are you there, Hébé?"

'Not knives, Jarry," said Hébé. "God, no."

He poured himself another drink.

"Would you mind if I used your tickets?" said Hébé.

"By all means take them, Hébé," said Jarry.

"Might I ask what fine young thing you were planning to take to the performance?"

"An agency made the arrangements," said Jarry. "A blond, I think it was."

"Shall I telephone to cancel her?"

"Certainly not," said Jarry.

"Thank you," said Hébé.

"It's the least I can do," said Jarry.

.　　　.　　　.

Hébé stared down into the canal. He took a step back. He examined the window frame.

"Where are the drapes?" said Hébé.

"The what?" said Jarry.

"Your window drapes," said Hébé.

"Those," said Jarry. "You won't find any."

"Out for cleaning?" said Hébé.

"There's an awning, actually," said Jarry.

Hébé twisted his head, pressed his cheek against the glass. He stared up and out.

"So there is," Hébé said. "I never noticed."

Jarry laughed. "All these years. Imagine that!"

Hébé opened the window, examined the awning. Green canvas, the edge fringed with frayed, braided rope.

"I am beginning to remember," Hébé said.

"Tell me, do," said Jarry.

"Your body ends up in the river," said Hébé. He looked out. "No easy throw," he said.

Jarry chuckled.

"That's a start," said Jarry. "Now we know the end."

Hébé poured a drink for himself, a drink for Jarry. He studied his watch.

"Was the sewing difficult?" asked Jarry, nursing his glass.

"I was afraid I had punctured your eye," said Hébé.

"No, no," said Jarry. "All in one piece, I assure you," he said. He rotated his eyes beneath their eyelids, felt the threads rubbing against them.

"You've been exceptionally understanding throughout this whole affair," said Hébé. "Very patient."

"What are friends for?" said Jarry, smiling.

.　　　.　　　.

"It's getting late," Hébé said, checking his watch. He removed his tuxedo jacket, sat down on one of the chairs.

"Why not telephone them?" said Jarry.

"I suppose I could," said Hébé. "I should have considered it sooner," said Hébé. "Thank you, Jarry."

"You will discover a public telephone on the ground floor," said Jarry. "My own telephone is dead."

"I severed the wires," said Hébé. "All in a day's work."

"I meant to ask if it was you," said Jarry.

Hébé put the tuxedo jacket on. "I wouldn't relish kicking you in the throat again, Jarry," he said. "But duty is duty."

"You can count on me," said Jarry, waving him gone.

Jarry stood, felt his way to the door. He fumbled for the bolt, slid it shut. He felt his way to the desk. He took a key from inside his mouth, unlocked the desk. He pulled the drawers open. He ran his hands through the contents, found scissors in the third drawer down. He brought the scissors out, pressed the cold metal to his eyelid. He began to cut.

Having cut one eyelid halfway through, he pried it open with his fingers until he felt the tightness of the threads. Before him he saw Hébé, elongated and skew in the distortion of his vision.

"I thought you had gone out, Hébé," said Jarry.

"I didn't go out, Jarry!" Hébé cried. "You have found me out. Eureka!"

Jarry stared through his half-eye. Hébé just grinned.

"I don't believe I care to continue tonight, Hébé," said Jarry. "Shall we postpone?"

"Jarry, dear Jarry," Hébé said.

He walked to Jarry. He pushed the hand holding the scissors delicately to one side. He put his arm familiarly around Jarry's shoulders.

"Isn't this really what you wanted all along?"

Jarry said nothing, simply observing Hébé.

Then he smiled.

"You are correct, Hébé!" Jarry said. "You know me better than I know myself!"

"No regrets, Jarry," said Hébé.

"None, Hébé," said Jarry.

Hébé reached out his hand, removed the scissors from Jarry's hand. He closed the blades, slid the scissors into the top desk drawer. Jarry shut the drawer, locked it. He presented Hébé with the key. He stood motionless as Hébé sewed his eyelid down.

Hole

Suddenly he no longer knew. In the darkness he woke and thought, One or two, one or two?

He got out of the bed slowly, listening to see if her breathing changed.

Or three? he thought.

He held his palms flat before him and plunged them through the open doorway.

He went through files without success. He switched off the light and sat in the dark, rubbing his face.

Why do I need to know this? he thought.

Why indeed?

I don't need anything, he thought. His arms gripped the arms of the chair.

When she awoke, she went downstairs, looking for what had been lacking. He was there, his eyes red, looking through them, one after another, looking at every page.

"What are you doing?" she said.

"It is a matter of discipline," he said.

He turned one page. Then another. Then another. He could not stop turning.

The Boly Stories

WHAT BOLY SEED

Boly seed her the first, her head all cave in and her leg-split hacked nigh up to her ribs, and said to hisself, Well, now. What have we? "Ye done good," he told to his dogs, and made for them to sat their buttholes flush to the ground and stay there for him until he tossed them shards of lint-covered jerky fished up from his pocket bottoms. He want too eager to call out for Rollins yet. He locked his triggers up, leaned the shotgun against a maple, and got down there on knees. He got hisself a twig and used it to lift the hair outta her face, and seed he didn't know this one, no how. Some quite a face on her, though, and he may could see what make a man to do her plain and simple, though the cutting and the head job, they want no reason for it, far as he could tell; they was mystery. But whatever be the reason of it, no how were this the reward girl.

He reached his hand out to touch to her with the veiny back of it and pulled his hand back like she was fire, so warm she still were. He sware and spat. He shooed the dogs away from her, and he were back quick to the gun, cracking it open for a check of the breech and booming it back together. He held it out afore hisself and pointed it around.

"Wherer ye be, mister," said he, "ye can come on out now."

Were no sound anywheres but them dogs apant and asniff at everything.

"I be going easy for you," Boly said. "If of you give yourself up now. Them others, they just as soon dead you as alive. Reward same either way."

He standed there a pace more, saying nothing. Then he collared one of the dogs and dragged it to the corpse-lady and whispered some junk to the dog. The dog sniffle all the way round the corpse but not find it, what he looking for. Boly left it snuffling around till it begun to licking blood off the corpse-lady's hair and then he given that dog a whap atop the skull hard enough to send it slinking. Boly pointed his rifle around.

"Don't think I haent seed you!" he cried out.

He await a spell and then cawed out at lung top, "Rawley!"

He shussed they's dogs and made for all alisten.

He heared Rollins call back and then come crashing his way. Boly cried out again, let Rollins get it closer, cried the third one.

"There's Boly," said Rollins.

"Here I be," said Boly. "Lookee this," he said, motioning with the gun.

Rollins took but a look, spat some chew.

"Haent her," he said.

"Know this one?" said Boly.

"Not from Satan," said Rollins. He nudged up her leg-split with his boot. "She were alive, bet," he said. "That got to have hurt."

Boly just standing. He watched one of the dogs fold his leg up like a cooked chicken wing and heave it up for to piss down a maple trunk.

"There a reward on this one?" said Rollins.

"Naw," said Boly. "None award I knows of."

"Leave her lie a few, and there bound to be," Rollins said.

Rollins given her a kick, watched her still supple limbs awobble. They began at kicking dead leaves over her.

"She still warm when I found her," said Boly.

"Well, now," said Rollins. He stopped at kicking and picked up his gun. "Dogs smell nothing?"

"Not a fart," said Boly.

"Want no trail?" said Rollins.

"Naw, Rawley," said Boly. "Haent nothing."

Rollins stooped hisself down for a squint at the ground. He gyred out from the corpse-lady, pushing branches aside all delicate.

"Here, Boly," said Rollins, asquat now. "You lazy."

Boly came on over, looked down between Rollins's boot tips, seed the bloodstreak on the mulchifying leaves. He seed Rollins's eyes move backward to the corpse-lady and up into the trees. The pair of them walked on over and stared up, hands shielding eyes.

Up there in the bare branches were a wiry little man setting astraddle over a branch. Were with him a bare and gagged-up woman astraddle the branch in front of him, her bare back against his front. He got a hacksaw to her throat.

"That her, my guess," said Boly. "Him too."

"We be rich, Boly," said Rollins.

"We seed you fair," said Boly. "Get ye on down."

"You gone and git yourselves," the man called down. "Or I kill this one too."

Rollins just standing. Boly turning antsy, starting to.

"Git, you hear?" the hacksaw man said.

Rollins leaned over at Boly and said all low, "He worth the same dead?"

"Same damn thing," said Boly.

"She too?" said Rollins.

"Dead or live don't make no different, finance speaking."

Rollins lifted his rifle, pointed it up.

"Hack away, mean fucker," he called.

Boly looked up and got a spatter of blood eyewise. He woped the eye clean and seed other blood red-spatter down on the leaves around him and on him too. He looked over

to Rollins. Rollins had lowered the rifle, but kept alook
up through his fingerblades.

"Handy with a hacksaw, gotta say," said Rollins. "Not
ever day you see it," said Rollins.

The dogs set to licking the blood off the leaves.

"I think that about do her," said Rollins.

He point up his rifle again and sighted up it, and shot
twice. Rollins and Boly both seed the bodies come down,
crashing branches.

Rollins opened the bolt and the shells kicked out.

"You a rich man, starting now, Boly," said Rollins.

Rollins stuck his hand down into a pocket, come up with
two more shells.

Boly seed him slip them in, drive the bolt home. Rollins
lifted the gun and pointed that barrel at Boly's head.

"I gone be set for life," said Rollins. "Make a head set to
spinning, just of pondering it."

They's dogs not doing nothing but sniffling around.

"I always fond for you, Boly," Rollins said. "Just business."

Boly just watch. It were the last thing he seed.

BOLY, SAVED OF DAMNATION

Boly spat blood gobs, watched the Rider come. He rubbed
Rollins's face into the gravel, get up off from Rollins. He
watched the dust billows the Rider made raise.

"Let the devil herself come," said Boly. "I aready."

He snorted up the bloody snot of his nose, hacked it out
into his mouth. He spat a viscous bloody string, wropped it
round the gatepost.

Rollins were breathing steadier now. He were getting up
to his knees, Boly saw out from his corner of eye. Rollins
shook his head clear, crawled about on the look for piece of
his tongue. He kept to his knees till Boly want given him
no heed, then scuttle off shackwise.

. . .

Boly spooked the old woman's mare way from the trough, plashed the silty water for his face. He primed the pump, shot a blast of fresh water down into the dirty. He stretched his mouth round the dripping pump cock, tasted lead. He reamed his tongue up the pipe, after the last drops.

The shack door banged. He whirled around, seed twere the old woman. She were astanding hardfaced, her arms afold cross her soggy chest.

"What to hell ye be doing Rawley like that?" she said.

"Rawley do hisself," Boly said.

"Ye asking to be birched?" she said.

"Naw," he said, kicking apart clods.

"You want your tongue cut like you done Rawley's?"

Boly shrugged. "Hell, I warn him to keep his mouth close," he said.

"He been mouthing again?" said the old woman.

Boly strike his chin out toward the road. The old woman shade her eyes, stare out at the dust the Rider raised.

"Could still turn off," she said.

"He haent about to turn off," said Boly.

She grabbed the birch from off the porch, strode back into the shack.

"Son of a bitch, Rawley!" she yelled.

Boly walked out to the gate and climb up the rails. He feeled the blood build up inside his nosehole and trickle down onto his lip. He could taste hisself in it, and he liked the taste of him.

From the shack come the crack of birch. Boly smiled.

The Rider come up to the fence, rode right up to him, rein in so close that Boly feeled the Rider's horse given a wheeze. Boly don't move. The horse drunk-stepped a mite, crazy-lathered and shivering.

"Looking for Thomas Shelton Garker," said the Rider. "Feller go by Boly."

"What ye want that one for?" said Boly.

"Haent none business of yours," said the Rider.

Boly squint up. "And were it?" he said.

"Open the gate or I gone jump it," the Rider said.

"Nag like that can't jump piss," said Boly.

"Haent nobody ever learnt you manners?" said the Rider.

"Naw," said Boly. "And haent nobody about to."

Boly left the Rider lying there, led the Rider's nag over to the watering trough. He gawked around for the old woman's horse but saw none of it. He seed Rollins and the old woman, though, asit in the door of the shack.

He warshed his face clean and then plunged his arms into the trough. He shaked the water off hisself.

Rollins and the old woman still there, watching him.

"What you staring at?" he said.

Rollins looked away.

"You being ignert again, Boly," said the old woman.

Boly wet his hair down slick, combed back through it with his fingers. He set down in the dirt, slipped his boots off, turn them tipsy-topsy. A bloody tooth fell out.

He picked the tooth up, turned it over in his fingers.

"This your, Rawley?" Boly said, holding it out.

Rollins looked asquint at the tooth, run his finger back in atween his lips.

"Naw," said Rollins. "Mine all there."

Boly pulled his boots back on, stood. He limped on over to the Rider, who were on the ground, breathing a mite shallow, eyes close. Boly squatted on down, reamed his finger into Rider's mouth, dragged it over the rotten teeth.

He take his finger out, slid it into his own mouth. He pushed the tip of his finger up into a gap, touch it to the tender gum. He popped the finger out, took a long stare at the bloody spit streaked on it.

"Well, I'll be jigged," he said.

He took the tooth, throwed it into the dirt. Rollins given a whoop and slap his knee. Then come the swack of birch. Rollins cry out.

"Manners, Rawley," said the old woman. "Haent nobody ever learnt you manners?"

The Rider were starting to come round. Boly spat into his face, gave him a good kick to the jaw.

"Ready for number two?" Boly said.

The Rider just rub his jaw and shake his head.

"Rawley?" said Boly.

"What you want, Boly?" said Rollins.

"Put 'em up, Rawley," said Boly, raising his fists.

"Naw, sir," said Rollins. "I had enough."

"I haent," said Boly.

He nudged the Rider with the toe of his boot. He grabbed the Rider aneath the armpits and pulled him standing. The Rider just cling to hisself and curl into a ball. Boly let him drop into the dirt. He kicked the Rider's head a time or few. The Rider don't do nothing for it.

He turned around, made after Rollins, but Rollins were already scurried off, God knows where. There were only the old woman, asit on the edge of the porch, birch in hand.

He grabbed the Rider's collar, hauled him backward over to the old woman.

"What we to do about this one?" said Boly.

"Ye plan to come back round here, Rider?" said the old woman.

"Naw," said the Rider. "I guess I haent."

"You warsh up in the trough and catch your breath, and then get," she said.

"Much obliged, ma'am," said the Rider.

"You gone to let me run him another round or few first?" said Boly.

"Ye heard me or haent ye?" said the old woman.

Boly pulled the man to his feet, shove him away. He watched the man warsh hisself in the trough. He waited till he think the old woman not alook, and get in a few good kicks.

"Goddam, this are boring," said Boly.

"What were that?" said the old woman.

"Nothing," said Boly.

"Who learnt you talk like that?" said the old woman. "Didn't I teach you not to take God vain?"

"I were just talking," said Boly.

The old woman stand up. "You gone tell me I reared myself a child devoid of religion?"

"Naw," said Boly.

"Bend yourself over," said the old woman.

"I haent nothing done!" yelled Boly.

"I heard that 'goddam' ring out clear as hell's bells!" she said. "Down with yer breeches," she said.

She made him count them as she gave him them, and there were Rollins and the Rider astraddle on the fence rails, seeing that he don't cheat the count. Boly gritted his teeth, feeled the stripes the birch were raising on his backside, on his thighs, on the leathery seamback of his scrotum.

"You got your father's no-good ass," the old woman said. "God, it an embarrassment to birth an ass like that."

Rollins and the Rider busted out laughing, almost keeled off the fence.

"No need for you laughing, Rawley," said the old woman. "You yourself got the same damn ass."

Rollins and the Rider quiet on down. They shared themselves a cigarette, passed it back and forth where they were asit on the rails.

The rhythm of the blows made waves in Boly's head. He counted up around forty and then lost count. She made him start back at one.

Said the old woman: "I want you telling me you thankful for how's I's saving you of damnation."

He felt his face go red. On the fence, the Rider and Rollins were alaughing fit to burst.

The old woman stopped midswing, turned, crossed her arms, looked at the pair of them.

"No need for laughing," said the old woman. "You two have your turn soon enough."

She leaned back down, lined the birch against Boly's bloody ass, raised it high, swinged.

Boly just smile.

DONE IN

She were feeding turkey broth tonight, and some stale bread for dipping, and for drink some water, maybe, if any damn thing at all. Rollins watched her through the window, her veiny, blotched-up old hands still quick with the knife. She gouged the meat out of the turkey neck, throwed it back into the pot. He skulked around outside apace, awaiting going in until he seed her set the three bent-up tin plates to table. Then Rollins slinked off the porch, come back up onto it, all full of noise.

"Boly?" the old woman said. "That be ye and Rawley?"

"Naw," said Rollins. "Just Rawley."

The old woman come out from the kitchen, the skirts of her apron pulled up in her hands for her to wope the turkey blood onto it.

"Boly still out there, alook out for that dead girl," said Rollins. "He plan to stay looking till he got her."

"I didn't hear that she were dead," said the old woman.

Rollins scratched his head. "They think dead," he said. "By now. But nobody know it but her."

She were gone, back to kitchen. She come again with tin bowls, slapped them down, clanging on the plates.

"Damn fool, Boly," she said. She were back to kitchen.

Rollins throwed his hat into a corner, set his rifle down along the bottom log. He took eight of the reward eagles from his pocket, slip the coins one after another underside the tablecloth, for her. He leaned hisself against the wall.

She come back in, hands to hips.

"Ye see what happen when a man get hisself too concerned with the worldly?" she said. "Ye have the tendency yerself, Rawley. Don't ye be forgetting yer spiritual uprearing, now."

"Naw," he said.

"When Boly come back I gone to kick his ass," she said. She just stood there.

"Yours need a kicking too?" she said.

"Naw," Rollins said.

He stoked up the fire, then stirred the broth while she hacked the last meat off the bones. He rised up the shards of turkey from the pot bottom, seed them stay afloat a minute before sinking back down.

She woped her hands off onto her apron, grabbed hold to the cutting board, lifted it, shaked it off. She woped the knife clean and picked up the stony bread, cut it into crust and crumb, swept it all into her apron.

He grabbed some rags for to carry the pot. He followed her out, seed her shake the bread crust out from her apron, in three pile. He set the pot down at table, grabbed the chair afore the biggest crust pile. She slapped his hand but hard.

"That be Boly's," said she. "Mine your manners."

He let the chair go, took hold to anothern afront the smallest pile.

She slapped at his face, but he blocked it with his forearm.

"Await your elders," she said.

"Yes'm," he said, and stepped back.

She used all her sweet time getting set, and then set there a pace afore giving him the nod. He set down, reach to the bread. He stopped midreach when he seed how she were eyeing him down.

"Ye godless, Rawley?" she said.

"Naw," he said. "Just hungered."

"Hunger be the different atween the heaven and the hell."

He done the praying hands. He bow his head and wait.

He don't hear nothing.

He looked up, seed her setting with her arms crossed, astare at him.

"Have at it, holy man," she said.

He looked behind him, don't seed nobody.

"Who, me?" he said.

"Unless you care to wait for Boly," she said.

"Naw," he said. "You speak it."

"I want to hear you do it," she said. "I want to see the religious in ye again."

"I haent about to," he said.

"You want me to kick your ass sore?" she said.

"Kick away, old woman," he said. "I haent got nothing to say to no God."

He played with his pile of crust, moved it about.

"We await for Boly, then," she said. "I'll for him to fix you a lesson or three."

"Haent no point to wait for Boly," he said.

She stayed all silent. She bored her old-womanly eyes into his skin till he turned away and not about to look back.

"I figured so," she said. She stood up. "Ye get out of here now," she said.

Rollins stood. He grabbed the stale crusts, crammed his pockets full, made for the door.

"If I not be doing you in," she said, "it only because ye all that left to me."

He popped the latch, pushed the door open, walk out.

"And you aren't so godawful much," she said.

He closed the door.

He leaned up against the split rail that ran edge for the porch and rolled a cigarette for hisself. He put the cigarette atween his lips, scratch a match aflame, brung the cigarette into glow. He smoked some. He stared out at the prairie, feeling the money grown heavy in his pockets.

He spat the butt out onto the porchboards, suffocated it with his heel.

He turned, took the last look at the house. Hanging out the window were the old woman, pointing the shotgun.

"Done change my mind, Rawley," she said. "I got to do ye, for Boly's sake."

She raised the gun. He stayed leaned up against the rail. He crossed his legs at the ankles. Very slowly, he took out a cigarette paper and his tobacco pouch, tap some grains of tobacco onto the paper, even them out.

Rolling the cigarette up, his hands begun ashook.

The Evanescence of
Marion le Goff

I

Marion le Goff imagines she has legs. Her stumps asway in dark water, she believes the legs are still there. She keeps still, sees visions within her skull. Creatures with legs, herself among them. In the darkness, she walks.

The two technicians open the tank, pull her forth into light. They stare into her dark pupils. What they see there is a function of the light. In darkness, they see nothing, say nothing. In strong light, their own selves, their ghosts swimming, silently speaking in her eyes.

They ask her series of questions which, after long pauses, she fails to answer.

The two technicians take notes, wait patiently for Marion le Goff to go mad. But she does not go mad: she walks.

One of the two technicians picks Marion le Goff up under the armpits, along the sagging edges of her breasts. He raises her over the lip of the hatch, lowers her into the dark water. She speaks all the while of her crimes, pleading for absolution. They are merely technicians, they inform her. They lack divine power.

Without legs she is twenty-eight inches tall, she tells them in confidence. By her reckoning, she is deserving of mercy.

The two technicians scribble on pads. They nod their heads, slowly, thoughtfully. Disturbed by doubts, one technician removes his tape measure. The other technician picks Marion le Goff up by the armpits, holds her, dripping, suspended over the water.

"Apparently, I am shrinking," says Marion le Goff, faced with the facts.

They lower her in, shut the tank.

Oh, the legs that Marion le Goff gains! Long slender machines that grow under her in the water to push her up through the top of the tank. Her wizened body perches atop them, the stride of the legs so long as to split her up the middle. In single strides, the legs cover leagues, landscapes spinning by, spreading forth below her.

The technicians lean forward, fascinated.

She walks through cities and towns, pads through craters of dust. She swishes through fields, steps over mountains, wades on the ocean floor. She feels her body lengthening, thinning to match the long legs she slips on. She feels the fibers of her stumps untangling, stretching themselves straight, their severed ends sprouting, entangling themselves in the fibers of the legs.

Something is changing. She feels her skin tightening, whitening, her crippled fingers straightening, stretching long.

Marion le Goff strides from city to city in long strides, a long beauty perched atop her long legs. There is the grating of a hatch somewhere, and she is tumbling down off her legs, falling, falling.

II

Marion le Goff rolls down the streets of Watts in a wheeled box, pushing herself along the pavement with her knuckles. She begs for money to continue treatment.

"Wait!" someone is crying. "Wait!"

"How does it feel?" one of the technicians at last asks her. "All that water!"

"Don't you know?" says Marion le Goff.

The two technicians glance at each other, querying each other on how to respond. They do not respond. They lift her out, dry her off. Her skin is pale and wrinkled, the tips of her fingers water-sodden.

Others start screaming in fifteen minutes, but Marion le Goff stays isolated for hours. When the technicians open the hatch, she shuts her eyes tight, presses her hands against the slick sides. It takes both technicians to drag her free.

She cannot help thinking that she is on the verge of a breakthrough, she says. She cannot help begging the technicians for additional sessions.

The technicians carefully write what she says on their notepads, noting the time of the utterance in the margin next to the words. They nod, their pencils at the ready, already considering how to analyze her statements.

The miles she covers, all with the greatest ease. Her legs still good for miles more, and herself becoming those legs. Those legs becoming herself.

The hatch opens, but her ears do not hear it.
The light streams in, but her pupils do not contract.
She is walking still, racing across worlds.

The two technicians drag her out. They take turns slapping her face until at last she shudders, falls from the legs. She cries out from the impact.

Eagerly, the technicians reach for their pencils.

III

The technicians leave Marion le Goff inside the tank for forty-eight hours. They sit together, pencils poised, observing the blank metal, observing their blank notepads. Without data to record, they feel deprived. They sit in their chairs, staring. They chain-smoke cigarettes, watch their thumbnails grow yellow, then brown.

The hours pass. They open the hatch. Inside, dark water. Inside, nothing.

Each technician writes some notes. The technicians compare notes. They stare into their own pupils. They take turns climbing in and out of the tank.

They pound on the hatch, begging to be let out. In the water, floating, they feel as if they have lost their legs.

Bodies of Light

He lay spread beside her, his body making itself felt until he was forced to acknowledge its presence. He folded the covers back. He crept from the bed, progressed from darkness to darkness.

He crouched, let a hand descend. His fingers brushed wicker, pursued the twisted fibers of a woven rimwork.

He pushed the hand within the bound, brushed his palm across a meager nimbus of hair. He slid it down to shape the maze of an ear, touched the swollen eye, allowed the hand to slide away.

The sheet was damp, lumped with bitter clotter and curdle. He lifted the fingers away, sniffed the sour milk upon them. He swabbed the hand upon the carpet. He moved the fingers back, spanned the palm across the whole of the back, found the flesh damp, chill. He took the hand away.

He turned the small body upward, pressed his fingertip into the fold of the neck. He brought his ear against the mouth. He raised the ear against the stiff nares.

He brought his hand to the mouth, cleared a sticky web, spread the web into the carpet. He pressed down upon the rib cage, caused a curdle to unrun from mouth and nose.

He entered the bathroom, closed and locked the door. He switched on the light.

He examined his fingers.

He washed his hands in the sink.

He examined his stolen face in the mirror.

He opened a drawer beneath the sink, removed from it a square of cloth. He soaked the cloth with water, wrung the water out, wrapped the cloth around his fist.

He turned off the light, unlatched the door. He felt his way along dark walls.

He cleaned the mouth with the cloth. He reached upward, groped along a wooden ledge, his fingers knocking against the spines of books to strike a rubber syringe into existence. He brought the syringe down, squeezed the air out of the bulb. He inserted the narrowed tip into each nare in turn.

He worked a hand beneath the loose neck, elevated the head. He folded the cloth in half, wiped beneath the skull. He allowed the head to fall.

The eyelids stuttered, split apart.

"Daylight come," he said.

She stretched her back, edged away from him.

He walked to the dresser. He opened the top drawer. He removed a black velvet case, broke it open to shake two silvered cuff links into his palm.

"A cloth," she whispered.

He removed a folded cloth from the pile beside the bassinet. He carried it to her, dropped it upon the bed.

She pushed her pillow back against the wall, sat up, the blanket falling away to reveal the panels of her brassiere dark and sodden. She opened the buttons, stripped back the panels to unbind nipples coursing with milk. She pressed the cloth over her breasts.

"Does she want to eat?" she said.

"I tried to wake her," he said.

"Try again," she said.

"I just tried," he said.

She climbed out of the bed, looked into the bassinet. She wandered into the bathroom, closed the door.

He dropped to his knees. He turned the body face up. He closed the mouth.

He manipulated the limbs with his fingers, broke the stiffness of the joints. His thumb coaxed the pupil of the open eye down from under the rim, pushed the eyelids shut.

He downturned the face. He left the room, drew the door closed behind him.

He entered the kitchen, poured coffee, poured milk. He took two bowls from the cupboard, stationed them upon the table. He plucked spoons from the dish drainer, carried them to the table. He slid a knife from the block, swiftly quartered an orange.

He attended the bathroom door until it opened. She appeared, a second cloth tucked badly inside the brassiere.

He occupied her hands with a glass of milk, a section of orange. He ushered her into the dining room.

"Still asleep?" she said.

"I will wake her," he said.

He widened his mouth, drew his lips over the nose and mouth as if to eat the face. He pushed his air into her. The chest rose. He drew back. The chest did not rise again.

He lifted the child, wrapped it in blankets, turned the face toward his chest. He balanced the swaddled form in one arm, manipulated the doorknob with the other hand. He slid the door open with his toe.

He gained the verge of the dining room, stood regarding her back split by the chair. The spoon moved up from the bowl, vanished to the other side of her head.

He cleared his throat.

She set the spoon down. She screwed the chair around toward him. She unbuttoned the panels, tugged out the cloth.

"Still asleep," he said. He tilted the baby toward her, keeping the face pressed against his chest. "See?" he said.

She clutched her breasts. The creases between her fingers grew dark, moist.

"Let me wake her," she said.

He shook his head.

She picked up the cloths, tucked them over her breasts. She licked off her fingers.

"She should wake now," she said.

He returned to the bedroom, placed the child in the bassinet, face down.

He sat at table, watched her throat constringe and swell as she swallowed milk. He lifted the coffee to his lips, sipped, found he could not bring himself to swallow. He allowed the coffee to spill silent out of his mouth, into the cup.

He looked up, found her to have emptied the glass. She set it upon the table. The milk-sheen faded from the sides, descended to ring the inner base.

She unbuttoned the panels, rolled them back. She unfurled the cloth, revealed her underwired breasts. Her flattened nipples stiffened, snouted up.

She lifted the glass from the table, held it beneath a nipple. She drew the milk out, her hand caressing small circles, the milk spurting off into the glass.

He lifted the coffee cup to his lips, pretended to drink.

He folded his napkin, placed it beside the bowl.

Her finger smeared a drop of milk over the aureole. She moved the glass to the other breast.

·   ·   ·

"Look at the time," he said.

"That was her?" she said.

He pretended to listen. He shook his head.

"Will you see if she is awake?"

"I have to go," he said.

She looked at him coldly, set the glass upon the table. He watched her cross to the back of the house, open the door of the bedroom.

He pushed away from the table. He removed his shoes, carried them in his hand. He gathered his satchel, tiptoed toward the door. From the back of the house, he heard her voice. He took his hat from the hook, placed the hat atop his head. He eased open the door, stepped into the light.

New Killers

Gous and Ramse took turns. Kline stayed in the bathtub, looking out from behind the shower curtain, planning retribution. He wrote what they did on a pad of paper, so as to remember all. *When Lux's legs were broken,* he wrote, *Ramse took Ping Pong balls, pushed them down Lux's throat.*

Gous and Ramse washed the blood off the bat in the tub. Kline naturally complained—sanitation, after all. They helped him out of the tub and gave him a towel. The three of them smoked cigarettes and talked. Listen to what the assassins said.

One of them said, "What did you think of that?"

One of them said, "A job well done is a job well done."

One of them pointed and said, "Do you recognize the finer points?"

One of them picked something up and said, "This will remain, no?"

Kline knows he should respond. They are waiting for him to respond. They have stopped talking and are looking at him, expecting him to respond. Their attention is focussed on Kline, in maddened anticipation.

All the while Kline is worried about how he will be able to remember this. He wants to get out the notepad and write. He keeps his hands where his accomplices can see them.

Mix, Mex, Somebody

Beneath the fur he felt the ribs—sharp, separate. Max, he thought, or perhaps Mix or Mex.

"Here, Max," he said.

Nothing but shudders.

He felt the bones above the eye, the orbit nearing a point of collapse. He crushed something hiding in the hairs of his forearm, leaving a black smear. He backed away.

At the edge of the hill, the top of a head, dark puffy hair, bobbed into existence.

He watched her body appear. He ran his finger along the rim of his eye socket. In the water shed's shadow he lit a cigarette. The match slowly smoldered on the dirt, aging. He flicked the butt over at the dog. It lodged in the fur somewhere.

She picked the cigarette end out of the fur, ground it out, prodded the carcass with her toe.

"It's his dog," he said. "Mix," he said.

"Mex," she said.

"Maybe," he said.

She took a look at the dog.

"What makes it do that?" she asked.

"Die?" he said.

They sat in silence, backs against metal.

Some places on the tank the paint had turned brittle—chalky—and had begun to crack. Birds began to gather above them, on the metal lip. Mostly sparrows. A few larger birds. His back was so cold.

"I found this," he said, handing her the paper.

She looked at it and set it aside. The wind made it tremble where she put it.

He saw something in the sky.

"You go ahead," he said. "I'll catch up with you."

"What about Mix?" she said.

"Max?" he said.

She shrugged. "Somebody."

Her Other Bodies

A Travelogue

Utah

He drove across the border, crossed into the barren northern stretches of Utah. Three miles into the state he killed his first, bashing her eyes in with his tire iron. In the back of the U-Haul he carved thirty-five stars into her back, rows of seven and eight. Flesh was not so easy with a penknife, he found, raising problems far beyond oak and pine. He hacked out a few early attempts, recut them on her thighs.

He locked the back up, drove the U-Haul back onto the highway, pushed his way into traffic. He turned on the radio, flipped the dial to gospel talk, 1450 AM band. Lights flashed by. He glanced at his watch. He dug the cigarette pack out of the crack between seats, ripped the wrapper off, tore away the foil with his lips. He shook the package softly until a few cigarettes broke over the edge. He gummed one free, lit it, watched the smoke curl and cloud up between himself and the windshield.

He wound the tight exit ramp down into Perry, taking it fast. The back tires slid for the emptiness of the truck. The near emptiness.

He parked the U-Haul back behind the pumps, between two semitrailers. He walked over to the café, skittering gravel ahead with his boots, breathing up the dust which his tires had raised.

The place was empty except for the waitress. He walked to the telephone, working out of his tight pockets fistfuls of quarters. He jammed a few quarters in, dialed Idaho. He looked around at the empty bar stools. The waitress loomed straight-armed over the counter, her hair loose, her apron crumpled and heaped before her.

"Closed, buddy!" she called out to him, as if she had just seen him.

He pointed to the phone, held up two fingers.

She shook her head, cursed.

He turned away. He stared out the window. The telephone kept ringing. He squeezed a few more quarters out of his pocket, stacked them atop the pay phone.

"Yeah?" said a voice.

"Hello," he said. "Honey? That you?"

There was a long silence.

"Marry me," he said.

The waitress had come around the counter. He could see her in the lit glass of the window, coming toward him. He hung up the dead phone, started gathering his quarters.

"No offense, pal," the waitress said.

"None taken," he said.

"Just I got to be out of here," she said.

He jammed his hands down into his pockets, quarters trickling through. He stopped before the door, turned.

"Don't suppose you care for a trip to Wyoming?" he said. "My treat?"

"What's Wyoming got?" she said.

"Nothing," he said. "I just done Utah already," he said.

The waitress smoothed her hands across the front of her jeans, so he saw her ring.

He shook his head, opened the door.

"Coming?" he said.

"Can't," she said.

He shrugged. "You never going to know what you missed," he said.

84 East, past Uinta, Peterson, Morgan. The air grew colder, the canyon closed in, threatened to swallow him up. He took it slow through the curves. The cars backed up behind him. The side mirror burned headlights into his eyes. He gripped the wheel tight, straightened his back, tilted his neck to keep the light out. On the straightaways they passed him, darting over the double yellow line, their headlights glaring in hard at him then vanishing. The mountain heaved itself up on his left, in the darkness inching its way closer to the road. To the right seemed a drop—sheer as far as he could tell—down to the dull river. Beyond, in the flat stretches on the other side of the river, a rim of light outlining the rails.

He moved over into the truck lane, slowed, wiped sweat off his palms and into his hair. He watched the cars spill past him and vanish up the road, their taillights diminishing then suddenly gone. He cracked his neck, shook his head, leaned back against the headrest.

He turned off at Devil's Slide, took a steep curve down across a river and onto a frontage road. He drove along the streets at the north end of town, stopped west of an old Chevron with one single-hose pump.

He climbed out of the cab, walked down toward the station. He rubbed his windburnt eyes, licked the dead salt off his lips. Putting his hands in his pockets, he walked around to the back of the station.

The rear of the building had three doors, unmarked and locked. He looked around, made out in the darkness a barren lot and piles of gravel, sorry scatters of some kind of long grass sprinkled between them. Halfway to the biggest one, he heard the clink. He stopped, listened to a few more links drag out. He took out his penknife, opened it. He held the knife almost swallowed up by his fist, then put it away. He ran his hands along the ground, gathering stones.

He whistled a few times.

Over the growl he heard the links of chain scuttle their way across the gravel, heard the chain leave the ground. He turned, saw a dark shape coming toward him. He leaped backward, felt it snap as it jerked back at the end of its tether.

He went close and threw the rock, hearing the crack as it struck home. The animal staggered, shook its head, went down. He threw a few more stones point-blank. He stepped forward and onto the dog's neck, pressing the windpipe shut with the heel of his boot. The dog clawed feebly at his legs. He stood there on the neck. He unbuttoned his jeans, pissed a strong, steady stream past its shoulder.

The boy didn't look at him as he came in. He sat on a stool near the register, his boots crossed out in front of him.

"What's a man got to do to see a bowl he can pour his troubles into?" said the man.

The boy slowly uncrossed his legs, pulled himself up. He reached above the cash register, ran his fingers down a row of empty hooks until he came to a hook with a key on it. He pulled the key off, stretched it out toward the man.

"You buying gas?" he said, drawing the key back.

The man looked at him. "I have to buy gas?"

"Supposed to," said the boy.

"I don't need none," said the man.

The boy fingered the key, looked at the man. He held it out. "Go on," he said.

"Real Utah hospitality," said the man.

The key opened the middle door. He shat, washed his hands and face. He crushed a silverfish against the sink with his thumb. He ran his wet hands through his hair. He opened the door wide, walked out in the shaft of light to the dog.

The dog was lying in its own blood, rocks scattered around it, flies crawling up and down the lacerations of the ruined head.

"Here, boy," the man said. He whistled.

"Hell, you can't start timing until she picks up the phone."

The boy kept staring at his watch.

"What about good old Utah hospitality?" the man said. "Hey, honey, it's me!" he said.

He heard the line cut and then the dial tone. He hung up.

"One twenty," said the boy, "on the nose."

"Horseshit!" said the man. "Two lousy seconds." He threw a quarter on the counter.

The boy looked at him. "It's one twenty," he said.

The man threw another nickel on the counter, made a fist.

The boy gathered the money, warily. "Supposed to be one twenty," he said.

The man walked over to the door, pulled his hands out of his pockets. He opened the door, turned back to the boy.

"That your dog back behind there?" he said.

"Suppose it is?" said the boy.

"Damn sorry sight what them boys did to that dog," said the man, stepping into the cool air. "Sorriest-looking sight I ever saw."

WYOMING

Croydon, Henefer, Echo, Emory, down out of the passes into a lower stretch of the Rockies. Wyoming brought mountains with smooth rolling slopes that the road cut through without winding. Snowbreaks, range fences. He smoked two packs of cigarettes, piling the stained butts on the passenger seat. The cab seemed bloated and immense, lolling down the road in slow motion, swaying. The motor roar sent the dead butts buzzing and leaping against each other, the slight curves rolling a butt or two off the seat and onto the floor.

He pulled over at an old Sinclair station and turned off his lights. The pumps were torn out, except for a few pieces of pipe sticking out of the cement. The windows of the station were broken out, the asphalt cracked by weeds. He sat on the edge of a raised cement slab. He stared out at the deserted roads. Feet on the ground, he lay down on the slab, staring up into the moonlit clouds, his arms spread back behind his head, against the cold concrete. He closed his eyes, lay still. He felt the cold creep up through his back, shooting slow tendrils up into his chest.

He stood, beat his arms against his body, stomped the needles out of his legs. He climbed into the cab, drove.

Miles of old billboards for Little America. The roar of the motor tried to lull him to sleep. Turns leading to Urie, Carter, Lyman. Dull lights in the distance.

He pulled the truck off to the side, turned on the four-way flashers. He popped the hood, stood out in the cold. Three cars passed in a half hour, none slowing despite his waving his arms. He felt beat and chilled through.

He sat on the back bumper, smoking a cigarette. He hadn't smoked half of it before a sports car passed, its motor revving down audibly. He stubbed his cigarette, walked toward the front of the truck. The car's taillights came on, and between them the white reverse lights. The car whined its way backward, toward him.

He flicked the cigarette onto the road. He opened the cab door of the truck, gathered the tire iron off the floor. The engine had warmed it a little. He tucked it through the back of his belt, walked out to the car.

He stooped down by the window. The woman was hanging her arm out, ducking her head to look up at him.

"Having trouble?" she said.

The tire iron caught on the door's upper rim, deflecting down, breaking her shoulder. He backhanded it up and across her eyes, and as she leaned forward to cover her face, he stepped back, took careful aim, and cracked the back of her skull.

He pushed his way into the store, walked past the clerks back into the trucker's showers. He took off his clothes and, standing naked, examined each garment for bloodstains. He had reached the right leg of his jeans when the head clerk pushed her way in.

"Two-fifty per shower," she said.

"I ain't taking one," he said, holding his clothes over his bare crotch.

"I'll add it to your bill," she said, and left.

"I ain't taking no shower!" he yelled after her.

He put his clothes back on, washed his numb face in the sink. He ran water over his comb, ran the comb through his hair. In the mirror, he saw the door open. The head clerk came in, threw a towel on the chair behind him.

"No shower," he said.

"Might as well take one now," she said.

"What say for a trip to Colorado?" he said.

"Fat chance," she said, and left.

He dialed, got a not-in-service message. He redialed, got a not-in-service message.

Green River, a meager stretch of populated land. Scattered houses, trees, street lights visible from the freeway for a two-

or three-mile stretch. Rock Springs, an upward sloping curve lined with hotels. He squinted to make out a Pizza Hut and a Wrangler Burgers, their signs turned off. Quealy, Point of Rocks, Bitter Creek.

He stopped in a rest area, walked himself awake. He bummed a cigarette off a constipated insomniac trucker who went on about his bowels so long that the man had no qualms about asking him for a second cigarette, then a third. Into Table Rock, skirting the edge of the Great Divide. Wamsutter, Red Desert, descending down to Creston, up to Rawlins. Sinclair and dawn.

He pulled into a rest area packed with Japanese, long lines of them waiting for the toilets. He unlocked the back of the truck, climbed in, rolled the door down tight behind him. Holding a penlight in his teeth, he carved five rows of ten, the middle row exposing the spine. The points of the stars came easier now that the body was rigid. He lay down to rest after each row of stars, stretching his body out against the cool aluminum.

He listened to the dogs sniff the truck, their nails clicking against the cement. He heard parents coaxing children into cars. He wiped his penknife on the girl's blouse. He sat up, took a deep breath, began the next row.

He bought two greenish hot dogs, slicked them with horse-radish, choked them down. He dialed Idaho.

"Irene coming at you," she said.

"Got a minute?" he said. "I need you, baby."

He listened to the dial tone awhile.

She spoke while smoking one of his cigarettes, little strands of smoke seeping out of her mouth.

"Walcott?" she said. "You don't want to live in Walcott. Even I don't live in Walcott."

"Where's home?" he said.

"Elk Mountain," she said. "It ain't much, but it's a heap better than Walcott. Laramie," she said. "Now that's a place you want to take a close look at," she said. "That's where the brains of Wyoming lie."

"Care to show me around Laramie?" he said.

"I got to work," she said.

"What time you get off?" he said.

"I'm doing books tonight," she said.

"You look like you might be worth waiting for," he said. "You got that look to you."

"Nothing personal," she said, "but don't wait."

An empty, sleepless stretch into Laramie. He pulled off I-80 and into a Conoco station, stopped at a green pump, pumped diesel into the tank until it was spilling out over his boots.

The cement front of the store was decorated with slanted shakewood strips. He searched through rows of boot mugs, cowboy-boot belt buckets, tiny tin spoons with bronco rider handles, until he found a packet of No Doz. He poured himself half a cup of coffee, filled it up to the top with cold water, dropped in four of the No Doz.

"You'll be lucky if you ever sleep again!" the kid at the counter shouted.

The man winced. He looked up, saw a big, semipudgy fellow wearing a HARLEYFEST shirt and a dirty black-and-gold baseball cap.

The man put the empty cup and the half packet of No Doz on the counter. "That's the whole idea," he said.

"Which pump you at?" said the kid.

"I don't know," the man said. "The green one."

The kid punched a few buttons. "Twenty-nine thirty-four of unleaded?" he said.

"I had diesel," said the man.

He grabbed a plastic-wrapped cookie covered with pink frosting, added it to his pile.

The kid punched a button. He banged on the register. He punched a few more buttons, shook his head.

"Free?" the man said.

"Mister, you just gone and put twenty-six gallons of unleaded gas into a diesel truck."

"Oh my God," said the man.

"Pour yourself another cup of coffee," said the boy. "It's on me."

Hands shaking and eyes wide, he watched the sun gutter out. He began walking. He started at one end of town, walking the north-south roads, working his way back on the east-west ones. It didn't take long. He took long empty farm roads out into the fields and past the occasional dark house. He flushed two men, naked but for their boots and Stetsons, out of the bush, and they pursued him down a deep rutted road, giving over the chase when he reached the edge of town and street lights. He walked past the closed stores, returned to the gas station.

"What in hell there to do in Laramie?" he asked the kid.

"I work nights," said the kid.

"What's for fun?" the man said.

"Harleyfest," the boy said. "The finest Harleys you ever set eyes on, from all over the world. Gathered right here for two heavenly days in Laramie."

"Point me to it," the man said.

The kid hitched his stomach up onto the counter, smoothed his shirt down over it.

"Read them dates and weep," he said.

"Maybe next year," the man said. "A bar, then."

"All that's closed," said the kid. "It ain't exactly early, you know."

"Not exactly late, neither," said the man.

"Up with the sun," said the kid. "This here's Wyoming."

He put a quarter in the slot, dialed, shouted a few words, hung up, picked up the receiver, put in a quarter, dialed again, shouted some more, hung up, picked up the receiver, put in another quarter, dialed again, got a busy signal, picked the quarter out of the coin return, put in the quarter, dialed again, busy signal, dialed, busy, dialed, busy, dialed, dialed, dialed, dialed, got a not-in-service message, dialed, not-in-service, dialed, not-in-service, dialed. He dialed and dialed, moving his quarter around the purgatory of coin return and slot, coin return to slot, until the break of day.

COLORADO

Tank drained and filled, filters cleaned, pads replaced, pump reprimed. Three hundred dollars poorer, No Doz wearing thin, U.S. 287 down to Tiesiding, over the border and into Colorado. He choked down four No Doz tablets at Virginia Dale, felt them burn against the lining of his stomach. The shoulder dirt went red. The trees contorted and hunched down into scrub oak. The landscape became folded, racked with dry, arthritic hills.

The traffic bottled in North Denver, narrowing to a single lane. He let himself count the plastic orange flags and the upside-down orange garbage cans wrapped with reflecting strips. The traffic became jerky, starting and stopping suddenly. His brakes stunk, the pedal getting closer and closer to the floor.

He smoked the cigarette butts heaped on the seat, getting a good puff or two from each, flicking them into the door-well once they were tapped out. The sun was bright and hot, blistering his burnt arms and neck. The rubber seal around the engine cover slipped out of its groove. Engine air began burning his left leg. In the motionless stretches he examined himself in the mirror, pursed his lips. He rubbed the blood bursts on his eyes, looked through blotches, waited for his vision to clear.

He followed a woman in a brown station wagon from Castle Rock to a rest area down past Larkspur. He pulled the truck in behind her, watched her climb out of the car. Blond, but not as young as he would have hoped.

She walked back and forth on the grass, bent down to stretch her legs. She read the advertisements outside the bathroom, climbed back into her car. He started the truck, followed her back onto the freeway, exchanged at Monument for a teenage girl in a baby blue Volvo.

The girl pulled off at the Air Force Academy lookout and he followed her. He walked up to her, stood close to her as she looked out across the installation and up at Pike's Peak.

"Very impressive," he said.

She half glanced his way. She nodded nervously, hugged her arms to herself.

"You from around these parts?" he said.

"No," she said.

He waited.

"Well, where you from?" he said.

"Look, I have to go," she said.

He travelled in the exit lanes, speeding ahead of the other cars, cutting in at the last moment. Finally, ahead, he spotted the baby-blue roof.

He lost her again near Fountain as traffic lightened and she began lane hopping. He put the truck into overdrive going up the hill, caught her a few miles later. He moved the truck alongside her car, waved. She pulled off at the last moment at the Piñon Rest Area and he cut quick to follow her. He watched her hurry into the bathroom, glancing nervously behind her.

He got out and walked around her car, trying each of the doors, peering in. A pair of fluorescent green sunglasses on the dash, some badly folded maps on the front seat, a Gucci bag tucked beneath the front seat. On the back seat, a plastic laundry basket full of neatly folded clothes, two beat-up suitcases stacked atop each other. On the floor a five-foot tall monkey-puzzle tree in a burnished ceramic pot, its leaves drooping in the heat.

He dialed Idaho, got a busy signal, dialed again.

"Hello?" she said.

"Just me again," he said. "God knows I'm doing my best to forget you."

"You sound like hell," she said.

"Haven't gone to bed these three nights," he said. He slid quarters into the machine.

"Where are you?" she said.

"Nowhere near," he said. "You can rest easy."

He could hear her whispering to somebody else.

"Why you so friendly sudden?" he said.

"Ah, well, just that you sound so godawful dragged out," she said.

"What in hell?" he said.

"Nothing," she said. "Nothing. Tell me how you feel. Stay on the line."

"Goddam you for this!" he shouted. "We're even now!" he yelled, and slammed the receiver down into the cradle.

He kept his eyes on her car, giving her space to breathe outside of the cities. Pueblo: smoke and chimneys. Old, beaten industrial plants, sharp curves, record heat. He licked his windburnt lips, spat phlegm onto the truck door. He held the accelerator down with his left leg, rolled up his right pant leg. The calf was red and numb from the engine air, warm to the touch.

He held an imaginary cigarette to his lips, took a long drag on it, hung it out the window.

He put his signal on and pulled over slowly, raising billows of red dust, watching the Volvo speed away. He put the truck in park, switched off the motor. He pulled his wallet out of his back pocket. The state trooper walked up through billows of dust.

"Anything wrong, officer?" the man said.

"License," said the trooper.

The man opened his wallet, took the license out, surrendered it. The trooper returned to his patrol car.

The man tilted his head back, closed his eyes. He felt the sun burn on his shoulders and chest. His skin felt sticky, his mouth dry.

The trooper was there, shaking him.

"Looks like you need some rest, buddy," said the trooper.

"I'm all right," the man said.

"Rest area, about eight miles down the road," the trooper said. "You pull over there."

"Thank you, officer," said the man.

The trooper touched his hat, looked away and across the roadway. He put his hands to his hips. Squinting his eyes, he looked back up.

"You know that woman in the Volvo?" the trooper said.

"No, sir," said the man.

"The baby blue?" the trooper said.

"No, sir," said the man.

"You know who I'm talking about, don't you?" said the trooper.

"I seen her on the road, I guess," the man said.

The trooper lifted his hand to shield his eyes.

"You following her?" said the trooper.

"Just trying to get myself and my things to Texas, by God."

"You sure you haven't been following her?" said the trooper.

"Now, who told you that?" said the man.

"This is Colorado. People watch out for each other here," the trooper said.

"I done nothing wrong," said the man.

"You take a good few hours at the rest area. Let that girl get to wherever she's going without worrying, hear?"

"Yes, sir," said the man.

"Pleasure having you in Colorado, sir," said the trooper, tipping his hat. "Enjoy your stay."

He pulled off into the rest area, drove through the parking lot, drove back onto the freeway. The needles on the dashboard climbed. He drove forty-five hot, empty miles through creamy rock, stopping for gas in Walsenburg.

He sprayed water over the radiator, over his face. The attendant shambled on out to the pumps, wrote down his license number.

"What you doing that for?" the man said.

The attendant hooked his thumb through his belt loop, shrugged. "Policy," he said.

He waited in the store until the attendant was out writing down another license, then walked back to the cigarette display. He slipped two packs in between the buttons of his shirt to lay against his belly, their plastic wrapping sticky on his damp flesh. When the attendant came in he carried another pack to the counter.

"What's the Colorado woman got?" the man said.

The attendant just rotated his hips, laughed.

"Any whores in Walsenburg?" the man said.

"Every one a whore," the attendant said. "Ask my wife."

They laughed.

"Any flesh nearby?" the man said.

He dialed.

"Where are you?" she said.

"Califuckinfornia," he said.

"Where, California?" she said.

"This here's Stockton, C-A," he said. "You want one more chance? I'll give you one more chance," he said.

"Stuff it," she said.

He sat on the slick toilet seat, eyes closed, muttering another woman's name.

"Baby, that was good for me," he said.

"Five bucks," she said.

He fished a crumpled bill out of his pocket, dropped it down onto the floor.

"There you go," he said.

"Hand it to me," she said.

"Let's see you bend for it," he said.

He reached into his pocket, threw down another bill. She looked at him close, crouched over in the cramped space between his boots, bracing her arm on the toilet rim between his legs.

He stared down at the back of her skull, considering.

Pryor, Aguilar, Ludlow, Hoehne, at full speed. He swallowed the rest of the No Doz all at once, chain-smoked a pack and a half of cigarettes. Stretching his legs, he felt the quiet ache between his thighs. The sun went out. His fingers turned sluggish, cigarettes falling into his lap.

He drove the streets of Trinidad, accidentally caught sight of a baby-blue Volvo at the Pizza Hut. In the back seat was a monkey-puzzle plant. He tried the doors, found them locked. He went back to the truck, got the tire iron.

It was a tight squeeze, none too comfortable once he was wedged under the car. He could only swing from his elbow down, and awkwardly. His head started to buzz.

He waited until she was jingling her keys and then broke her ankles. He watched her legs shudder and stutter-step as the ankle gave out. She cried out and fell down on all fours, like a dog. He dropped the tire iron, reached out from under the car to grab her by the throat. Squeezing her windpipe shut, he dragged her head under the car.

He banged her head up against the underside of the car awhile, letting her arms and legs flail where they would. He crawled out, cracked her skull with the tire iron, dragged her by the feet over to the truck. He opened the back, threw her in, closed it, drove.

NEW MEXICO

Two thousand feet up to Raton Pass, the truck laboring, down into New Mexico for seven miles of narrow-lane traffic. He burned his flesh to stay awake, holding a cigarette to his wrist. He took a long drag on the cigarette, tasting himself in it.

He stared long at the wisps of smoke. He scraped the side of the truck along the cement divider, jerked it away to mow down cones, then back into the cement. The truck shuddered and skidded, gave a half-leap. A headlight went dead.

He grabbed the wheel hard with both hands, held on and kept his arms stiff. He stared straight through the windshield, sweating death all twenty-five miles to Capulin.

．　　　．　　　．

He regained consciousness midincision, his knife poised
against flesh Lord knows how long. Flashlight between his
teeth, nine stars hacked, eighteen to go. Shining the light
told him he had been cutting stars into the wrong girl. He
scraped the cut skin away, mutilated out the stars.

He felt around for the freshest flesh, began to cut.

He knocked his head against the dashboard, shook it, yelled.
He drove, watched the country flattening out. He turned off
the headlight, tried to divine the approach of morning. The
truck felt swollen and lifted, as if on tires pumped as high as
mountains, the cab teetering, airy, the road far, far below him
and inconsequential. He was on his way to heaven. He traced
his name into God's prayer book with his cigarette coal.

He made the ninety miles from Capulin to Des Moines,
drifted off the road, down a gentle grade. He came out onto
a farm road, drove before realizing he wasn't on the highway. He drove a dirt road back, wheels spitting gravel up a
loose grade. He knocked through a mileage sign, bucking
the wheels sharp enough to start something whining under
the hood. He sang "The Spirit of God Like a Fire" the last
eight miles into Grenville, belting the words out, his head
shaking and swaying from side to side, a metronome.

He pumped the tank full, kept pumping until his shoes were
soaked and he was standing in a puddle of gasoline. He shook
his head, cut off the pump.

He went into the station.

"How much?" he said.

"Forty-two twenty-three," said the attendant, a woman.

．　　　．　　　．

"Sir?" The attendant was shaking him. "Sir?"

He lifted his head off the counter, ran his hands over his bloody eyes.

He found himself in an aisle, confronted by pharmaceuticals, the woman shaking him. He gathered all the No Doz boxes up, carried them to the register.

"You got to sit down and take a rest," said the attendant, following him.

"Don't tell me what I got to do," he said.

He got two cartons of cigarettes, a liter of Coke. He opened two of the No Doz packages, poured all the pills into the foamy Coke, drank all down.

"Let's have the damage," he said.

"Sixty-eight dollars and sixty cents," she said.

He pulled out the last wads of bills from his pockets, smoothed them out, pushed them across the counter to her. She took them, counted them.

"Where's the rest?" she said.

"Ain't that enough?" he said.

He told her there was cash in his truck. He went out to get the tire iron. He stumbled up to the counter and swung the iron up above his head and down at her, crashing through the sign and racks and down into her temple, cigarette boxes raining down upon her. He went back behind the counter and stomped upon the woman's skull with his heels until it went pulpy and caved in.

He slipped the tire iron through a belt loop, grabbed the body under the warm, damp underarms. He pulled her up to him, squatted, folded her over his shoulder. He stood, grabbed cartons of cigarettes.

He stood listening to the dial tone until the weight of the dead woman collapsed him. There was something wrong with his stomach. He lay on the floor with the woman on top of him.

"Hello?" he was saying to the receiver. "Hello?" But the receiver was far above him, out of reach.

He dragged her by her heels out the back way, in stages, her pulped head leaving a bloody swath. He stood swaying on the gravel, looking out at the distant truck, at the pumps, and then staggered toward them. He had to stop for rest on the way. His stomach was knotted up. He had to fall down in the gravel and hold onto himself, moaning. His head started to buzz. He crawled the rest of the way, hooking her foot through his belt, pulling her behind him.

Her leg got hooked on the pumps. He lay there until the No Doz made him human. He unhooked her from his belt, stood, fumbled the back of the truck open.

He tore her skirt in extricating her, saw her bare white skin through the hole. He pushed the skirt up, ran his hands along her thighs. He dragged her up onto the bumper and from there heaved her into the back, laying her down and lowering the door so that her shoulders and head were in the darkness, her legs and hips dangling off the back.

He got out a cigarette, got it lit, took a few drags. He pulled the silk white panties down around her knees, ran his fingers up past them. He prodded her with his tire iron. With his cigarette he burned her up one thigh, down the other. He crawled on top of her, kneed her back along the floor with him, back among her other bodies.

He cut stars in the darkness, tracing over them afterwards with his index finger. He placed his thumb on the spot he wanted to serve as the center of the next star, cutting the star around the thumb, lacerating his thumb. Thirty seven stars hastily hacked, six uneven rows of six along her back, a seventh over on the front between her breasts, centered, as far as he could tell by touch, in the darkness.

In the sky was a pale light, announcing the sun. He swallowed another box of No Doz, vomited it up over the cab. His head slipped down, banged the steering wheel. He drifted from one side of the road to the other. The sun came up in front of him. He drove into it.

Mt. Dora, and he not knowing how he had arrived there. He rolled the windows down, let the wind knock him around the cab. He unbuttoned his shirt, let the fabric flap against his chest, his sides. He licked his fingers, ran them back into his tangled hair, holding up his head. He shook his head, felt the car drifting again, shook his head.

TEXAS

He lit a cigarette, burnt himself with it on the stomach, drove forward a mile or two, burnt himself again, higher up.

By his nipple, he was in Clayton, ten miles from the state line. He drove.

The long line of pain along his torso kept him awake. He lit another cigarette, kept it ready, but ended up smoking it mostly. He held the wheel with both hands, the cigarette dangling from his fingers, watched as the cigarette slipped slowly out of his fingers and tumbled down to land on his gasoline-soaked shoe. Flames spread up into a half-invisible blue flicker that licked up his legs. He crossed the state line. WELCOME TO TEXAS he read, and then DON'T MESS WITH TEXAS. He beat at the fire, watched the flames spread up onto his thighs. He ran the truck up against a light pole and through it, watching the cab crumple in on him, the glass shatter against his face. He was thrown out and slid across the gravel down into the coarse grass. The grass around him started to flame. He kicked his boots off, rolled away from them, beat at his legs with his hands until they stopped burning. He climbed to his feet, stumbled away from the lines of flame shooting out all across the grass.

The truck lay on its side, leaking a river of gasoline from the back and onto the roadway. The cab smouldered. He kicked the broken glass out of the windshield and crawled his way in, groped around behind the seat until he found the tire iron. He picked it up, felt it sear his flesh.

A burnt, barefoot mile to Texline. Oil wells, refineries. He threaded the narrow streets until on the side of a gas station he found a pay phone. He dialed.

"How will you pay for the call, sir?" the operator said.

"Person-to-person?" he said.

"Your name, please," she said.

He told her. He stayed on the line, listened as the call went through. The woman answered. He listened to the operator state his case to her.

"Absolutely not," said the woman.

"Baby!" the man yelled. "Honey! Lamb!"

He left the receiver dangling. He turned around and bashed in the face of the first woman he saw. She staggered, fell to her knees, and he hit her in the back of the skull. She tried to stand but he was already on top of her, cutting her blouse from her back with his penknife, pushing her skull down into the cement.

He had just time to slash a huge lone star across her back before hands dragged him off, knocked the knife away, knocked him down. The hands picked him up off the ground, knocked him down again. The hands lifted him up and held him up, striking at him in earnest. He let himself go limp, let the even rhythm of the blows lull him to sleep.

Eye

He came close enough to her to see the webbed stresses on the surface of her eye spreading out from the minute white pocks of crushed glass. He wondered how it felt for her to have the roughness of the glass scratching against the insides of her eyelid, damaging it.

"Don't look at me like that," she said, from where she was beneath him on the bed.

"Like what?" he said.

"My eyes," she said.

"Eye," he said.

The lashes that moved down to cover the eye were thickly spread. The top layer of them obscured the bottom layer. There was a flaw on the edge of the lid, the upper lid, a gnawed-away lashless gap.

He moved his hands to her eyes. His thumb on the lower lid, his pointer on the upper lid, he pried the eye open, held the eye open.

"Don't," she said, contorting her face.

She squirmed underneath him.

"Hold still," he said. "Bug or something."

Her lid relaxed. He let go of it and touched the eye itself, moved his littlest finger in tiny spirals over the glass of the eye. The pocks caught against the grooves of his fingerprints, interrupting the smoothness of his finger's motion. He moved his finger away. He saw himself reflected in both her eyes—seeing, unseeing.

She tried to close the lid, fluttering it and rolling her good eye about. She struggled underneath him.

"Get off," she said.

He kept his weight on her. He spread his legs wide and braced his feet like outriggers far out on the bed to either side of her.

"You are crushing me," she said.

She shook her head from side to side. He reached out with his free hand. He forced his fingers in her mouth, hooking on to her bottom teeth, pulling down until her mouth was wide and her bottom jaw pushed down against her collar bone. He held it there as he looked, and looked.

"This is one hell of an eye here," he said, and let her jaw free.

"I am screaming," she said, "swear to God."

He smiled down sadly, as if hurt.

He stayed on her but shifted some of his weight back onto his knees. She breathed in deeply. He kept her eye pried open as wide as it would open.

"You can pluck it out?" he said.

"Another time," she said.

He grabbed her cheeks, squeezed. He made her look at him. "Yes or no?" he said.

She wriggled. He squeezed.

"It comes out," she slurred past his hand.

"Take it out," he said.

"Let me up and I'll take it out," she said. "I have to get up to do it."

"Take it out from here," he said.

"I have to stand up," she said.

He let go of her chin and eyelid. He placed his open palms

on both sides of her head, covering her ears. He pushed in and held her head still while he moved his face down against hers. He opened her eyelid with his tongue and sucked until the eye popped loose.

He rolled the eye around on his tongue. He spat the eye out onto the bed. It bounced slightly, rolled a little. Pupil half-down, the eye came to a stop. She began to make sounds he had never heard out of her—out of anyone—before. He pried her lid open, stared into the puffy of the almost-hole.

"Will you look at this," he said. "Nobody will ever believe this."

He fluttered her flat lid open and closed quickly. He opened and closed it over and over.

"Peep?" he said, knocking on her skull. "Peep, peep?"

He put his jacket on, removed from his pocket a crumpled plastic ziplock bag. He shook the bag out, smoothed it flat on his palm.

She hissed at him something he could not hear from where she was facedown on the bed.

"You want to know what your problem is?" he said. "Your problem is the company you keep," he said.

He moved toward her, toward the bed which she was groping around on. He moved his head down until his lips were at her ear.

"On the house," he whispered.

He picked up the eye, rolled it around on the back of his hand. The eye vanished. He reached out and pulled the eye back into existence from her ear. He put the eye in the plastic bag. Expressing the extra air out, he sealed the bag. He stuffed it into his jacket pocket. He waved, shrugged, went to the door.

"Ah, what the hell," he said. He went back to the bed. He rummaged through the sheets until he had in his possession the other eye, the false one, as well.

"Be seeing you," he said, and then took his leave of her in fact.

The Sanza Affair

romanzo breve,
racconto lungo

From every realized amount of fact some other
fact is *absent*.
                —*William James, "A Pluralistic Mystic"*

When we say we do not know, we are not to say it
weakly and meekly, but with confidence and content. . . . Knowledge is and must ever be *secondary*.
    —*Benjamin Paul Blood, letter to William James*

I

THE DEATH OF SANZA

Inspector Sanza was conducting a reinvestigation into the particulars of the Hadden case when, one mild October night, after ten but not later than two, according to various testimony and to the autopsy, they killed him. He was found two days later in a suburban alley, his jaw clenched tightly, his skin going gray, the base of his skull crushed to paste. He had been killed with a hard object which, splinters in the tissue samples suggested, was made of a lacquered wood of some sort—probably, though not certainly, oak. His fingers had been broken after his death between the first and second knuckle by an instrument which had left a crosshatched scoring upon the upper and lower portion of each finger. Perhaps a spanner or a nutcracker. Two coins had been slipped between his lower eyelids and his eyes, each pushed far enough below the rim of the orbit to stay in place, leaving a circular indentation on each eyeball.

Sanza's corpse wore a green-plaid button-down shirt and tan slacks—though when he had left Graca's house earlier that evening, he had been wearing, according to Graca, a white knit shirt and loose cloth pants. He had been wearing as well his off-white panama hat, a hat which was either "his absolute favorite" (Graca) or "one of his favorites" (Sanza's wife). The panama hat was now missing, having appeared neither at his home nor at the scene of the crime, nor was there any physical evidence to suggest that he had been wearing the hat at the time of his murder. Perhaps it had blown off in the wind and had been lost earlier in the evening (Sanza's wife), or perhaps when they killed him they first snatched the hat from his head, for reasons of "assassination etiquette" (Inspector Lund) or because one of the killers "fancied the hat" (Graca).

Sanza's jaws were locked so tightly that during the autopsy it was necessary to slit open his cheeks and peel them back to the ears in order to cut through the muscle tissue and dislocate the hinge of the jaw. Cutting the tongue free, the pathologist found hidden beneath it a single scrap of paper, plastered to the inside of his bottom teeth. The paper had been clipped from an unidentified magazine, the word "anamnesis" printed on it. In italics. *Anamnesis.* A word with which Sanza was not familiar (Sanza's wife). A word Sanza knew very well indeed (Graca).

Perhaps the paper was a note of some sort (Inspector Lund, Graca) or, perhaps, merely "a scrap of paper, meaningless, accidentally lodged in his mouth" (Sanza's wife). If a note, possibly it had been cut from a magazine or journal by Sanza shortly before his death and was meant as a clue to the identity of his murderers (Lund). Though it might also have been placed there by his murderers either as an obscure jest, a trademark, a clue, a taunt, or an intentional misdirection (Graca). In any case, it was indisputably a piece of paper, indisputably found in dead Sanza's mouth. It was a scrap of evidence to be noted, categorized, filed away.

On the evening of his murder, Sanza returned from his office an hour late, because he was "making a little progress on the Hadden case" (Sanza's wife), because he had had a "breakthrough in the Hadden case" and had made shocking discoveries which were "likely to lead the case to the swiftest and most surprising of resolutions" (Graca). Sanza ate the meal his wife had prepared earlier and had left covered on the sideboard for him. He did not bother to heat the meal, being already late for his hebdomadal visit with Graca. The dinner was "cold *vitello ripieno*, a salad of greens and shallots, a glass of red wine" (his wife). Sanza's stomach contained "*vitello ripieno*, a salad, creamed peas, pistachio nuts, traces of chardonnay" (pathologist's report).

As he ate, his wife read to him from the national newspaper, from the front page. She read aloud a small article beginning at the bottom of the page, an article which discussed Sanza's reopening of the Hadden case after so many years—the first moment the reinvestigation had entered public knowledge. The article referred to Sanza's interest in the case as "obsessional" and "pointless." The reinvestigation, it said, was a "waste of taxpayers' money" and a "waste of valuable time."

Sanza smiled as he chewed. He did not comment. When his wife finished reading the piece and demanded his opinion, he informed her that he was making progress on the Hadden case, progress which would certainly prove the national press wrong.

Sanza carried his empty dish to the sink, running tepid water over the plate, the silverware, his hands. He left the dish and utensils stacked in the sink. He dried his hands surreptitiously on his shirt front and was reprimanded by his wife—either "mildly" (Sanza's wife) or "harshly, out of all proportion" (Graca, quoting Sanza)—for misusing his shirt, for having failed to employ the *torchon* hanging from a hook above the sink.

He left his wife reading the newspaper, climbed the stairs to his bedroom. He changed out of his professional clothing and into an off-white (Graca) or light gray (Sanza's wife) knit shirt and a pair of cloth pants. He removed his panama hat from its hook in the closet, carried it downstairs with him. He set the hat down on the table next to the newspaper, which his wife had folded into a small, neat rectangle. His wife was leaning against the sink, smoking a cigarette, tapping the ashes down onto the scratched porcelain. He plucked the cigarette from between her fingers, sucked until the cigarette's tip was fiery and crackling. He let his wife snatch the cigarette from his lips after the second suck "or perhaps the third" (Sanza's wife). He pulled his chair out from the dining room table and sat on it, his back toward his wife, holding "that horrid hat" (Sanza's wife) in his hands, rolling and unrolling the canvas brim of it, "ruining the hat" (wife).

Sanza continued this project of rolling and unrolling the hat until the telephone rang. He directed his wife to answer. She blunted out her cigarette, dropped the butt into the ashcan, unhooked the receiver from the telephone. Discovering that the person speaking on the other end of the connection spoke neither English nor German, she passed the receiver to Sanza, who spoke into the receiver briefly in French then at length in Italian, neither of which languages his wife spoke. While speaking into the receiver, Sanza checked his watch twice, which caused his wife to glance at the clock on the wall. 6:43. 6:48. As he spoke, his gestures were reserved, perhaps because of the nature of the telephone call or the nature of the caller herself (Sanza's wife), perhaps because his wife was in the room (Lund), perhaps as a function of the language he was speaking (Graca).

When he restored the receiver, his wife asked him who had been at the other end of the line.

"I do not exactly know," said Sanza, his forefinger touching his nose.

He was "lying" (Sanza's wife), perhaps lying (Lund), perhaps telling the truth (Graca). Sanza looked around the dining room without meeting his wife's gaze, checked his watch a third time, picked up his hat, embraced his wife, and hurriedly left the house.

.   .   .

The walk to Graca's house was a five-minute walk (Sanza's wife), an eight-minute walk (Graca), an eight-and-one-half-minute walk at a rather brisk pace (Lund). Sanza arrived at twenty minutes after seven, according to the clock on Graca's kitchen wall (twenty minutes later than usual), leaving fifteen minutes unaccounted for (Sanza's wife), ten to twelve minutes unaccounted for (Graca), five to eight minutes unaccounted for (Lund). Possibly Sanza, despite being already late, had taken his own sweet time (Sanza's wife). Perhaps he had encountered an old acquaintance and had stopped to chat (Graca). Perhaps he had a brief rendezvous with the woman he had spoken to on the telephone (Lund) or had met with another unknown (to the police, not to Sanza) individual to discuss either the Hadden case or private, unrelated matters (Lund).

When Graca answered the door, Sanza had already removed his hat and was holding it in his hands, rolling the brim nervously.

"He depressed the doorbell button once and then, before I answered the door, depressed it again, impatiently," said Graca. "I have never known Sanza to depress the doorbell button twice."

Said Sanza's wife: "Sanza has often complained about how long it takes Graca to answer the door, though he has consistently overlooked Graca's more serious flaws of character."

"She has always resented me," said Graca, "for the simple reason that I have known her husband longer than she. It has been I rather than she who has served as her husband's confidant, both in public and private affairs. She cannot help being jealous."

Sanza stepped inside, and Graca and Sanza moved directly to the table in the kitchen, on which the chess match was arranged in the same combinations in which they had left it the week before. Together they executed the move that their correspondent/opponent had mailed to Sanza, briefly discussing their opponent's possible motivations. While Graca poured himself a cognac, Sanza studied the game. They spent the rest of the evening staring at the game, discussing the possibilities of their impending move, the ramifications which that move might have on the future course of play.

"It has been years since either Sanza or myself has looked at anything but the game pieces while conversing. Even in those rather rare instances when we do regard one another face to face, we see not one another's faces but the arrangement of the chess pieces gridded over our faces" (Graca).

Near the end of the evening, shortly before ten, Sanza and Graca came to a decision as to their next move, as they always did, as they had always managed to do one evening each week for the past several years (Graca), "for too long now" (Sanza's wife).

Graca stood, walked out of the kitchen, down the passage, into the bedroom, across the bedroom, to his desk. He opened the desk drawer, removed a lacquered teak case. He opened the case, removed a silver pen (a gift from Sanza), and replaced the case in the drawer. From a lower drawer he removed a cream-colored envelope and a sheet of stamps. He tore a stamp off the sheet, affixed it to the envelope. Atop Graca's desk was a stack of thick paper, weighted by a handful of coins sprinkled over the top sheet. Graca slid a sheet from out of the middle of the stack, realigned the stack when he finished. Pen, paper, and envelope in hand, he walked away from the desk, out of the bedroom, down the passage, back to the kitchen.

Sanza had found a bag of pistachio nuts and was eating them, cracking the shells open with his teeth, smoothly, quickly. The cracking of the shells between Sanza's teeth reminded Graca of the sound of cracking knuckles. The shells of the nuts stained Sanza's lips dark red.

Graca placed the writing tools on the table. He swept the

pile of cracked shells off the table and into a hand. He dumped the shells into the ashcan.

Graca wrote down his and Sanza's chosen move, folded the stationery, sealed it in the envelope, addressed the envelope. Sanza tried to telephone his wife to tell her he would be home "in a little while" (Graca) but his wife had not answered the telephone. Hanging up the receiver, Sanza stood with his arms crossed, leaning against the kitchen counter, eating pistachio nuts. He at this point talked to Graca not only about their tenth chess game with their unknown correspondent—a game which both he and Graca believed they had, for all intents and purposes, won—but also about the Hadden case, which he believed he had, for all intents and purposes, solved.

"Bungled," Sanza kept saying. "The original investigation of the Hadden case was miserably and intentionally bungled."

Sanza mentioned a bowl and the underlip of a counter.

"An unexceptional bowl. A rather ordinary counter," Sanza said. "Similar to this counter," Sanza said, rapping on Graca's kitchen counter with his knuckles. "Everything is available, everything collected—too much collected. A matter of sifting and sorting, bringing evidence to the fore of the mind readily, expunging evidence from the mind readily, anamnesis, oblivion, oblivion, anamnesis. One must possess a fluid mind, willing to conjoin, willing to disjoin."

Sanza uncrossed his arms, pushed himself away from the counter, walked to the door. Graca followed, letter in hand. He opened the door, ushered Sanza out. Graca slipped the letter into the letter box, slid the red stick forward to benefit the letter carrier. He watched Sanza affix the panama hat solidly on his head, wave, turn away, walk away. Graca closed the door.

.　　.　　.

Since Sanza's death, Graca had received no subsequent chess move from the unknown correspondent. He had at one point mailed the last move he and Sanza had made a second time, but had received no response.

Graca had none of the postcards the chess correspondent had sent to Sanza. Sanza had always taken the postcards home at the end of each visit.

Sanza's wife had never seen the postcards. Sanza, she believed, had never brought the postcards home. She had no idea where Sanza would have hidden them had he brought them home. A search of the Sanza house discovered no postcards whatsoever.

The post office revealed that the post office box number given by the unknown correspondent had been registered to J. A. Sanza, Inspector. Investigation of the signature on the registration card suggested that it was either Sanza's genuine signature (third handwriting expert), a very good forgery of Sanza's signature (first handwriting expert), or perhaps the one, perhaps the other (second handwriting expert). Only the fingerprints of postal employees appeared on the registration card, two sets of prints in all, one probably made when the card was initially placed into the file, the other when Inspector Lund ordered the postal service to find the registration card and to surrender it to the police.

The first set of prints was matched to a young, male postal employee who claimed to have no memory of accepting the registration card. The card might have been mailed in, might have been left anonymously at the *guichet*, might have been handed to him in a pile of registration cards accepted by another employee.

The signature was "obviously a forgery" (Graca), a joke played by the correspondent, who had expected Sanza to investigate the ownership of the post office box almost immediately, "though to my knowledge he never investigated it at all" (Graca). The signature was, in all probability, Sanza's genuine signature, "nearly definitive proof" that Sanza had been mailing chess moves to Graca and to himself for several years now (Lund). That Sanza operating individually could have beat Sanza and Graca operating together was inconceivable (Graca). Unless Sanza had consciously encouraged Sanza/Graca to make moves which Sanza, operating alone, was able to counter (Lund). Sanza would not waste his time sending himself ridiculous moves for an equally ridiculous game (Sanza's wife). But the chess game was not a waste of time: it ensured Sanza one evening a week with Graca—one evening a week away from his wife (Lund).

What part the correspondent (the chess player) acted in Sanza's actual murder, however, if any part, remained unclear. There seemed no easy path for Lund to trod from Sanza's chess playing back to Sanza's crushed skull. But the lack of direct paths did not for Lund preclude the existence of convoluted paths. Quite the contrary.

If Sanza had been mailing the chess moves himself, then aside from the possibility that Sanza mailed them to escape his wife or to see Graca, Lund reasoned, there was the possibility that the chess game was an excuse to meet, on a weekly basis, either before or after chess, another individual. Perhaps the foreign woman who had telephoned Sanza on the night of his murder. Though that telephone call, according to Sanza's wife, had been an isolated occurrence. Sanza had never spoken into the telephone in Italian before.

"In fact," said Sanza's wife, "it surprised me to hear him speak Italian at all. I did not know he spoke Italian."

Nor had Graca known, though he was aware that Sanza could read Italian. Yet speaking and reading a language are two different processes, and Sanza had never done anything to suggest to Graca that he spoke Italian fluently. Sanza had never even repeated a sentence from one of the Italian novels Graca knew he read.

Sanza had a "veritable fear of uttered Italian" (Graca).

He might have spoken Italian but had not made known that he spoke it, even when he and his wife had travelled through Italy (Sanza's wife).

Perhaps Sanza's knowledge of spoken Italian was not as meticulous as his wife (who spoke absolutely no Italian) believed—assuming he had spoken in Italian, and not simply a language which, to his wife's ear, resembled Italian, such as Romansh (Inspector Lund). To Lund, it made perfect sense that a woman Sanza met with weekly (assuming he did) would call on the night of Sanza's death, since Sanza, despite his normal punctuality, was behind schedule that night and she, if she were in the habit of meeting him regularly, might have been concerned enough to risk a telephone call.

Sanza's having mailed the cards with chess moves written on them to himself (assuming he was the one to mail them) might have been an attempt to send another message (Lund). A sort of code, perhaps to the police to be solved after his murder with the aid of the paper hidden under his tongue, perhaps to an unknown individual as the chess match progressed—someone who had been able to examine Graca's chessboard on a regular basis, either "through Graca's kitchen window with a pair of field glasses" (Assistant-Inspector Masten) or by "gaining entry into Graca's house" when Graca was absent (which was seldom), "by means of a stolen key or by picking the doorlock" (Lund).

Yet to what degree can repeated chess games, strictly regulated by the moves each piece can make, convey a distinct, coherent message? What might a chess match allow Sanza to convey that he might not convey with infinitely more ease through other methods?

Possibly the chess playing had originated with Sanza's love of chess, and only over the last few months had the games begun to take on a vague significance. There might well be types of messages for which the form of the chess game might be particularly appropriate, certain meanings more likely to spring from chess matches, though Lund could not imagine any. In the last game, or in the last sequence of the last game, perhaps Sanza had realized the usefulness of a chess match to convey secret information, and this vague significance had quickly been specialized by Sanza into a codified system to convey, to an unknown individual, definite information.

Any attempt at making a chess match a message was made doubly difficult by several factors. First, Sanza, in playing chess, was forced to follow a system of fixed and definite rules; second, he was not playing alone but in combination with Graca, and Graca had to be made to believe they were choosing the best move rather than conveying a code. Each chess move Sanza performed with Graca had to be utterly relevant and responsible, both in the context of the game itself and in the context of the code which Sanza had invented (a code which might not exist).

Unless, to simplify matters, Graca too was aware of the code and fully complicit in Sanza's use of it. Assuming there was a code at all.

"Sanza had a great love of chess," said Graca. "They were games for our pleasure, nothing more."

Beginning with the last chess move he and Sanza had executed together, Graca was able to reconstruct the sequence of moves directly preceding the last move, regressing three moves for each color.

White, the color Sanza and Graca were playing together, had first moved the queen to QB2, then a rook to KR5, then the queen to KR2, without any pieces taken.

Black had castled, followed by the advance of a pair of pawns—the queen's bishop pawn, then the queen's knight pawn, without any pieces taken.

White's three pieces travelled a total of thirteen squares. Black's travelled eight.

All the white pieces moved had ended their turn on white squares. Black had ended with the two pawns on black, with the king and the rook involved in the castling on black and white, respectively.

Neither set of moves had substantially advanced the game. In both cases, there were better moves to be played.

To search for meaning in such a sequence of moves, in an utterly meaningless game, was a sheer waste of time (Sanza's wife). As chief inspector, Sanza surely had more effective ways of surreptitiously conveying messages at his disposal (Lund). Is there anything unusual about a man having a passion for a particular game, a passion which is unmotivated by secondary consideration? (Graca).

There seemed to be no pattern to the moves the correspondent mailed to Sanza/Graca, excepting the patterns dictated by the development of each particular game (Graca). Nor were there any provable connections between the chess matches and the telephone conversation Sanza had had with the "Italian" woman, the Italian-speaking woman. Nor any evident connection between Sanza's death and the game of chess he was conducting at the time of his death.

No connection, except for the fact that, shortly after making his final move, Sanza had been killed.

II

GUILTY

Sanza's wife viewed the death of Sanza as "a great loss, not only to the Bureau of Police, but to us all—and to myself in particular in having lost a marvelous husband." Sanza's wife had been disappointed in her marriage from the start (Graca). She had married young, either with "a full knowledge of what she was stepping into" (Sanza's wife) or "foolishly, on a whim" (Graca). She was a member of a prominent Northern family and had never managed to lose the shibboleths that set her apart from the Southerners. She was at ease neither with Sanza nor with the Southern style in general (according to Graca)—which she (like Lund) found pushy rather than endearing, crude rather than vital.

In her fifth year of marriage, Sanza's wife boarded a train while Sanza was asleep, travelling north to her family. When she arrived and demanded asylum, her family refused to speak to her. They dragged her down to the station and sent her home on the next train (Graca).

"In the long run, our occasional differences strengthened our love" (Sanza's wife).

Sanza had no feelings of intimacy for his wife by the time of his death—he never had (Graca). Though, initially, he had been fond of her physically (Graca). Now there remained "nothing to be fond of—a body with which to avoid intimate connection" (Graca).

Belonging to an orthodox Northern family, it would have been easier for Sanza's wife to kill Sanza than to gain the support needed to justify a divorce (Lund). Though there was no reason she would have suffered thirty-two years before killing Sanza.

Sanza's wife was "a sly one" (Graca), an "ordinary woman" (Sanza's wife), a woman with neurotic tendencies, but no more so than any childless woman who has been estranged from her family and her husband (Lund). Sanza's wife had always silently despised Sanza (Graca). Sanza's wife had had a deep love for her husband (Sanza's wife). Sanza had as few (as many) feelings for his wife as a husband can muster after thirty-two years of mutual indifference (Lund).

On the night of Sanza's murder, Sanza's wife had stayed home alone, awaiting her husband's return. She read a mag-

azine—perhaps *Der Spiegel*. She had not, from the time her
husband left the house to the time she realized he was missing, left the house. Nor, for all intents and purposes, had she
left the settee upon which she had sat shortly after his departure. She had, she said upon reflection, read first *Der Spiegel* and then turned through the pages of a back issue of
Vogue. She had, she now remembered, left the settee twice,
once to pour herself a glass of bottled water, a second time
to visit the water closet. In the water closet she had read *Der
Spiegel*, and, at one point, thought she heard the telephone
ringing. No, she had not looked at a clock either time she
had left the settee, nor was she wearing a watch.

After reading the two magazines, she entered the kitchen
to pour a second glass of Volvic. The clock read 10:30. She
drank the mineral water, then telephoned Graca's to ask ("to
demand rudely"—Graca) if she could expect Sanza home
within the next twenty minutes.

"Sanza left more than thirty minutes ago," said Graca.

She hung up the receiver, sat down at the table. She
brewed some coffee, drank a cup black, then a second cup.
She examined with distraction a copy of the London *Times*
a fortnight old.

At 11:30, she telephoned the Bureau of Police.

Sanza's wife had "personal motives" for killing Sanza
(Graca). She, among others: in moving upward to his position as chief inspector, Sanza had insulted many people, both
criminals and officials, Lund among them.

Sanza's wife was the type of woman who had the *froideur*
to pursue her husband into an alley in order to break his
head open (Graca). She could never have hit Sanza hard
enough, nor for that matter have effectively dragged a suit-
able murder weapon across town to the alley in which Sanza
was slain (Lund).

If she had killed Sanza, Sanza's wife had had an accomplice.

.   .   .

Graca and Sanza had been "companions since childhood" (Graca), though since that time they had become increasingly distanced, until their friendship was now a "mere formality, a mere excuse for a game of chess" (Sanza's wife). If Sanza had been his own chess correspondent (which, claimed Sanza's wife, was unlikely), he had mailed the moves first and foremost because of his interest in chess, and second to assuage his guilt over the change in his feelings for Graca— to force him to meet with Graca once a week (Sanza's wife).

"Sanza and I have never had an argument of any kind, either violent or verbal," said Graca. "We have forever been amicable, our friendship fattening with the years."

Graca was a man of reason (Graca). Graca was well known for his furious temper (Sanza's wife). Graca was incapable of harming the quick or the dead (Graca). Graca was neurotic, unpredictable (Sanza's wife).

"He does not care for me," said Sanza's wife. "He believes I am a usurper."

"I have never liked her," said Graca. "In truth, I do not care for many people, yourself included."

"Our animosity is mutual," said Sanza's wife. "But Mr. Graca remains the instigator."

Graca had little reason to kill Sanza, his "only genuine friend" (Graca). Graca was unmarried and possessed neither a wife with whom Sanza might have slept nor a girlfriend whom Sanza might have stolen. Graca was, "quite frankly, asexual" (Graca's physician), never interested in "matters in flesh" (Graca). Graca was "latently gay, enamored of Sanza from his earliest years" (Sanza's wife). Graca was neither homosexual nor heterosexual—he had no sexual preference for the simple reason that he possessed no mature sexuality (Graca's psychoanalyst).

Graca had lived alone in his parents' house ever since the death of his parents, supporting himself on the insurance money their deaths had brought. He associated with nobody on a regular basis, excepting Sanza. Graca left his house only rarely—to purchase groceries and supplies, to walk to the White Owl for a drink, to walk the public gardens near his house. He had no profession. He spent his days reading magazines and newspapers.

Graca's body had been made rotten by an idle life, and he was far weaker than the average. One of his legs had been crippled in a fall down the stairs at a young age, the ankle shattered and improperly reconstructed. He walked with a cane when he walked at all and was unable to cover distances without frequent rest.

His cane was not made of lacquered oak—which he soon would have tired of lugging—but consisted rather of burnished, hollow-core aluminum.

A search of Graca's house revealed two other aluminum canes identical to the first but nothing wooden which might have been used first as a cane, second as a murder weapon.

"Though indeed I did possess a wooden cane once," said Graca. "A thin, knotty thing. As a boy."

The autopsy report suggested that the pulping of Sanza's head had been carried out with a wooden, roughly cylindrical object twice the diameter of a cane—perhaps a baseball bat, a small club, or the thick end of a walking stick.

Graca would have been unable to travel through the streets rapidly enough to catch Sanza. But Sanza's wife, armed with a walking stick of the kind neither she nor Graca possessed, might have managed (assuming she knew how to manipulate a walking stick properly) to catch Sanza. Having caught up to him, however, the chances she had of killing him with the stick, even if his back was turned, were slight. She possessed neither the strength nor the coordination. Graca, on the other hand, though weak, would have been able, or slightly more able, to knock Sanza on the skull with the walking stick, perhaps hard enough to stun him. Once stunned, after sufficient blows had been rendered, Graca would eventually have caved in Sanza's head. Graca, however, because of his limp, would have had extreme difficulty catching Sanza. Once he did catch him, Sanza—a "naturally cautious fellow" (Sanza's wife)—would have been disturbed by Graca's using a wooden walking stick in lieu of the habitual aluminum cane and even more disturbed by Graca's appearance after dark on streets he never travelled. Nor would Sanza have been less surprised to discover his wife in a dark alley at a late hour. The sudden appearance of either the one or the other would have placed him immediately on his guard. The appearance of the two together would have positively alarmed him. . . .

. . . even had Graca managed, somehow, to walk to the spot where he would kill Sanza, he could not have returned to his house in time for Sanza's wife's telephone call. It took twenty minutes to travel from Graca's house to the murder site, thus forty minutes for a complete voyage out and back— not considering Graca's increased slowness because of his injured leg, which might extend the voyage to an hour or longer. Telephone company records verified that Graca's residence had been telephoned by Sanza's residence at 10:28, and someone in the first residence had spoken to someone in the second for a period of almost a minute. Graca would not have had sufficient time to kill Sanza and to return to answer the telephone. Assuming that he had located a taxi almost immediately, he still would have been hard pressed, after stopping to pay the taxi driver, to make it home from the murder site in eight minutes.

If he had driven his own car, however, he might have just made it. Graca, however, did not have a car. He had never learned to drive.

If, however, Sanza's wife had driven Graca to the murder

site, where he leaped out to kill Sanza immediately and then leaped back into the car without letting the body cool, driving rapidly and dangerously home, Graca would have reached his house in time to receive the telephone call from Sanza's wife. Yet Sanza's wife would have had difficulty driving from Graca's house to her own soon enough to *place* the telephone call to Graca.

And how might Graca and Sanza's wife have known that Sanza would appear in that particular alley?

And why might they have allowed Sanza to travel twenty minutes afoot before slaying him?

Sanza's wife, Lund discovered, had never learned how to drive. Of the three, only Sanza could drive, and he was unlikely to drive to his own death. But surely she (Sanza's wife) and Graca both had friends who drove and who, for a fee, might be willing to drive them out to an alley and wait for them, without asking questions.

Neither Sanza's wife nor Graca, when asked, was able to assemble a list of friends. As acquaintances, Sanza's wife listed a saleswoman working at a local goods shop and the previous owner of her house, a Mrs. White, who now lived in an apartment complex several kilometers distant.

Graca's list consisted of four of his parents' friends, none of whom he had seen in the last two years, and the proprietor of the White Owl.

The saleswoman did not know Sanza's wife by name. She did, with some prompting, finally select a photograph of Sanza's wife from among a group of black-and-white photographs. The saleswoman knew nothing about Sanza's wife's personal life, except that she came to the shop regularly, though the saleswoman could not, offhand, remember on which days Sanza's wife habitually came.

Mrs. White had mailed greeting cards to Sanza and his wife once a year for the last nine years, ever since selling her house to them. She had received, yearly, in return, a note of acknowledgement and gratitude from Mrs. Sanza. Mrs. White had spoken briefly with Sanza's wife twice in the last six months. The first time Sanza's wife had telephoned to tell Mrs. White that she had found an unidentified and sealed wooden crate in the corner of the basement—did Mrs. White desire to examine it? Mrs. White had agreed to examine it the next day; however, she had received a call from Sanza's wife that evening telling her that, no, Mrs. White did not need to come after all. The crate had, it seemed, belonged to Sanza all along. The police investigation had revealed no such crate in Sanza's basement, and Sanza's wife claimed not to know anything about a crate.

One set of Graca's parents' friends described Graca as a quiet but bright lad, solitary, but a good sort on the main. The couple had not seen him for nearly two years, but couldn't imagine he had changed, for he had not changed in the last thirty years.

The other set of Graca's parents' friends had been dead for several years. Graca was not aware of their demise.

The proprietor of the White Owl had seen Graca frequently and had, on occasion, spoken to him briefly. Even when intoxicated, Graca avoided speaking of himself or of his life. He enjoyed speaking of mental games, rugby, mathematics, music. He was tolerated as a harmless eccentric by most of the other patrons of the bar. He claimed no friends among the patrons.

Sanza's wife's neighbors knew her by appearance, Lund's inquiries indicated, but few knew her by name. None spoke with her on a regular basis. Graca's neighbors revealed that they were familiar with Graca's parents and their reputations, but few were personally acquainted with the son, whom they found "evasive and solitary, lacking in the all of the social niceties."

Neither Sanza's wife's neighbors nor Graca's neighbors had ever seen either Sanza's wife or Graca leave their houses or return to their respective houses with anyone except Sanza. Neither could be said to be gregarious.

Without Sanza, Graca and Sanza's wife remained isolated. Sanza was the only link to connect them to the rest of society, and as such was the most valuable person in the world to them (Lund). To kill Sanza was to give the final twist to their loneliness.

To resolve Sanza's murder through speculation on the culpability of those closest to him was, according to Lund, a dead trail.

III

THE HADDEN AFFAIR

Sanza's reinvestigation of the Hadden affair had been motivated by an overactive imagination (Sanza's wife), by a devotion to the law (Sanza's secretary, De Jaen), by a malignant devil (Lund), by sheer curiosity (Graca), by love of a difficult puzzle (Inspector Masten), by God-knows-what (Commissioner Kniffen). Sanza had been obsessed with the Hadden case continually ever since it first went to trial (Sanza's wife), though he had not made his obsession known to the members of his department and had stopped speaking to his wife about the case soon after the verdict was reached. Indeed, it was quite a surprise for Commissioner Kniffen when Sanza, directly after being appointed chief inspector, informed Kniffen that he had every intention of reopening the Hadden case. Kniffen had either strongly discouraged him from reopening the case (De Jaen, Graca), had been simply noncommittal (Masten), or had shown himself doubtful but affably tolerant (Kniffen). Sanza had persisted, insisting there existed evidence which proved the culpability of "people of conse-quence" in the Hadden affair.

"What people?" Kniffen had asked, a question which "went unanswered" (Kniffen).

Claimed Sanza (so reported Kniffen): "I am the only one prepared to solve the Hadden case," stating that the resolu-tion of the case was in fact as simple as its primary clue, a simple fact—which, Sanza said, was, in fact, "not as simple as it appeared."

"What Sanza meant, I never knew," said Kniffen.

There had been a bowl in the Hadden case—indeed, several bowls. The first had been the porcelain bowl of the toilet in the Ramsay apartment, under the rim of which had gathered a substantial quantity of blood. The blood was almost evenly distributed in a film, giving the impression that the bowl of the toilet had been filled at one time to overflowing with blood. The blood type corresponded to Ramsay's (a common blood type), and further investigation revealed microscopic particles of blood of the same type throughout the wash-room, though essentially nowhere else in the apartment.

The Hadden defense argued that Hadden "had not killed Ramsay in the street in a knife fight over an old slight, and then dragged the body to the nearby field where it had later been found, but rather Ramsay had been held down, over the toilet bowl, by an unknown number of men, while a final man slit his throat" (court transcript).

The bowl of the toilet had been the more famous bowl, the one whose evidence had been dismissed when Ramsay's doctor revealed "the fact" (Masten) that Ramsay had had extremely volatile hemorrhoids—or when a doctor was found who would "testify to the lies promulgated by the prosecution" (De Jaen).

But there had been another bowl, a second bowl, a small

shaving bowl. This bowl had been the bowl Sanza had been most interested in, oddly enough (Masten), rightfully so (De Jaen). When the police had broken down the door of the Ramsay apartment, the bowl had been full of cold water with a sheen of collapsed foam peppered with whiskers on its surface. Neither the defense nor the prosecution had made anything of this second bowl in the trial, though "according to Sanza, it was an important piece of evidence" (Masten), though it was "the only important piece of evidence" (De Jaen), another one of "Sanza's crazy schemes" (Kniffen).

The importance of the latter bowl—its "alleged importance" (Masten)—consisted for Sanza in a number of "loosely connected factors" (De Jaen):

• The length of many of the whiskers found in the bowl had reached one centimeter, though Ramsay himself had always been clean-shaven.

• The residue of the soap in the bowl had been identified as a hard soap, of the kind used most frequently to scrub sidewalks (a variety of soap not discovered in Ramsay's apartment), though powder for mixing shaving cream had been available in an inset cabinet behind the mirror.

• The razor itself—a cutthroat affair—had several hairs clinging to it and wedged into its hinge. None of these hairs, however, was more than 3 millimeters long.

Ramsay himself, when his body was discovered, was clean-shaven. His face was smooth to the touch, though he had reportedly died in the evening. His habit had been to shave in the morning (his maid), though "there is no law which keeps a man from either breaking his habits or choosing to shave twice on a given day" (Masten).

The perfect smoothness of Ramsay's face seemed to Sanza (according to De Jaen) too phenomenal to be believed. Ramsay had been seen walking through District XII, almost fifteen kilometers from his house, three hours before being allegedly killed by Hadden. There was not time for Ramsay to return home and to shave and still return to District XII to have his throat slit (De Jaen). Unless he took a taxi (Masten). Ramsay had never been considered an impulsive man—this postulated thirty-kilometer vacillation was certainly non-characteristic (De Jaen), though not impossible (Masten). Perhaps he had shaved elsewhere (Masten), though no trace of whiskers were to be found on any of the clothing his corpse was wearing (De Jaen).

Witnesses testified that Ramsay had spoken with Hadden at length, for almost two hours, directly before his murder. Surely, Sanza had thought (De Jaen reported), that would leave a roughness to Ramsay's face.

Besides, facial hair grows for several hours after death.

But Ramsay's corpse was utterly clean-shaven, freshly shaven. His dead cheeks smelt of shaving cream.

The color of the long whiskers in the shaving bowl was slightly different from the shorter whiskers on the razor's hinge. To whom did the longer whiskers belong?

Sanza's postulations concerning the bowl were "ridiculous theories, mere speculations" (Masten).

Sanza had discovered that "Ramsay had been shaved after his death, hardly the first act a man who had killed him in a rage with a knife would think to do" (De Jaen). In fact, "Hadden was innocent" (De Jaen)—Ramsay's death, Sanza believed (reported De Jaen), had been more than a simple knife fight over old feuds.

Three months after beginning his reinvestigation into the Hadden affair, Sanza had either been "ordered to drop the case immediately" (De Jaen) or had been "politely queried as to whether he considered the Hadden case to be worth continuing" (Kniffen).

Sanza had indicated that there was much in the Hadden case worth exploring.

"Why should we continue?" said Kniffen (according to De Jaen). "Hadden has been hanged; there is no raising of the dead. Why disturb stagnant waters only to raise mud?"

Said Commissioner Kniffen to Inspector Lund (according to Kniffen): "I suggested to him not exactly that he drop the Hadden case, but that he consider giving the case slightly less of his attention. The Hadden case was interfering with his more pressing responsibilities."

Indeed, Sanza was "obsessed" with the Hadden case, to an unhealthy degree (Sanza's wife). But with good reason, for "one of the people of consequence thrown into doubt by the latest developments in the Hadden case was his own immediate superior, Commissioner Kniffen" (De Jaen).

Sanza's theories were "no more than theories, a result of real paranoia, nothing more" (Assistant Inspector Masten).

"After seeing what his findings were, I realized that Sanza had been wasting his time" (Kniffen). "Please examine the findings for yourself," he said to Lund. "Nothing of interest. You will see immediately that Sanza discovered nothing of real consequence."

The contents of the Hadden file were sparse (Lund); were normal for a straightforward case, which the Hadden case was (Masten); were unnaturally slim because of the file having been doctored (De Jaen). Though Sanza had apparently worked "obsessively" on the Hadden case, the file contained only two new typewritten sheets besides the original Hadden trial transcripts and the evidence reports made in preparation for the Hadden trial. Two double-spaced sheets were reportedly typed by Masten from Sanza's written pages, at Sanza's request (Masten) or without Sanza's knowledge (De Jaen).

Masten had been assigned to Sanza either to assist him until he became comfortable with the job of chief inspector (Commissioner Kniffen) or to allow Kniffen and those above Kniffen to keep an eye on Sanza's progress (De Jaen).

It was astounding that a chief inspector of such reputation had been able to accomplish so little (Masten).

It was astounding how much paper Assistant Inspector Masten had shredded (De Jaen).

"Sanza's investigation was most unfortunate. His death even more unfortunate," said Commissioner Kniffen. "Profoundly felt by all."

He picked up his paperweight, set it down again on the other side of the desk. "You don't see anything to connect Sanza's death to the Hadden case, do you Lund?"

Unblinking, Inspector Lund said, "Absolutely nothing."

"There's a good fellow," said Kniffen, smiling. "You know to ignore the inessential. You will go far, Lund."

Though, according to Masten, Sanza had "read the typed sheets of commentary he had asked Masten to add to the Hadden file," and though, according to Kniffen, Sanza had approved these pages by placing his official stamp at the bottom of each page, nowhere on the document could Lund discover either Sanza's fingerprints or those of his assistant, De Jaen. Besides a profusion of Masten's and Kniffen's fingerprints, there were a number of partial, overlapping fingerprints—most clear enough to be identified as belonging neither to De Jaen nor to Sanza, but many not clear enough for any positive identification to be attempted. A clear thumbprint imposed to the left of a line that read, "By dint of the authority invested in him he took the opportunity," seemed with reasonable certainty to belong to the left thumb of the minister of culture. A right index fingerprint midway down the second page resembled remarkably that of the provincial senator.

Odd, mused Lund, considering "nobody outside the office had seen the file" (Masten).

Not so odd, considering that the two pages had first surfaced only several days after Sanza's death, and that both the
minister and the senator would have found themselves "most
seriously at risk" because of Sanza's original ("and now destroyed") findings (De Jaen).

What most interested Lund about the two typewritten pages
was the sanitized quality of the prose, substantially different
from Sanza's usual florid style. Unfortunately, Sanza's original handwritten version of the two pages had been "misplaced" (Masten) or "never existed" (De Jaen). Comparing
the two typed pages to Sanza's report on the Moglo-Bejerano
case (the case which gained Sanza his position as chief inspector), Lund identified thirty-two obvious stylistic and
syntactic differences. He had no doubt that a qualified specialist would discover several score more—had Lund been
able to employ such a specialist without attracting Kniffen's
attention. The differences were manifold: ranging from
Sanza's prevalence of subjunctive forms in the Moglo-
Bejerano case report to the absence of the subjunctive in
the Hadden pages, from Sanza's multisyllabic vocabulary in
the former to a stripped and simple vocabulary in the latter,
from a prolixity of compound and complex clauses in the
former to an absence of compound and complex sentence
structures in the latter.

Yet the sentences had reportedly been copied by Masten
"in exactly the way Sanza gave them to me."

"Sanza," said De Jaen, "never gave Masten any papers.
Sham creation."

Lund wondered if it might not be prudent for him to keep
two separate files, one official, one private, the two not entirely in accord.

•   •   •

When Commissioner Kniffen was given word by "anonymous sources" (Kniffen) or "by Masten" (De Jaen) that Sanza had continued to conduct a surreptitious investigation of the Hadden affair, despite his promise to drop the case, he had "seriously threatened Sanza" (De Jaen), "mildly reprimanded Sanza" (Masten).

"I merely informed Sanza that in this department we do nothing privately. We do nothing in darkness," said Commissioner Kniffen. "We have nothing to hide, Lund?"

Kniffen leaned back in his chair.

"You yourself are no longer pursuing Sanza's connection to the Hadden case?" Kniffen said.

"A few last details for the report," said Inspector Lund. "Strictly technical matters."

Several days before Sanza's death, Kniffen "shouted at Sanza and threatened to stab him with a letter opener" (De Jaen), "mildly suggested to Sanza that if he had any reason to pursue the Hadden case, he should, of course, do so—but if there was no clearly defined reason for such a pursuit, it was perhaps time to close the case" (Kniffen).

Sanza had agreed to stop the investigation and, indeed, for all intents and purposes seemed to have done so by the time he died (Masten). In actuality, Sanza had redoubled his efforts, spending all his time mulling over the Hadden case, although he had become extremely tight-lipped about the case around everybody but De Jaen (according to De Jaen). Despite this, on the day before Sanza's murder, someone had indicated to the national press that Sanza was continuing to investigate the Hadden case. Perhaps De Jaen. Perhaps Masten. Perhaps an unknown, Italian-speaking woman. Perhaps Sanza himself.

The other cases Sanza was working on at the time were "of such complexity that Sanza would have had no time to work on the Hadden case" (Masten). The national press was, "as is often the case," misinformed (Kniffen).

Sanza had only cursorily investigated the other cases assigned him, "leaving the brunt of the work to Masten," at the same time "maintaining for Masten's sake the illusion that Sanza himself remained extremely busy with related issues" (De Jaen).

"Sanza was extremely busy with two other cases at the time of his death" (Masten).

Sanza in fact was busy with only a single case—and only unofficially (De Jaen).

Said Commissioner Kniffen to Lund, confidentially: "I would caution you against accepting anything De Jaen calls truth as unmixed truth. She had certain attachments to Sanza, extending—how shall I say—'beyond the pale of normal secretarial responsibilities.' "

Said Masten: "De Jaen is not a first-rate secretary in any sense of the word. Sanza allowed her to stay only because she made certain concessions to him, concessions of the most carnal kind."

Said Commissioner Kniffen: "De Jaen knows she will not be in our employ for long. This knowledge has transformed her into a malicious devil. Her performance as a secretary is, quite frankly, far from adequate. Her performance between sheets, I imagine, is worth the price of admission. But you would have to ask Sanza about that."

Said De Jaen: "Sanza and I were friendly. One thing led to another. Neither of us had regrets."

Said Sanza's wife: "Impossible. Sanza was absolutely faithful. Our affection for each other did not wane from our first day to his last."

"Sanza had not slept with his wife in years," said Graca. "He could not help but be repulsed by her. But, as to another woman: no. He would have informed me."

"A simple case of jealousy provoked to extremes," said Masten. "A woman scorned. . . ."

"My husband had no lovers," said Sanza's wife. "I was his only true love."

An inquiry at the telephone company indicated that the volume of telephone communication between Sanza's house and Graca's house had not decreased since Sanza's death. If anything, it had increased.

"I despise her," said Graca. "But one must speak to another human being occasionally in order to stave off madness."

"He is detestable," said Sanza's wife. "But better Graca than a silent night in a dead man's house."

Said Masten to De Jaen and Lund: "We have discovered our motive."

"We both know what happened, the real motive, the elaborate politics behind Sanza's death," whispered De Jaen to Lund later, in confidence.

One of Sanza's wife's neighbors reported seeing Sanza's wife, on several recent occasions, leave her home accompanied by an elderly gentleman carrying a cane. A handsome but dour old fellow, the neighbor said. The proprietor of the White Owl, when shown pictures of Graca and Sanza's wife, indicated that the pair had come to the pub together once or twice in the last week, but never before that time.

"Romance at that age," said the proprietor, shaking his head. "What a horrid thought. You think they would have learned their lesson."

"Why should I not spend the evening with her?" said Graca. "It is natural Sanza's wife and I should spend time together, despite our mutual hatred. Each of us provides the catalyst missing from the other's formulae for conjuring up memories of Sanza. Together we raise the dead."

Lund filed his findings in his private file, submitting a routine report to the public file. When asked by Masten when they were planning to arrest the "elderly lovebirds," Lund responded, "Never."

Masten furrowed his forehead.

"Appearances are deceptive," said Lund.

"Are you certain?" said Masten.

"I must ask that you trust me," said Lund. "Sanza's death lies elsewhere."

Lund spent a full day searching Sanza's office, finding neither a second file on the Hadden case nor clues that a second file had existed. Behind the filing cabinet were a pair of pennies and a larger, foreign coin, sticky with cobwebs. There were crumbs in the corners of the room. Stuck to the underside of the desk was an old ball of chewing resin. In Sanza's middle desk drawer were two fountain pens, two Le Cassât pencils, a stack of blank business cards, a pair of black-handled scissors, a German screwdriver, an adjustable set of vise grips carrying a herringbone pattern on its pincers.

Lund discovered Masten's fingerprints on the paper shredder (and no one's but Masten's), though Masten had claimed that De Jaen had been the only one of them ever to use the paper shredder. In De Jaen's desk, Lund discovered a long and narrow strip of paper, a shredding, rolled around a pencil and taped down to it. He peeled the tape off, unscrolled the paper. The paper was single-spaced, wide enough to hold four characters:

```
          i n c l
          h e   r
          n   t h
          v e l y
          a n i ,
          Gram
          d   a s
          s h o
            n e d
```

```
i t h e
.  O
r a t e
c c u r
,  h o
c o n t
an  a
h e m
d  w i
 d a y
o w l
namn
```

Lund brought De Jaen in from where she was waiting with Masten in the adjoining room. De Jaen sat down. Lund straightened out the strip of paper, dropped it on the desk between the two of them.

"I wondered when you would ask," said De Jaen.

"I am asking," said Lund.

"It has to do with the Hadden affair," she said.

"In what way?" said Lund.

But she smiled, shook her head, said nothing.

He had descended the steps of the Bureau into the dark streets when an unknown woman walking past grabbed his hand gently, tugging him with her down the street, through an alley, onto a main street, into a parking lot.

She bowed low, vanished.

Lund looked around. Far down the row a car fluttered its yellow headlights.

He took his gun out of his holster, loaded it, pushed it into his coat pocket. He kept his hand in the pocket, finger on the trigger. The car lights fluttered again. He walked toward the car.

Lund knocked on the dark window. De Jaen opened the door, climbed out. She moved around the car to the back, threw the trunk open. Inside were two large bags made of thick black plastic.

He untied the knots that held the bags closed, peered in with caution. Nothing but cut bits, thousands of strips of paper. Two gigantic Gordian knots.

He plunged his hands deep into a bag, felt the paper swallow his fingers.

On the morning of his murder, Sanza "appeared distracted" (Masten), "as if something were consuming him" (Kniffen). He arrived at the Bureau several hours later than was usual. He spent most of the day in his office, tracing mathematical figures on his desk top with a piece of chalk and then wiping them away (Masten). He spent the morning thinking through the information he had gathered for the Hadden case, a task doubly difficult in that, because of Masten's presence, he had to do so without the aid of notes and without referring to the case files (De Jaen).

When asked by Masten what he hoped to perform with his chalk equations, Sanza had said dryly, "A sort of mathematics." When asked by De Jaen in Masten's absence, he whispered, "Solving the Hadden case."

At noon, he sent De Jaen down the street to buy a *tournedo* with extra salt while he examined Masten's latest report on the Marcello burglary/battery. He ate the meal at his desk, wiping away the grease that dripped onto the desk with an old handkerchief. Between bites, he dictated to De Jaen an official response to Masten's report on the Marcello burglary/battery, specifying a continued course of investigation, reprimanding Masten for having failed to pursue witness Gardner on the inconsistencies of his testimony.

Masten sat at his desk, observing Sanza, without expression. At times, Sanza dictated the words of his report while staring Masten in the eyes. Though the reprimand was "unjustifiably harsh" (Masten), Masten did not ask Sanza to rephrase the report.

After finishing his report, Sanza turned to Masten. He said, "Have I covered everything, Masten?" A comment which Masten answered only with a curt nod of his head.

Sanza brushed the crumbs off the table and onto the floor. He tucked the old handkerchief back into his pocket, stood to crack his knuckles. Without a word to Masten or De Jaen, he made his way out of the door and to the washroom, in which he spent "a minute or two" (Masten), twenty minutes—"much longer than normal" (De Jaen).

In the early afternoon, Sanza announced to De Jaen that he had solved "the immediate and intermediate particulars of the Hadden case." He had not yet completely determined the "external particulars" and the "originary motivating factors"—though he had a general idea as to who and what those might be.

Shortly thereafter, Sanza crossed the hall to Commissioner Kniffen's office, knocked once on the door, entered, closed the door behind him.

"Sanza was frequently meeting with Commissioner Kniffen in the former's capacity as chief inspector. It was not unusual for him to do so on a given day" (Masten).

The meeting was highly unusual in that "Sanza never instigated a meeting with Kniffen, but only met with Kniffen at the commissioner's request" (De Jaen).

From behind the door came shouting, primarily that of Kniffen (De Jaen). There was nothing of the meeting that could have been overheard (Masten).

"It was a conference similar to any other conference, Lund, no more, no less," said Kniffen. "The Hadden case was not even discussed."

Said Masten: "Official business."

Said De Jaen: "The Hadden case, certainly."

Said Commissioner Kniffen: "We discussed a few ques-

tions Sanza had on the cases Masten and he were just beginning to pursue, particularly the Marcello case and Masten's
role in that case. Sanza then spoke briefly about his wife,
who, he said, was quite pleased with his new appointment
as chief inspector."

"I made it quite clear to Sanza," said Sanza's wife, "that I
did not care one way or the other about his new position. It
made no difference to my quality of life. He rarely discussed
his work, excepting the Hadden case."

When the door was thrown open and Sanza exited, he was
grinning slightly. "Behind him a red-faced Kniffen stood
shaking with rage" (De Jaen). Or perhaps Sanza and Kniffen
had shaken hands cordially across the thick oak desk and
then, as Sanza left, Commissioner Kniffen "returned to the
document I had previously been reading, a report on the
Voegel burnings" (Kniffen). A completely ordinary inter-
office encounter, of the type which occurred daily without
fail (Kniffen, Masten). A significant encounter, perhaps an
error in judgement on Sanza's part, a premature accusation
which had sealed Sanza's fate (De Jaen).

At 5:00 Sanza buttoned his coat and left with the others.
They walked together (Masten, Kniffen, De Jaen, Sanza) to
the Castellan metro annex. While Masten descended to the
lower level to board the west suburban metro, and Kniffen
bought a ticket for the Châteauredon run, Sanza and De Jaen
continued on in company to De Jaen's residence. After
speaking with De Jaen momentarily, the two of them standing together in the lower doorway, Sanza kissed De Jaen
once, lightly, commenting favorably on her perfume (De
Jaen). He released her, turned, watched her enter the building, and then (De Jaen assumed) "he must have returned the
way he had come, back toward the metro annex."

At 5:20 Sanza reappeared at the Bureau, where he surprised the caretaker in the act of lighting a cigarette. Sanza

went into his office, telephoned his wife to tell her that he was "working late" but would be home directly. He then made another telephone call—to whom, the caretaker could not say. Sanza was still on the telephone several minutes later when the caretaker passed by on his way to sweep Commissioner Kniffen's office.

Having finished Kniffen's office, the caretaker removed a large sack made of black plastic from his pocket. He unfolded it, smoothed it out on his belly, dumped Kniffen's rubbish bin into it. He walked down the hall to do the same with the washroom rubbish bin. There, he discovered, crinkled into a ball, thrown behind the bowl of the toilet, a piece of paper with some writing on it; he didn't know what, he hardly looked at the words, he simply threw it away. He thought it curious that someone had been doing some writing in the washroom, since, as far as he knew, it wasn't anybody's regular habit.

When the custodian returned, Sanza was gone.

Between the time when he was seen by the custodian and the time when he arrived home that night, later than usual, there might have been, apart from travel time, almost thirty minutes unaccounted for—at the least twenty minutes. Sanza might, in that time, have returned to De Jaen's apartment, "as he often did when 'working late' " (Masten). De Jaen claimed not to have seen him.

Perhaps he had simply taken his time walking home (Sanza's wife). Perhaps he had met someone: a friend (Kniffen), a business associate (Graca), his killer (Masten), or the unidentified person whom he had spoken to later in Italian over the phone. But whom he had met (if anyone) and where they had met (if anywhere), were questions Lund could not answer.

Looking for clues, Lund reached down Sanza's throat, pulled up his stomach.

IV

REGURGITATION

Lund crammed his pockets with small, clear plastic bags, took his meals at the several restaurants between the Bureau of Police and Sanza's house. His selections varied according to restaurant but always included creamed peas. He never ate the peas, only scooping a sample into a plastic bag, sealing the bag tightly, labelling the bag with the name of the restaurant and of the chef who had prepared the peas.

Of the twenty-three restaurants in the city known to serve creamed peas, only eight were within Sanza's range on the night of his murder, assuming he was travelling afoot. Only three of these restaurants claimed to have served creamed peas on the night Sanza was killed. Each of the restaurant proprietors, without exception, claimed never to have seen Sanza before, and the headwaiters who had been on duty were fairly certain (though two—at the Hungry Paysan and at Casa Torrence—were not absolutely positive) that Sanza had not attended their restaurant on the night in question.

A waiter at the Sbasta claimed that Sanza often ate there but never had ordered the creamed peas. A waitress at Herr Altmann initially claimed that Sanza had eaten there either the night of his murder or the night prior to his murder, but had eaten alone and had not ordered creamed peas. When pressed, she claimed she must have mistaken the man.

Laboratory analysis of the creamed peas found in Sanza's stomach indicated that the cream did not precisely match any of the samples which Lund had collected from restaurants. However, three of the eight samples were close to the original sauce. Since the sauce of the original had been subjected to unusual conditions, and since there had been only a small sample extracted from the stomach, there was a possibility the creamed peas might be the same as one of the three other creamed peas. Or might be from the same recipe, made by a different chef (official report).

But none of the three samples which the laboratory report favored belonged to restaurants which claimed to have served peas on the night of Sanza's murder. And none of these restaurants' employees remembered ever having seen Sanza.

Sanza had eaten out "only rarely" (Sanza's wife). He had eaten out surreptitiously and frequently because he "hated his wife's cooking—if you can call it cooking" (Graca). Sanza despised creamed peas (Sanza's wife), would not have eaten peas "had his life depended on it" (Graca). Sanza loved legumes of all varieties, cooked or raw, including peas (De Jaen). Graca had never seen him eat vegetables, though vegetables had been offered to him "on countless occasions." Sanza's wife had never cooked creamed peas for Sanza, nor had De Jaen, nor had either the one or the other seen him eat creamed peas *per se*, though Sanza's wife had thrice seen him turn down creamed peas, and De Jaen had at Li-Bau Chang seen Sanza eat "an Orientalist dish" of snow peas and chicken in a sauce with a consistency similar to the sauce of creamed peas.

Perhaps Sanza had stopped at a restaurant on the way home to order a plate of creamed peas (De Jaen), though none of the three most likely restaurants claimed to have served creamed peas on the night in question. Perhaps Sanza had had the peas crammed down his throat after his death by his killers (Graca) or had been offered the peas by those who planned later to kill him (perhaps before he knew they were going to kill him), and had been offered them in such a way that, even though he hated creamed peas, he "found himself incapable of a refusal" (Sanza's wife).

A third variant, offered by Lund in his official report to Kniffen: "It is not beyond the realm of possibility that Sanza ate the peas by choice, not in a restaurant but in a private residence, at a location unknown to De Jaen, Sanza's wife, and this inspector."

A further query of the staff of the eight restaurants obtained no results. Interviewing waiters and waitresses, chefs and kitchen support, uncovered vague indications Sanza had attended several of the restaurants on more than one occasion, perhaps even regularly—though Lund was never able to extricate more than the vaguest hints.

Lund called in the proprietors of the restaurants, made accusations, bluffed them into thinking he knew certain things. He uncovered an informal gambling association which played whist in a back room at the Saltero on Wednesdays and in the kitchen of the La Hanabera late on Sundays. Among the waitresses of the Cicorico, prostitution had sprung up in the back of the cloakroom, informally and clumsily operated, the project of poor waitresses rather than of a pimp. But nothing to do with Sanza. Nothing at all.

Neither Graca's suggestion that the peas had been crammed down Sanza's throat after his death nor Sanza's wife's suggestion that he had accepted the peas at an earlier time from the same killers, willing or unwilling, seemed either provable or entertaining (Lund). If the peas had been crammed down Sanza's throat after his death, the throat would still be coated with cream sauce, and several of the creamed peas might have ended up in Sanza's throat instead of his stomach. Nevertheless, a tube forced into Sanza's throat and down into his stomach, similar to the type of tube used to suck toxic substances out of a stomach, with a funnel attached to the end of it into which previously masticated peas could be poured, and a device to force them down, would bring the peas cleanly into the stomach (Graca).

Yet the peas had been found not on top of the stomach

contents, but rather beneath the remains of Sanza's dinner, the dinner he had eaten at home, alive, just before having visited Graca.

Despite this, Graca insisted on the unlikely possibility that the peas might have been consumed thereafter. The end of the tube might have been located by someone with a knowledge of medical practice, not in the stomach, but, by forcing open the stomach valve, in the top portion of the large intestine. The tube's contents, Dr. Alosh demonstrated on a fresh cadaver, might have been injected beneath the top mush of food, even far into the intestine.

But why would the killers trouble themselves to insinuate the peas into a certain part of the digestive system? What difference would it make to them if it was believed that the creamed peas were eaten at a certain time, instead of not eaten at all? It was not only farfetched and meticulously planned out, but, if it was true, had failed to throw suspicion on any particular restaurant or group of individuals. Why would they bother to pump anything into Sanza's stomach in the first place? And why, of all possible substances, creamed peas?

If the peas had, on the other hand, been fed to Sanza by his killers before they had killed him—perhaps even before he knew that they were going to kill him—why had Sanza chosen to eat them? There are ways of declining food (particularly a food as banal as the creamed pea) without rendering offense, and Sanza, who seemed not to have cared for creamed peas, might have graciously declined them, and done so in such a way as to satisfy the demands of etiquette. However, Sanza had either (if Sanza's wife was right) chosen for whatever reason not to decline the peas or had had the peas forced upon him in such a way that he could not possibly refuse them. What was at stake was the degree of complicity on Sanza's part in swallowing the peas. This, the corpse chose not to reveal.

In all probability the peas themselves were not prepared

in a restaurant. Rather, they might have been from a personal recipe, served at a private residence of one of the several million people in the city. Even had Lund been able to narrow the number down to the roughly twenty thousand or so people living on or near the path Sanza had walked from the Bureau of Police to his house every day, a viable investigation would have been impossible (official report). Besides the twenty thousand people of fixed domicile there were the hotels, the rented rooms, the tramps, the guests of residents, the individuals who had leased private residences for short periods. There was no point pursuing the investigation of Sanza's stomach further (official report).

Two days after submitting his official report to Commissioner Kniffen, Lund received a telephone call from a woman named White, the owner of an apartment complex. She claimed she had seen the progress of the Sanza case in the newspapers and was "interested in doing all she could to help solve the horrible murder." She indicated to Lund that she had matters "of the utmost importance" to discuss with him, matters concerning Sanza and, in particular, concerning the creamed peas in his stomach. She claimed to have discovered "tangible proof" of Sanza's connection to the creamed peas in one of her (currently vacant) apartments.

Lund sent Masten with an official photographer to examine Mrs. White's "tangible evidence," while he himself again traversed the complicated issue of where Sanza had eaten the peas, assembling and arranging his speculations for a confrontation with Mrs. White's tangible proof.

Masten returned with a bowl. The bowl's interior was lined with a creamed pea mixture which had cracked and dried along its interior. Analysis showed that the bowl's contents approximated the creamed peas discovered in Sanza's stomach.

. . . .

Mrs. White claimed to have discovered the bowl containing the creamed peas in the apartment leased by Alderico Zayas, a middle-aged *homme d'affaires* who had been renting the apartment for a year as a place to stay when in town for business. Though, Mrs. White said, "more than just business" had gone on in the apartment—or so the "steady flow of ladies" Zayas brought to the apartment led her to imagine. Lately, the stream had dried up, narrowing to a trickle: a blond-haired woman who wore the most recent fashions and who spoke with an Italian accent. This was the only woman Mrs. White had seen attend Zayas during the past nine weeks. Or rather, during the seven weeks preceding the last two weeks, for she had not seen him at all during the past two weeks, alone or accompanied. And Zayas's name, she knew when she had seen the Sanza cadaver on television, hadn't really been Zayas at all, but Sanza.

Directly after the television broadcast, Mrs. White had gone to Sanza's/Zayas's apartment, knocked on the door. Nobody had answered. She called out. Employing her spare key, she let herself in.

The apartment was unoccupied. The bed was unmade. In the sink she saw a dirty bowl, which she realized contained dried creamed peas. The first famous bowl of the Sanza affair, thought Lund. The peas had shrivelled, and the sauce they were in had dried, solidified, cracked.

Mrs. White had at first thought that she should telephone the police, but had hesitated. Perhaps, she had thought, there was merely a superficial similarity between Zayas and Sanza, to which future images of Sanza she would see on television might give the lie. But with each news broadcast showing Sanza's corpse, she became more certain Zayas was Sanza. Several days later, she read about the creamed peas in Sanza's stomach, about the line of evidence which Lund had first pursued and then (some papers said, "unwisely") dropped. Perhaps, she rationalized, still coincidence.

Having failed to see Zayas for quite some time, she re-entered the apartment to search for "clues." She had found in Zayas's closet a number of white shirts, each with the name *Sanza* written in black ink on the tag inside the collar. She locked the apartment, called the police.

Sanza never labelled his name on his clothing, had "never had any clothing with names written on it" (Graca, Sanza's wife, De Jaen). An inventory of the Sanza closets revealed no markings resembling those found on the shirts in the Zayas closet: indeed, only two series of shirts in Sanza's home had any markings at all. In the first (five white shirts with long sleeves and tin cufflinks, purchased, according to Sanza's wife, almost eight years earlier), a red *S* was marked on the heel of the shirt, an *S* which differed substantially from the *S* found on the Zayas shirts. The second series of shirts (two shirts which Sanza brought into the marriage thirty-two years before, one cream and the other a bright yellow) had the initials *A.S.* sewn into the pocket in white thread.

Comparison of the *Sanza* written on the Zayas shirts with examples of Sanza's handwriting, culled through the years, suggested that the markings on the shirts had not been made by Sanza. Comparisons of the Zayas markings to the hand-writing of Sanza's wife and the handwriting of De Jaen in-dicated a similar dissimilarity.

It was not difficult for Lund, returning to the Bureau one morning, to riffle through the outgoing mail in Mrs. White's letterbox, stealing one which had many of the same charac-ters found in the name *Sanza*. Preliminary analysis suggested that the writing on the Zayas shirts might belong to Mrs. White, though there were notable differences between the Zayas apartment *A* and the *A* of Mrs. White. A surreptitious, unskilled comparison of the Zayas markings with Masten's handwriting suggested that the markings on the Zayas shirts might also have belonged to Masten. Though Lund could not be certain without having a sample of Masten's handwriting written with a pen as thick as a clothing marker on a textile with a thread count and fabric consistency identical to that of the Zayas shirts.

Analysis indicated that the Zayas creamed peas were quite close in chemical content to those in Sanza's stomach, though not identical. The variation might have been the result of additional ingredients being added to the original batch or of an uneven mixture of peas with varying content (Masten), or it might have been the result of a batch being made from the same recipe as the peas in Sanza's stomach but by a new chef who did not know the slight variations the chef who usually made the recipe had introduced—a too meticulous following of a written recipe (Lund). It was likely that the peas had either been made from the same recipe or by the same chef, and probably they were the same peas which Sanza had eaten (Masten). Or that they had been mixed by someone with an awareness of the chemical content of the peas in Sanza's stomach (Lund).

The bowl containing the creamed peas had no fingerprints on it, as if it had been washed directly before receiving the peas and had been touched only while wet—as if the peas had been eaten quickly and the bowl placed immediately in the sink (Masten). Or as if the bowl had been wiped clean of fingerprints (Lund).

There was no spoon accompanying the bowl in the sink. There were, however, several spoons lying on a serviette beside the sink, all without fingerprints. But if Sanza (assuming it had been Sanza) had chosen to wash the spoon he had used, why had he not washed the bowl as well? Perhaps he had "taken the spoon out of the apartment with him after eating the peas" (Masten), but all six spoons of the silverware set which furnished the apartment were present, and there were no other spoons of other types found.

Might it have been a matter of a single renegade spoon Sanza carried with him habitually, perhaps "Sanza's favorite spoon?" (Kniffen).

Might Sanza/Zayas, after washing his spoon, have been forced, for whatever reason, to leave off washing the dishes, never to return to them? (Lund, official report).

Might it be that these peas were placed there by others, that Sanza had never been Zayas, because there was no such person as Zayas—that Sanza had nothing to do with these peas? (Lund, unofficial report).

Lund's own examination of the Zayas apartment's silverware revealed a fact which Masten's official report had failed to notice: none of the silverware was tarnished, bent, scuffed, water-spotted. All of it appeared completely new, even those spoons lying on the dish cloth beside the sink. There was not the slightest indication that they had ever been used.

Lund could not resist, when alone, plucking a spoon off the towel, slipping it into his pocket.

A fingerprint sweep of the Zayas apartment revealed virtually no fingerprints on the flat surfaces of the room, and no readable prints at all. The surfaces of the apartment had been wiped clean by someone with a damp rag, probably not Sanza (Lund). Sanza had taken the greatest care not to leave any markings to connect him to his love nest (Masten). Why might Sanza go to such extremes, but then bring shirts into the apartment which had his name written on the collar?

There were relatively few strands of hair and fabric on the floor and on the bed; what was there matched neither Sanza's home clothing nor samples of Sanza's hair. There were, the report indicated, neither filaments of hair nor flakes of skin between the bed sheets—perhaps because Sanza had recently changed the sheets (Masten); perhaps because Sanza, never having entered the apartment, had never slept in the bed (Lund). If Sanza had been in the apartment, to leave it as clean as it was he would have had to wear a bathing cap and to dress in clothing not prone to losing fibers, clothing made of leather, plastic, or rubber.

There was nothing which seriously suggested Sanza had been in the apartment (Lund's unofficial report).

"What was found of fabric threads and hair strands was similar to Sanza's hair and to the material of his coat—it seems possible that Sanza had been there on occasion" (Lund's official report to Kniffen).

Using a list of ingredients derived from the laboratory report, Lund mixed his own recipe for creamed peas. He measured out a quantity, dolloped it into a bowl. He placed the bowl in a sink, taking careful notes as it dried.

Registration records indicated that no lodgers by the name of Alderico Zayas were in the official files. Nor was Sanza listed as a lodger, being listed only as the owner of a home.

It was not difficult for Lund to lever open the window of Mrs. White's office and, once inside, to pick the lock on her filing cabinet. The rental files for Room 3a said nothing of either Zayas or Sanza. No contract had been filed. It appeared that the apartment had been vacant for nearly two years.

Lund reached under his arm, pulled out the pistol, loading it as Mrs. White looked on. He grabbed the old woman's loose-fleshed throat, shoved the gun barrel between her teeth. Shortly thereafter, Mrs. White became cooperative.

She had received fifteen thousand in new currency for renting the room for one month. There was an additional twenty thousand for memorizing the provided script and improvising said script into believability.

Of course she had been frightened, but thirty-five thousand was thirty-five thousand.

No, she never had heard of a Hadden. She knew a Haldenne, though, from the North.

Why they had thought it necessary to create a room in which Sanza might have eaten peas, she claimed not to know.

They had contacted Mrs. White only several days previous, only shortly before Mrs. White had made her telephone call to the Bureau of Police, speaking in the manner in which the script instructed her to speak.

She claimed not to know any names. They were two men, of "ordinary features." She had not seen either man before or since.

With Lund's assistance, Mrs. White's memory was refreshed. She recollected that one of the two had been a tall blond. The other man was short and dark-haired, with a high-pitched voice, an Italian accent.

With Lund's further prompting, Mrs. White conceded that the short man's voice had been high enough that he might, over the telephone, have been mistaken for a woman.

The tall man was not terribly tall—only tall relative to the short man, who had been very short indeed, she admitted.

The shorter man had said to the taller man at one time, "Already missed her, Ranns?" Or perhaps it had been, "Are you ready, Mr. Ramse?" Or perhaps, "Are you red-eyed, Mr. Brance?" She had not heard the taller man's response. Ramse/Ranns/Brance had indeed been red-eyed, Mrs. White could not help noticing. Though she could not say for what he was ready or whom he was missing.

Had she ever seen these gentlemen before they had approached her about the apartment?

No, she had never seen either one before.

Did she imagine she might see them again?

No, she did not. Though she did not know for certain.

Did she know that if these two men discovered she had spoken openly to Lund they would kill her?

She shook her head dubiously, slowly. No, she had not known that.

Did she know that if she breathed a word to them of Lund's visit, that Lund himself would kill her, with the pistol he had in his hand?

She claimed not to have known that.

Was there anything else she cared to tell him?

No, there was nothing else.

Were there things she had not told him?

No, nothing.

Did she have anything else left to tell him?

Reported Lund, officially: "There is no reason to suspect that the creamed peas found in the Zayas apartment are not the same peas that Sanza ate, though his motivation for eating them remains obscure. It is almost certainly tangential to the real difficulties of the case."

(Yet though the creamed peas in the apartment and those in Sanza's stomach were unimportant, Lund thought, there was much to suggest that someone was doing their best to make the creamed peas mean something. Beneath the surface, forces were operating which suggested to Lund that there was more to Sanza's murder than even he had guessed.)

V

BODIES

Kniffen asked Lund if he would care to set aside the Sanza case temporarily, in favor of a more recent case. This case also a murder, the slaying of a woman who let apartments, a woman by the name of White. Did Lund know whom he meant? Kniffen wanted to know. The White woman, name of White, the woman who had known Sanza or at least had claimed to know Sanza. But who, Lund's report claimed, had had little relevance to the Sanza case. Did Lund, Kniffen wished to know, care to revise his opinion?

Lund indicated that he did not care to give up the Sanza case. There were a number of possibilities still untried, a number of trails which would soon grow cold.

Kniffen shrugged.

"Please examine the White body. I would like your opinion of the White corpse, even if you choose not to accept the case." He waved his hand, dismissively. "I invite you to think upon it, Lund."

Lund sent Masten inside to examine the White corpse while he himself stood at the gate, smoking a Gauloises. He looked out over the yard, looked from one end of the street to the other. He butted the cigarette against the iron gatepost, flicked it into the flowerbed. He walked down the road, away from the White apartments.

"Inspector Lund! Inspector Lund!"

Lund turned, squinted back through the sunlight at Masten standing on the concrete steps of the White complex, waving. Lund waved, shouted that he would soon return.

Masten came off the steps, moved toward the gate. Lund made windmills of his arms, sending Masten back.

Lund turned right down a side street, went a few blocks, turned left onto a narrow cobbled lane running along the back wall of a candle factory. Inside the factory, beyond the wall, came a rhythmed crashing. He turned, looked behind him. There was nobody.

He took the gun from the holster under his arm, slipped it into his jacket pocket, moving a second gun from his other pocket and into the holster under his arm. He wiped the first gun clean with his handkerchief, dropped the weapon into a rubbish drum.

He walked a few blocks, glancing back over his shoulder. He couldn't help patting his side to assure himself that the second gun was there, slung in its holster. He wandered a few streets then turned back, returning to the White complex by a different route.

Masten, when he saw Lund wending up the street, walked out to the gate to wait for him.

"What was that concerning?" said Masten.

"What?" said Lund.

"Your departure?" said Masten.

"Nothing," said Lund.

"Where were you, Lund?" said Masten.

"Business," said Lund.

They went up the stairs, down the hall to the apartment, found Mrs. White's body collapsed on the floor just inside of the door.

An exit hole for a bullet appeared in her temple, just below the hairline. Her legs had been broken slightly above the ankles by a flat heavy object approximately seven centimeters wide.

Lund and Masten stood watching as a uniformed member of the national police fell to his knees beside her. He began tracing her outline on the parquet floor with an ungainly, deformed lump of white chalk.

Masten and Lund slipped on their plastic gloves.

Lund examined her hands, found that the fingernails of the left thumb and forefinger were nicotine stained. He asked the chalker what cigarettes Mrs. White smoked. The man looked up dully, shrugged.

Masten thumbed through the inventory list, the plastic gloves crumpling the pages of his notebook.

Lund stuck his fingers into the woman's mouth. He pushed the upper lip back, examined the teeth.

"No cigarettes were discovered," said Masten, pocketing the notebook.

Lund sent the national policeman upstairs to see if any of the other tenants knew what cigarettes Mrs. White smoked.

"Oh," Lund said, absently. "Please ask them if they have seen Mrs. White with either a tall blond man or a short dark-haired man, the latter probably Italian."

Lund kneeled over the body, poking at the mouth. He made a U of his thumb and forefinger, plunged them into the mouth along the outside of the upper teeth. He ran his fingers back along the dry insides of the cheeks, stretching the sides of the mouth. There was a crackling sound then a pop and he pulled out the upper set of dentures. He reached in again, drew out the lower set.

He handed the dentures to Masten, who held them pinched awkwardly between two fingers.

Beneath each of the eyelids Lund could see round circles, pushing the lids up strangely. Pennies or pfennigs or centimes or other foreign coins. He left the eyes closed.

He stood, stared down at the corpse. Next to him, Masten began to click the dentures together.

There was no sign of a struggle, no windows or doors forced, no papers displaced, no files obviously missing, the cash box still locked and untouched atop Mrs. White's desk.

This suggested to Lund and Masten two scenarios. First, that the thieves had known exactly what they wanted and where it was, and, after having murdered Mrs. White, they had "taken what they had come for, leaving directly" (Masten). Second, they had entered the apartment solely to kill Mrs. White (Lund). In either case, further investigation of the White murder was "justified" and "was likely to force a reconsideration of the relation of Mrs. White's Zayas apartment to the Sanza case" (Kniffen).

It was evident that Sanza had been "involved in illegal dealings" (Masten). It was evident that someone was interested in creating links between Sanza and the White complex "in order to hide the actual links" (Lund), which, were the truth to be known, was much more shocking than mere "illegal dealings" of Sanza (De Jaen). The White affair needed to be investigated in its own right, and was now the "key piece of evidence" in the Sanza affair (Kniffen, Masten). The revelations of the White affair were "mere sidetracks—not clues leading to Sanza's death but events which had been set in motion after Sanza's death" (De Jaen).

The White affair, were it to be handled in the way Kniffen and Masten advocated handling it, would reveal nothing of importance about the Sanza affair (Lund). Only by working against the grain could one hope to make any use of the White murder—though it was still unlikely to give much satisfaction in and of itself (Lund).

To handle the White case in a way other than Kniffen and Masten's way could place Lund, and perhaps De Jaen, in jeopardy. The White case was likely to have a profound effect on Lund's future, more than was justified by what it could reveal (Lund).

More intriguing than the White murder as an individual phenomenon was its interest as a variation on a theme: Why a bullet instead of a crushed skull? Why broken ankles instead of broken fingers?

The pathologist reported that the White ankles had been broken after death, well after the bullet had slain her, by an unknown instrument constructed of steel.

Nobody in the White complex had heard a shot, nor was there tangible evidence, besides the body, to suggest the

murder itself had taken place in the White apartment. If Mrs.
White had been shot there with a silencer, the murderer(s)
had scrubbed the place thoroughly afterward to remove any
splatter, and had dug the bullet out from where it had lodged,
puttying over the bullet hole.

The White body itself had been scrubbed meticulously
clean. Lodged in its flesh were the bristles of a brass wire
brush. In several places, most notably the neck and the
thighs, the flesh had been severely abraded.

The bullet had entered the back of her head, passing from
the base of the skull up through the left temple, exiting just
below the hairline. She had been killed instantly.

Masten read him the note signed by Commissioner Kniffen
requesting that Lund surrender his firearm for "routine examination." Lund stood, removed the jacket, lifted his arm.
Masten reached into Lund's armpit with a yellow handkerchief, removed the pistol.

He dropped the pistol into a plastic bag, sealed it.

"Please surrender your own pistol to me," said Lund.

"Why do you want my pistol?" said Masten.

"Why do you want mine?" said Lund.

Masten shrugged. "Routine examination," he said.

"Might you be more precise?" said Lund.

Masten shrugged. "I proceed in the fashion in which I am
told to proceed," he said. He held up Kniffen's note.

Lund held his hand out. "I am leaving the office," he said.
"I need a pistol."

"Going where?"

"Out," said Lund. "Surrender."

He struck off down a cobblestone street, cutting into a back
alley that curved left slightly to burst into a cul-de-sac. He

knocked at a door with a wooden sign depicting a knife and fork hanging over it. He stood, waited. He knocked again.

An old man came to the full-length window next to the door, folding over the volets to stare out at him. Lund took his official certification out of his pocket, unfolded it, held it against the glass.

The man opened the door a modest crack.

"You sell silver?" Lund said.

"Among other things," said the old man. "I have a license. I harm no one."

"See that you continue," said Lund.

"Would you care to examine my license?" said the man.

"No," said Lund. "Your wares."

"You are here to buy?" said the old man.

"Not exactly," said Lund.

The man closed the door. Lund heard him fumbling with a chain. The door opened and the elderly man put one foot out, took Lund by the arm, drew him gently but firmly across the threshold.

Lund wandered the narrow aisles, moving from case to case, examining the silverware. Twice, he paused long before a velvet-lined case, examining spoons, reaching into his pocket to bring the spoon out, holding the spoon against the glass of the case. He moved down the rows. A third time he stopped before a set of silverware, spread on black crêpe, in the open air. He fingered the utensils, called the owner over.

"I am interested in these," Lund said.

"A popular line," the old man said. "Quite affordable."

"Do you sell a lot of these?"

"Oh, yes," said the old man. "Though they are by no means my finest line. The silver is impure."

"Have you sold any recently?" said Lund. "In the last week perhaps?"

The old man squinted at him. "Shouldn't I have?" he said.

"I don't know why not," said Lund.

"Yes," said the old man. "Three or four sets this week."

"To whom?" said Lund.

"I do not take names," said the old man. "I am not required by law to do so."

Lund removed a folded-over manila envelope from his coat pocket, unfolded it. He worked free the frayed end of the dyed brown string, unwound it from around the two brown circles. He peeled the adhesive flap back, pulled the envelope open. Removing a picture of Sanza, he passed it across to the old man.

"Do you know this fellow?" said Lund.

"No," said the man, handing back the picture. "Only on television, rather."

Lund showed him a picture of Kniffen.

"I have never seen the man," said the old man.

Masten.

"No," said the old man. "Handsome fellow, however."

"That pattern can be bought throughout the city," said the old man. "Nobody keeps records. It is not required."

"Thank you," said Lund. He replaced the photographs in the manila envelope, stuffed it back into his pocket.

"As you can see," said the old man, spreading his hands, "My business is entirely legitimate."

The old man shook Lund's hand, led Lund by the hand back to the door. "Such diligence in investigation is not the infant of wisdom," the old man said.

Buttoning his coat, Lund suddenly realized that the old man was staring at him.

"But you," said the old man, tapping a queer, crooked forefinger on Lund's cheek. "I know you from somewhere."

Lund dropped the spoon onto the asphalt. It lay there, glistening. He kicked it, watched it stutter across the road and into a sewer opening. He started walking.

The street was crowded with people, but none of them

looking at him, not even when he turned. He saw behind him a short man and a tall man, arm in arm, chatting.

He felt under his arm for Masten's gun. He ran his fingers over the rough grip. He turned down into an alley. Sprinting a few steps, he threw himself behind a pile of large sacks made of black plastic, full of garbage and knotted shut.

He drew his gun. He crouched there, catching his breath.

When nobody came, he holstered the gun. He straightened his suit, walked out onto the street. He let the traffic swallow him.

Lund had been at his desk only a few moments when Masten returned. The latter laid the plastic bag with the gun in it on the desk, held out his hand. Lund reached under his arm, pulled out Masten's gun, returned it to him.

"Well?" said Lund.

Masten looked at him, turned and left.

Smiling, Lund opened the plastic bag. He popped out the clip of his gun, spread the bullets in a semicircle on the desk top. Two of the bullets were the standard issue, different from those Lund had originally loaded into the gun. He picked them up, cut Xs in their tips, reloaded.

The sky was threatening rain when they arrived. With a mallet she pounded wooden stakes into the ground at regular intervals, while he unravelled the string. He removed the site report from his pocket, unfolded it. He measured from the fence over to the spot where Sanza's body had been found, marking its location with several large stones. She had outlined a large square with the stakes and was spreading dark string from stake to stake now, charting a grid of sixteen smaller squares.

He took out a notebook, flipped it open, wrote on the top piece of paper: *Sanza site: Re-evaluation.*

He slipped on plastic gloves. He got down on his knees, crawling to the edge of the square, peering into the string square. He began in the corner, picking up clods of dirt, peering underneath them. He scraped dirt away carefully. He held the clods outside of the confines of the string, squeezing them until they dissolved in tiny showers of silt.

He held his face close to the ground, his chest pushing down the string, scanning the surface of the earth. He saw blades of grass, a beetle. Filaments, roots, buried stones.

"2D. A wooden matchstick," she called out. "Head gone, shaft charred."

He looked up to see her drop the remains of the matchstick into a plastic bag.

He finished scanning his square, moved forward to the next square, began again.

Night coming on, and a matchstick all to be had. There were slight impressions in the earth as well, but nothing they found readable.

Dragging the mallet sideways, Lund scuffed out his and De Jaen's footprints. De Jaen wound the string back onto the spool. Lund gathered stakes, slid them into the sack.

He slung the canvas sack over his back, took De Jaen by the hand. He pulled her to him, embraced her. He kissed her, feeling the sack weigh on his shoulder, feeling her body against him. He opened his eyes, saw in the falling darkness her closed eyes.

In his mind Lund reconstructed the grid they had cut, locating their bodies in relation to that of Sanza.

He dropped the sack onto the desk, picked up the envelope. It was from Commissioner Kniffen, the cover officially sealed, signed, stamped. He opened it, read the note within, handed it to De Jaen to read.

"That's it, then," she said.

"Officially," Lund said.

"You intend to continue?" she said.

"Unofficially," he said.

"Consider Sanza," she said.

"That is the point, is it not?" said Lund.

"Consider him dead," she said.

"What other can one do?" said Lund.

"What of me?" she said.

He turned to her. "What of you?" he said.

"Consider me," she said.

He turned, stared at her without moving any part of his face. He shrugged.

"We are involved in life," Lund said. "People get hurt. When your turn comes, there is nothing to be done."

VI

WORDS

After dusk, he took the two large, black plastic bags out of his trunk, carrying them surreptitiously across the asphalt and into his apartment complex. He climbed the steps, silently mounting the four flights to his apartment.

He slit the bags open with a pruning knife, tore the plastic open, pulled out in handfuls the twisted strips of paper. He kept the contents of the two bags separate, heaping up two piles to either side of him until they threatened to collapse in upon him.

He sat between piles, staring from one pile to the other, holding the eventrated sacks loosely in his hands.

"My apologies," said Lund.

Kniffen spun his letter opener. "I am pleased to see we are

in agreement," he said. "You are too valuable to us to waste time repeating tasks which have already been accomplished."

"Consider it my mistake. A Saturday pleasure outing. It will not happen again," said Lund.

"Promise me," said Kniffen.

"It is finished," said Lund.

"If there is anything more to be found in the Sanza case, Masten will discover it." He looked up at Lund, the letter opener arrested in midtwirl. "Which I doubt there is," said Kniffen. "Anything more, that is."

"No more than I, sir," said Lund.

Kniffen shook his head. "Lund, if only I believed you."

He extricated paper strips from the piles, creasing them slightly to keep them from curling. He spread the strips out over the parquet, long rows of them spread side to side, many more still left to spread.

He removed a strip from one of the two piles at random. He carried it down the rows from strip to strip, holding it to both sides of each strip before moving to the next one, trying to match the letters on the one with the letters on the others. It took him eight minutes to travel the rows.

He made it through the rows with the first strip without discovering a match. The second, too, revealed near matches, but nothing matched with exactitude. Lund crawled down the line with the third and fourth strips. His knees and back started to ache. He sneezed, blew up a flurry of strips, wasted minutes rearranging them. He chose a fifth strip, began again.

"You look none too good," said Masten, not looking up from the typewriter.

"I did not sleep well," said Lund. "Have you seen De Jaen?"

"The commissioner wants a word with you," said Masten. "I told him you would see him the moment you arrived."

"Where is De Jaen?" said Lund.

Masten shrugged. "The commissioner is waiting," he said.

"Lund!" said Kniffen, rising, all smiles, from his desk. "To what do I owe the extreme pleasure?" He came around from behind the desk, took Lund by the hand, shook it, looked Lund in the eyes, as if concerned. "You don't look well, Lund," said Kniffen.

"I had difficulty sleeping last night," said Lund.

"Nothing serious, I hope. An isolated occurrence." said Kniffen, turning away. "I am concerned about De Jaen," Kniffen said.

"De Jaen?" said Lund.

"You know whom I mean? The secretary?" said Kniffen. "Something awry with her. Job dissatisfaction. Depression. Instability, perhaps of the psychological kind. Could do something rash. Perhaps she would be happier elsewhere. Investigate, Lund, investigate."

"Yes, sir," said Lund.

"I mean it," said Kniffen. "We shan't have our employees unhappy, shall we?"

He led Lund back to the door, ushered him out.

"Still staying clear of the Sanza case?" said Kniffen.

"Entirely Masten's," said Lund.

"Good, good," said Kniffen.

He turned his smile off, closed the door.

Lund rang the bell at the outer door, received no answer. He stepped back from the door and into the street, staring up the side of the building to her window. The light was on, he saw through the volets; there was a light on. He depressed the button, waited.

He depressed other buttons by other names, travelling from button to button until the doorlock buzzed and he

pushed his way in. He made his way past the first landing
and the three doors there, winding his way up the staircase.
A door on the second balcony was open, a hunched old man
standing in the doorway, his eyeglasses aglow in the light of
a naked bulb suspended in the stairwell.

Lund nodded to him, smiled. Lund continued up the stairs.

"Perhaps it was you who rang?" said the old man.

"Yes," said Lund.

"I don't know you," said the man.

"I don't know you, either," said Lund.

The man said something else Lund didn't hear as he hurried up the stairs. The third balcony. He went to De Jaen's
door. He knocked. He slipped his gloves on, tried the door.
The door was locked.

The old man was suddenly there behind him, shuffling up
the creaking stairs and onto the wooden landing.

"I don't know you," the old man said, in a hoarse voice.

"Our ignorance is mutual," said Lund.

"What are you doing here?" said the old man.

"I have come to see Miss De Jaen," said Lund.

"What?" said the old man. "She works for the police, I
will have you know."

Lund knocked on the door again.

"I doubt you should be here," said the old man. "Should
you be here?"

"Yes," said Lund. "Should you?"

The old man shrugged. "I live here," he said.

Lund knocked again.

"You should leave," said the old man, tenuously.

"You should leave," said Lund.

"She works for the police, I'll have you know."

"So do I," said Lund. He took out his official certification,
unfolded it, flashed it at the old man. "Inspector Masten,"
Lund said. "Official business concerning the Sanza case."

He watched the old man shuffle to the edge of the wooden

landing, disappear step by step over the edge of it. When he heard the man's apartment door shut, he forced the lock.

The apartment was ablaze with light, every switch on. Lund closed the door, locked it behind him. He took his gun out, switched the safety off.

"De Jaen?" he said.

The bedroom was empty, the sheets stripped from the bed and heaped on the floor. He kicked through them, spread them about, examined their stains. He opened the closets, closed them again.

The sitting room was bare, dead flowers lying on the table.

In the kitchen, on the counter, a ball of raw ground meat, stinking and going black.

The washroom mirror had been cracked, a vertical and neurotic line running through it. Lund took off one glove, ran his finger under the rim of the toilet, found only filth. He examined the sink closely, washed his finger off. He explored the tub. He got down on his hands and knees on the floor, examined the tiles.

"Did De Jaen come in?" said Lund.

"No," said Masten. "Probably sick." He looked up, dropped his pencil onto his desk. "Kniffen would like to have a word with you."

"Again?" said Lund.

Masten shrugged.

"Lund, here you are," said Kniffen. "Don't bother sitting. Masten tells me De Jaen didn't show up today. True, Lund?"

"Probably sick."

"Probably sick, Lund, probably sick. Words of wisdom, Lund," said Kniffen. "Sick of what, Lund?"

Lund shrugged. "I haven't any way of knowing," he said.

"Nor have I, Lund, nor have I," said Kniffen. "But I suggested something was wrong, did I not?"

"You did indeed," said Lund.

"Imagine," said Kniffen. "I was the first to guess."

"You are the commissioner," said Lund.

"Well put, Lund," said Kniffen. "That will be all."

Lund grabbed hold of the door handle, turned to go.

"Flowers, Lund," said Kniffen.

"Flowers?" said Lund.

"Flowers do wonders, Lund. Send the girl flowers. Straight from our hearts."

He chose a strip of paper, unthreaded it from the pile, smoothed it out. He dialed De Jaen's telephone number. No response. On his knees, strip pinched between his fingers, he moved down the rows of strips, comparing. He stood halfway through the strips, dialed her telephone number.

He dialed the office, let the telephone ring until the janitor picked the receiver up.

"Might I speak to De Jaen?" said Lund.

"Well . . ." said the janitor. "Who is this?"

"Lund," said Lund. "You know me. The inspector?"

"De Jaen is not here," said the custodian. "Nobody here but me."

"Hasn't she been there?" said Lund.

"Her rubbish can was empty."

Lund hung up the phone, returned to the strips.

"Lund!" said Kniffen. "How are things, Lund?"

"Nothing special," said Lund.

"Quite," said Kniffen. He took Lund by the arm, drew him in close, whispered to him confidentially. "This De Jaen matter," he said. "Is it resolved, Lund?"

"On the verge," said Lund.

"Get cracking, Lund, get cracking," Kniffen said, releasing his arm. He walked away, walking down the hall and away from Lund, walking, waving.

When at last he matched two strips he glued them to the wall, touching one another. After checking sixty more strips, he had six pairs and one of three strips together—a triple strip twelve characters wide. In this narrow space there was no mention of Hadden, nothing to reveal Sanza's true opinions of the Hadden case.

Lund kept matching, kept gluing.

"I'm a reasonable man, Lund," said Kniffen. "Lund?"

"I have no doubt," said Lund.

"But De Jaen has to go, Lund," said Kniffen. He looked up. "She has to go?"

"It appears she has already gone," said Lund.

"Talk to her, Lund," said Kniffen. "Terminate her. I'm counting on you, Lund."

"Where might she be?" said Lund.

"Lund, Lund, Lund," said Kniffen. "Use your powers of deduction, Lund. For what is the inspector paid?"

The first page which formed itself out of the strips had nothing to do with the Hadden case, being merely the shredded fifty-second page of the police manual. Nor did the second page. Nor the third, Nor the fourth. All being pages from official manuals. Lund assembled a few dozen more pages with the same results.

He rolled and smoked a cigarette. He thought.

He peeled the strips off the wall, one by one, crammed them back into the bag.

.   .   .

He carried the two black plastic bags down the stairs, out to his car. He set the bags down, opened the trunk. He lifted them up to stuff them in, found they wouldn't fit. He dropped the bags on the ground, looked into the trunk. Inside were two black plastic bags.

He untied the knot around the neck of one of the bags. He opened it. He had to step back because of the stench. He breathed in, breathed out, until he stopped smelling the decay.

Through the plastic of the bag, he traced the sockets of her eyes. He felt along that half of her body to try to know how it had been done. He felt along the other bag, her lower half.

He twisted the neck of the first bag shut again, knotted it off. Cramming in the bags with the papers as well, he closed the trunk, went back inside.

VII

THE LUND AFFAIR

He spent the day at his desk, typing in triplicate a summary of his findings regarding the Sanza case, culled from his private report. Masten came in and out, looking at him curiously. Lund did not look up, just kept on turning the pages of his private report, kept on typing page after page of his "Circumstances of the Sanza Affair, Assembled for Immediate Publication."

"Have you seen De Jaen?" said Masten.

"No," said Lund, without stopping typing.

"Have you any idea what has become of her?"

"None," said Lund.

"Do you want me to type that?" said Masten. "I am quite handy with a typewriter."

"No," said Lund.

"What are you typing?" said Masten.

"Confidential," said Lund.

Masten kept coming in, questioning him, going out. Lund kept typing. The telephone rang. Lund let it ring.

"Do you plan to answer that?" said Masten.

Lund sighed, straightened up, reached for the telephone. The line was dead—a dial tone.

"Kniffen wants a word," said Masten.

Lund stood, cracked his knuckles, wandered toward Kniffen's office. He stopped, hesitated halfway there, turned back to gather his unofficial report and his newly typed triplicate sheets, unrolling as well the paper in the typewriter, taking all with him.

"Lund," said Kniffen, unsmiling. "Do come in, Lund. Come in. Have a seat."

Lund sat, his documents in his lap. Kniffen came around the desk, pushing his chair around until it was opposite Lund's. He shook Lund's hand, sat down. They were close enough that their knees touched.

"Are you happy here, Lund?" said Kniffen.

"Yes," said Lund, without hesitation.

"I mean happy," said Kniffen.

"Yes," said Lund.

"Open your soul, Lund," said Kniffen, taking him by the hands. "Be honest with me. I sense you are troubled."

"Not at all," said Lund.

"Nothing?" said Kniffen. "Lund?"

"Not a thing," said Lund.

Lund sealed the three copies of the report, addressing one to the national newspaper, the other two to the best city newspapers. He sealed them, stamped them. He took his hat and coat, walked toward the door.

"Wait a minute, Lund," said Masten. "I'll walk with you to the metro."

"No time," said Lund, holding up his watch. "Late's the word. Have to run." He darted out the door.

He mailed the letters at the post office, then backtracked, walked toward his car.

People done for the day began to pour out of offices. Lund turned off the busy street, walked down a few streets into a residential area of curving lanes, devoid of life. He charted an erratic course leading roughly in the direction he wanted to go. He came to intersections, hesitated, checked the position of the sun. He looked back at the way the street behind him had curved its way there. He looked forward. He backtracked, guessed at routes, found his steps choked by second thoughts.

He checked the signs, found only street names, the names of famous generals and politicians. No numbers. He continued on. The houses all looked the same, simple—cheaply made boxes.

Before him the street stretched out, threw itself straight. Numbers began to appear on the curbs. The houses, he began to think, seemed familiar.

He saw from the numbers on the curbs that he had travelled many blocks too far north. He turned left down an alley, headed south past the backs of houses.

The houses were interspersed with small buildings. He exited the alley, crossed a largish street, zigzagged down into another alley. He had walked a little way down when the asphalt of the alley petered out and vanished, turning for several meters into gravel, then dirt the rest of the way down. He began looking for covered-over holes, and thought, in passing, in the low light, that he saw tiny swells in the dirt that might once have been they.

He stopped, lit a cigarette, flicked the match into the dirt. He kept walking.

He was nearing the end of the alley, where it spilt out onto a larger street. On that street, crowds of people were walking past. On that street, three people walked halfway past the alley, then stutter-stepped, stopped, conferred, returned to stare at him. They started walking toward him.

"Lund!" he heard Kniffen's voice call. "There's someone here I want you to meet."

Kniffen put his hand on one of the two men with him, on the one of the two who was not Masten. A short man wearing a white panama hat, smoking a cigarette. The three of them kept coming at him, striding forward. Lund could hear their boots scuttling over the dirt. Smiling, they kept coming.

He wheeled, began to run backward down the alley. Behind, he could hear them call to him loudly, feigning surprise. He kept running. He reached under his arm and pulled out his gun. Still running, he twisted around, started firing.

He saw the three of them scatter, throw themselves to the ground. He kept running, kept firing.

Two Brothers

I

DADDY NORTON

Daddy Norton had fallen and broken his leg. He lay on the floor of the entry hall, the rug bunched under his back, a crubbed jag of bone tearing his trousers at the knee.

"I have seen all in vision," he said, grunting against the pain. "God has forseen how we must proceed."

He forbade Aurel and Theron to depart the house, for God had called them to witness and testify the miracles He would render in that place. Mama he forbade to summon an ambulance on threat of everlasting fire, for his life was God's affair alone.

He remained untouched on the floor into the evening and well through the night, allowing Mama near dawn to touch his face with a damp cloth and to slit back his trouser leg with a butcher's knife. Aurel and Theron slept fitfully, leaning against the front door, touching shoulders. The leg swelled and grew thick with what to Aurel's imperfect vision appeared flies but which were, before Daddy Norton's pure spiritual eye, celestial messengers cleansing the wound with God's holy love. Dawn broke and the sun reared suddenly up the side of the house and flooded the marbled glass at the peak of the door, creeping across the floor until it mottled the broken leg. Daddy Norton beheld unfurled in the light the face of God, and spoke with God of his plight, and felt himself assured.

When the light fell beyond the leg and Daddy Norton lay silent and panting, Theron called for his breakfast. Mama had risen for it when Daddy Norton raised his hand and denied him, for *He that trusteth in the Lord is nourished by his word alone.*

"Bring us rather the Holy Word, Mama," Daddy Norton said. "Bring us the true book of God's aweful comfort. We shall feast therein."

Theron declared loudly that he loved God's Holy Word as good as any of God's anointed, but that he wanted some breakfast. Daddy Norton feigned not to hear, neglecting Theron until Mama returned armed with the Holy Word. She spread it before him, beside his face, tilting the book so her husband could read from it prone.

Daddy Norton tightened his eyes.

"Jesus have mercy," he said. "I can't find the pages."

Mama brought the book closer, kept bringing it closer until the pages were pressed against Daddy Norton's face. "Closer!" he called, "Closer!" until his head rolled to one side and he stopped altogether.

"Make me some breakfast, Mama," said Theron.

"You heard what Daddy Norton said," said Mama.

"I'm starved, Mama," said Theron.

She took up the Holy Word and began to read, though without the lilt and fall of voice which Daddy Norton had learned to afflict on the words. Aurel could not feel the nourishment in Mama's voice, sounding as it did as mere words rattling forth without the spirit spurring them. He made to listen but in a few words paid heed only to Daddy Norton's leg. Crawling closer, he looked at it, watched God's love seethe.

"Goddamn if I don't make my own breakfast," Theron said, standing.

"Theron," said Mama, marking the verse with her thumb. "Be Mama's good boy and sit."

Theron ventured a step. Mama heaved her bulk up and stood filling the hallway, the Holy Word lifted over her head.

"Damned if I won't brain you," she said.

"Now, Mama," said Theron. "It's your Theron you're talking to. You don't want to hurt your sweet child."

In his dreams Daddy Norton gave utterance to some language devoid of distinction, spilling out a continual and incomprehensible word. He lifted his head, his eyes furzing about the sockets, his tongue thrust hard between his teeth. He tried to pull himself up, the bone pushing up through the flesh and the blood welling forth anew.

"Listen to what he's saying, Theron," said Mama. "He's talking to you."

Theron listened, carefully sat down.

Daddy Norton continued to speak liquids, his mouth flecked with blood. Aurel and Theron stayed against the outer door, silent, watching the light slide across the floor and vanish up over the house. Aurel's mouth was so dry he couldn't swallow. He kept clearing his throat and trying to swallow for hours, until the sun streamed in the window at the other end of the hall and began its descent.

"Tell Daddy to ask God what time lunch is served, Mama," said Theron.

Mama glared at him. She opened the *Holy Word of God as revealed to Daddy Norton, Beloved* and read aloud from the revelations of the suffering of the wicked. As she read, Daddy Norton's voice grew softer then seemed to stop altogether, though the lips never stopped moving. The light made its way toward them until they could see, through the glass at the end of the hall, the sun flatten into the sill and collapse.

Mama clutched the Holy Word to her chest and rocked back and forth, her eyes shut. Theron nudged Aurel, then arose and edged past Daddy Norton. He skirted Mama, his boots creaking, without her eyes opening. He strode down the hall and into the kitchen, the door banging shut behind him.

Mama started, opening her eyes.

"Where's Theron?" she asked.

Aurel pointed to the kitchen door.

"That boy is godless," she said. "And you, Aurel, hardly better. A pair of sorry sinners, the goddam both of you."

She closed her eyes and rocked. In the dim, Aurel examined Daddy Norton. The man's face had gone pale and floated in the coming darkness like a buoy. Theron returned, toting half a loaf of bread and a bell jar of whiskey. He edged around Mama and straddle-stepped over Daddy Norton, seating himself against the door. He ripped the loaf apart, gave a morsel to Aurel. Aurel took it, tore off a mouthful. Mama watched them dully. They did not stop chewing. She closed her eyes, clung tighter to the Holy Word.

"Holy Word won't save you now, Mama," said Theron. "Like all God's children, you need bread."

"Shut up," said Aurel. "Leave her alone."

"Won't save Daddy either," said Theron. "Nor angels neither."

"Shut up!" shouted Aurel, hiding his ears in his hands.

Unscrewing the lid of the whiskey, Theron took a swallow. "Drink, Mama?" he asked, holding the jar out.

She would not so much as look at him. He offered the jar to Aurel, who removed his hands from his ears long enough to take and drink.

"Aurel knows, Mama," said Theron. "He don't like it, but he knows."

Turning away from them, she lay down on the floor. Aurel swallowed his bread and lay down as well. Theron took the remainder of the whiskey. He leaned back against the door, whispering softly to himself, and watched the others sleep.

In the early light, Aurel awoke. Daddy Norton, he saw, had risen to standing and was leaning against the wall on his whole leg. In one hand he held a butcher knife awkwardly, trying to hack off his other leg just above the broken joint, crying out with each blow.

He stopped long enough to regard Aurel with burning, red-rimmed eyes, the knife poised, his gaze drifting slowly upward. Shaking his head, he continued to gash the leg, the dull knife making poor progress, at last turning skew against the bone and clattering from his fingers.

Bending his good leg, he tried to take the blood-smeared knife off the floor. He could not reach it. He cast his gaze about until it stuck on Aurel.

"Aurel," he said, his voice greding with pain. "Be a good boy and give Daddy the knife."

Aurel did not move. They looked at one another, Aurel unable to break Daddy Norton's gaze. He began to move slowly backward across the floor, pulling himself until he struck against the door.

"Aurel," Daddy Norton said. "God tells you to pick up the knife."

Aurel swallowed, stayed pressed to the door.

"You're a sorry sinner," said Daddy Norton.

Daddy Norton extended an arm, pointing one finger at Aurel, his other hand raised open-palmed to support the heavens. Stepping onto the injured leg, he listed toward the boy and fell. His leg folded, turning under him so that he looked like he was attempting to couple with it. He lay on the floor slick-faced with sweat, his eyes misfocused.

"Give me the knife, Aurel," he said.

He began to pull himself around by his fingers, twisting his body around until it became wedged between the hall walls. Grunting, he rolled over, twisting the broken leg, and fainted.

Aurel shook Theron. Theron blinked his eyes and mumbled, his voice still thick with liquor. Aurel motioned to Daddy Norton, who came conscious again and stared them through with God's awful hate.

"Stop staring at me," said Theron.

Daddy Norton neither stopped nor moved. There was a smell coming up from him, from his leg too. Theron stood, holding his nose, and stepped over him, taking up the butcher's knife, Daddy Norton's eyes following him almost in reflex. "Stop staring," Theron said again, and pushed the blade in.

Aurel closed his eyes. For a long time he could hear the damp sound of Theron working the knife in and out, and then the noise finally stopped.

He opened his eyes to see Theron leaning over Daddy Norton, holding the remains of the man's eyelids closed with his fingertips, though when he released them they crept up to reveal the emptied sockets. Theron twisted the man's neck and rolled the head, directing the face toward the floor. He wiped the knife on Daddy Norton's shirt. Putting the knife into Daddy Norton's hand, he stood back. The fingers straightened and the knife slipped out. He folded the fingers around the haft, watched them straighten again.

"Theron?" said Aurel.

"Not now, Aurel."

"What about Mama?" asked Aurel.

Theron seemed to consider it, then stood and took the knife in his own hands and approached Mama.

"Don't kill her, Theron," said Aurel. "Not Mama."

"Be quiet about it," said Theron. He prodded her head with his boot. "Wake up, Mama," he said.

She did not move. Theron pushed her head again.

"Daddy needs you, Mama," he said.

"I can't bear to have you do it," said Aurel.

"You don't know at all what you can bear," said Theron.

Kneeling down beside her, he took the Holy Word out of her hands and dropped it aside. He placed the knife into her hand, carefully, so as not to awaken her. The knife fit, held.

"You can have only one of us, Aurel," said Theron. "Me or Mama?"

"Mama," said Aurel.

"It's me you want," said Theron. "You aren't thinking straight. Let me think for you."

He picked up Mama under the shoulders and dragged her closer to Daddy Norton. He took her wrists and pushed her hands into Daddy Norton's body until they came away stained, the knife gory too.

"Besides," said Theron. "You don't have a choice. Mama gone and died while we were jawing. You got only me."

II

THE FUNERAL

For the funeral, Preacher Thrane collected from his congregation enough for a shirt and a pair of presentable trousers for both boys—though, he said, they would have to secure collar and cravat of their own initiative, did they care for them. This he suggested they find the means to do by taking up the cup and pleading door for door to members of Daddy Norton's former congregation.

"But," said Thrane, "I want you to give by any plans you have of being prophets after the manner of Daddy Norton. You aren't Daddy Nortons. You come worship with me from now on."

"We're Daddy Norton's boys," said Aurel.

"What?" said Thrane.

"We got to carry on Daddy Norton's work," said Aurel.

"You don't got to nothing," said Thrane.

"Don't listen to Aurel," said Theron. "We had enough of Daddy to last a lifetime."

Thrane hesitated then patted them both on the shoulders, passed to Theron a brown paper package wrapped in twine.

"There are good boys hidden in you somewhere," Thrane said, touching their hair. "All you got to do is let them out."

They took a tin cup from beneath the sink and left it on the porch of the house beneath a hand-lettered placard reading "Comfort for the Bereav'd" with a crude arrow pointing down. They wore their new clothes to loosen them a little before the funeral. They wore the clothes in the hall, sitting on the floor, admiring what they could see. Each time the clock chimed they stood on their toes and looked out the panes along the top of the door, but never saw that anyone approached the cup to give into it.

"Thrane should damn well have the decency to buy us some collars and cravats too," said Theron. "I have a mind not to attend their funeral at all."

Aurel said nothing. Theron strode up and down the entry hall. Snatching his hat and coat from their pegs, he went out.

Aurel stood tiptoe at the door and watched his brother pick up the tin cup, stare into it, put it back down. Theron put his hat on, then his coat, then stood on the porch looking out over the fields. He stood like that for a long while, then came back inside.

"Hell if I'll beg," said Theron. "You?"

"I don't want to go to any funeral," said Aurel.

"What?" asked Theron.

"I don't want to go," Aurel said.

Theron stripped off his hat, his coat, hanging them from their pegs. He sat down on the floor, began to work off his boots.

"I am not going," said Aurel. "Theron, you heard me?"

"I heard you, Aurel," said Theron.

"We could stay here," said Aurel. "Nobody would know the difference."

"Preacher Thrane would," said his brother.

"What do we care about Preacher Thrane?" asked Aurel.

"He gave us these clothes, didn't he?"

"He only wants us coming to his church," said Aurel. "He wants us to be his boys."

"We aren't nobody's boys," said Theron.

"We are Daddy Norton's boys," said Aurel.

"No," said Theron. "Don't say that, Aurel."

He looked briefly into his boots, then set them to one side. Sliding back, he leaned against the door.

"I am not going," said Aurel, "I mean it."

"Nobody said you were," said Theron. "We'll stay," he said. He stretched his hands toward his brother. "Come sit with me," he said.

Aurel looked at him carefully, but came and sat down next to him.

Theron made a point of looking up and down his brother's body.

"Fine clothing," said Theron. "But if we aren't attending no funeral, take them off. They reek of Thrane's God."

Aurel began to unbutton the shirt, stopped.

"You aren't taking yours off," he said.

"All in time, brother," said Theron. "You lead the way."

Aurel stood and turned into the corner. He unbuttoned the shirt, stripped it off his shoulders, let it fall. Unbuttoning the trousers, he stepped out of them.

"Briefs, too," said Theron.

"The briefs are mine," said Aurel. "No preacher gave them to me."

"You got them from Daddy Norton, didn't you?" said Theron. "You better do all I say."

"I don't want it," said Aurel.

"Doesn't matter," said Theron. He stood and shook loose his own belt. "This is all my church now. I take what I want."

They sat against the door, touching each other, staring down the hall. Preacher Thrane came and pounded on the door and cursed them, but they did not open for him, and once they dropped the clothes he had given them out the window he took his leave. Others came by, and knocked, and called out, but the two brothers remained silent and holding each other and did not respond.

Near evening someone knocked, and, when they did not answer, tried to turn the knob, then began to throw a shoulder against the door, weakly.

Theron stood and looked out to see a woman there, rubbing her shoulder. She stood rubbing it for some time then turned the other shoulder to the door and started again.

"By God," whispered Theron, crouching. "She thinks she can break down the door."

"Can she?" asked Aurel.

Theron snorted. "Not the likes of her," he said.

"I heard that!" the woman yelled from the outside. "Open the door!"

"She knows we're here," whispered Aurel.

"Let's see her do anything about it," Theron said.

"You got to let her in," said Aurel.

"Let her in?" said Theron. "And then what are we going to do with her?"

Aurel looked. Theron, he saw, was bare of body, his sides scarred where Daddy Norton had beat the devil out of him and made paths for the penetration of God. He looked down at himself, saw his red hands fidget and swim on his pale thighs, his belly slack, the dull tip of his sex prodding the floorboards between his body.

"I am naked," said Aurel.

"I want to know what you think you are going to do to her after we get her in."

"Don't let her in," pleaded Aurel, covering his sex with his hands.

Theron stood and turned to the door. "Just a minute," he called. "A moment please."

"No," said Aurel. "Please, Theron."

"Who do you love, Aurel?"

"What?" said Aurel.

"Do you love her?"

"I don't love her," said Aurel.

"Nobody said you did, Aurel," said Theron. "But who?"

Aurel brought his head down against his knees, tipped over onto his side. "Don't ask me that, Theron," he said.

"Think about it," said Theron. "Think it through."

The thumping at the door resumed.

"Who do you love? Who is all you have in this world, Aurel?" asked Theron. "With Mama and Daddy Norton dead and gone?"

"God?" said Aurel.

"In *this* world," said Theron, kicking Aurel in the side. "God isn't in this world. Think, goddamn it."

Aurel remained silent a long time, his side darkening where Theron had kicked him. He kept touching his ribs and pulling his fingers away and staring at them. Theron took Aurel's hands, held them away from his body, stilled them.

"You?" asked Aurel. "Is it you?"

Letting go of Aurel's hands, Theron cupped his own hands around Aurel's face. He drew the face forward, kissed it on the mouth.

"Yes," said Theron. "Me."

He let Aurel's head go and watched Aurel collapse, his eyes rolling back into his head. He went and unlocked the door. He opened it.

"God almighty," said the woman outside.

Aurel came conscious and tried to crawl out of line of the woman's voice, but Theron kept opening the door wider until the door was pressed against the wall and there was nowhere left to crawl. Aurel got up and stumbled down to the far end of the hall, covering his sex, then came stumbling back, moaning.

"You come on in," said Theron.

The woman seemed to be trying to keep her eyes on his face. "Will you put on some clothing?" she asked.

"Not me," he said.

"We are clothed in God's spirit," said Aurel.

"Shut up, Aurel," said Theron. He rendered his best smile. "What can we do for you?" he asked the woman.

She looked at Aurel, then back to Theron, then at Aurel again, her eyes drawn down then quickly up. "It's about the property," she said.

"Won't you come in?" Theron said.

He stretched his hand toward her, his palm opening and closing. Aurel came up behind Theron and hid behind his body, his sex beginning to exert itself more severely. He peered over Theron's shoulder at her. He tried to push the door shut, but Theron kept it blocked open with his foot.

"No," she said, stepping backward, "I don't think I can."

"What's thinking got to do with it?" said Theron. "Just come on."

She took a few more steps backward until she stepped off the edge of the porch and fell hard.

"The property," said Theron. "We'll pay you whatever you want. We have it inside."

"We don't have any money, Theron," said Aurel.

"Shut up, Aurel," said Theron. "Soon," he said to the woman. "We'll pay you soon. Is it money you want?"

She sat in the weeds holding her ankle, rocking back and forth, her face grimacing.

"I think she likes you, Aurel," said Theron.

Aurel just watched until Theron nudged him. "What's her name?" Aurel said.

"What's your name?" asked Theron of the woman.

She had taken the shoe off and was rotating the foot manually and with care, wincing. She did not choose to answer.

"My name is Theron," said Theron. "This is my brother Aurel. Our Daddy and Mama are dead."

"Pleased to meet you," Aurel said, trying to shut the door.

"Maybe you have a name too?" said Theron. He stared at her, watched her stand and put her weight tenuously on the foot. "Looks like she's hurt, Aurel," he said. "She won't get far."

"I bet her name is Arabella," said Aurel. "That's a pretty name, all right."

"Is that your name?" asked Theron.

She looked at them. Slowly, as if to avoid startling them, she began to limp away, flimmering her hands for balance.

"Go fetch her, Aurel," said Theron. "Bring her back here."

Aurel did not move.

"I mean it, Aurel," said Theron.

Aurel went to the far end of the hall and crouched there, shaking, hugging himself around the knees. Theron watched the woman stumble away for a while and then came back into the hall, closing and locking the door.

He came down the hall toward his brother.

"You'll have to do," said Theron.

He sat on the floor beside him, leaning in, putting his hand inside his brother's thigh. He kissed Aurel on the shoulder, the cheek, the neck.

"See now," he said throatily, "we only got each other. Nobody in the world but you and me."

III

The Dog

Aurel would hardly leave the hall, at most taking a step out onto the front porch or going through the extreme door into the bathroom. He would not enter the kitchen and Theron had to bring food out to him, though he swore each time that he would not bring it the next.

Theron left him so as to rummage through the rest of the rooms—excepting Daddy Norton's private room, the door to that room being locked and he (though he dared not admit so before Aurel) not having quite the nerve to kick it down. Had it been open, he told himself, he would have entered. But he could not bring himself to break in.

The sprawling house was even larger than he had imagined, running into a half-dozen levels and half-levels, and strung into labyrinths of makeshift rooms, especially on the upper floors, that Theron could not make sense of or later recover. He at first made some effort to restrict himself to the two lower floors, as he had done when Daddy Norton was alive, but as the days passed he went farther up. To make sense of the upper levels, he tried to trace his way in and then out of a floor along the same path, but always seemed to lose his way. Often he found himself in trying to leave passing through chambers that did not seem to have existed before.

He searched through the rooms and found clothing which seemed to belong neither to him nor his brother, nor Mama, nor Daddy Norton. He could make no sense of it nor piece it together in complete outfits, for no matter how many times he coupled articles, they seemed mismatched in color, style, size. He abandoned clothing and took to gathering objects that interested him, carrying them with him for fear of never finding them again. He gathered them and then, when sufficiently burdened, tried to find his way back, in the process discovering more than he could ever hope to carry. He heaped what he could in kitchen and hall, dividing objects into piles according to an interior logic he could not fathom but felt compelled to obey.

Aurel sat almost entirely still, seemed hardly to breathe. He could still arise and walk up and down the hall when he chose, though he moved now with an excess of precision, as if even his most subtle motions were the result of a tremendous and impeccable focusing of the will. He spoke in a similar way, his voice measured and taut, his inflection oddly spaced but so well controlled as to impact upon the words much harder.

"You have begun to talk like Daddy Norton," said Theron. "Are you thinking of reopening the ministry?"

"No," said Aurel. "Daddy Norton has begun to talk like me."

Unable to puzzle through what Aurel meant, Theron came to

watch his brother more closely. He noticed that when his brother moved it was as if he were hardly resident within his own body, or was resident only in a strictly mechanic sense. When Aurel was motionless, he did not seem present at all.

Watching him like that made Theron conscious of a strange kinship between himself and Aurel, and between the two of them and the dead, a kinship that made it difficult for him to keep always in mind who he was. He took to nudging Aurel when he came into the hall, prodding him gently until the eyes focused in. He kept this current for a few days, until Aurel learned to ignore it.

In one of the upper rooms, under a blanket, Theron found an air rifle and a box of hard plastic pellets. He pumped the gun and shot it into a rat-eaten mattress, raising puffs of dust. Taking the rifle downstairs, he brandished it before Aurel.

"Where was it?" asked Aurel.

"Upstairs," said Theron. "One of the rooms."

"Daddy Norton's room?" asked Aurel.

"No."

"What is in Daddy Norton's room?" asked Aurel.

Theron claimed that he had entered the room but could not remember precisely what was there. Nothing important, he told Aurel. The next time, he thought, I will go in.

The next time, he did not go in. He stood for some time beside the door and even tried to twist the knob again, but it would not turn. Bending down, he applied his eye to the key-hole, but found the aperture blocked. He shot the doorknob with the air rifle, listening to the pellets ping off and roll about the floor.

He began, to please Aurel, to imagine Daddy Norton's room, to flesh it forth out of nothing in his head and then regurgitate it. It was, he claimed, a simple room, spare in decor, austere, little substance to it, a few books, a few ordinary objects. When he described Daddy Norton's room, Aurel seemed almost attentive and even asked a few questions. It became so that Theron had to keep a series of notes in the kitchen and review them frequently, for Aurel noticed any inconsistency. He seemed to remember every detail, even to the point of requesting certain items from the room itself, asking for the private trinity of holy books that Theron claimed Daddy Norton had written: *Unaccustomed Sinners*, *Fathers of Light*, *Body of Lies.*

"I won't bring his rubbish to you," said Theron. "Get it yourself."

Aurel came to his feet, his knees crackling, and swayed down the hall. Before he got to the door, he slowed, sat deliberately down.

"What's the matter?" asked Theron.

"I am not ready," said Aurel. "Not yet."

At times Theron left the hall not to wander the upper rooms, but to remain behind one of the five doors leading off the main hall, his ear pressed to the door or the door cracked open slightly and he peering through, observing Aurel. Aurel did not appear to notice him, nor in fact to notice anything at all. Each time Theron returned to the hall and shook him conscious, Aurel would say, "You've been to Daddy Norton's room?" and, when Theron shook his head, "I'll have to go myself."

"Why don't you go?" Theron asked.

"I am going," said Aurel. "Here I go," he said, but could not rise.

The pantry was nearly empty. Creditors and bastards of the slickest varieties took to coming to the door and posting legal notices and other formal threats. The brothers did not answer. A wet-haired man in a tightbuttoned shirt tried to crack open the door with a crowbar until Theron opened it himself and threatened him with the air rifle.

"You can't shoot me," said the man. "You're naked."

Theron jabbed the man in the belly and pulled the trigger, the pellet burying itself in the fat. Wheezing, pressing his hands to his belly, the man backed away.

The food in the kitchen ran out. Theron grew hungry. He searched the upper rooms for food, found nothing.

Returning to the entrance hall, he grabbed the air rifle, pulling Aurel to his feet and toward the front door. Aurel leaned against him, moving languidly, as if drugged. He allowed himself to be propelled through the door, onto the porch, and then began weakly to resist.

"Where are we going?" he managed.

"To kill something," said Theron.

"We need clothes." Aurel said.

Theron bent his brother over the porch rail, went back into the house. Kicking through the piles in the hall and kitchen, he uncovered a pair of bathing trunks and a pair of briefs. He slipped into the former, carried the briefs outside.

Aurel had fallen off the porch, was lying curled up and hardly moving in the dirt.

"What's wrong with you, brother?" asked Theron.

"What do you mean?" asked Aurel.

Theron stepped off the porch and slipped the briefs over Aurel's feet, working them up to rim about the knees. He lifted his brother off the ground, pulled the briefs up until they caught on his sex, then lifted the elastic out and over.

"I have to go back inside," said Aurel.

"We need something to eat," said Theron.

Supporting Aurel, he dragged him forward until he began to move his legs of his own accord. Theron slowly slacked his support, Aurel tottering forward on his own.

"I want to go home," begged Aurel.

They traveled alongside the town road for a time then cut away into the fields. They waded through a vacant plot, the ground dawked and uneven. Theron stuffed Aurel through a barbed wire fence, the wires combing his body with lines of blood, then crawled through himself. Passing through wheat fields, they fell onto a dirt track and were led to a house. They went around to the back. In the shade of one of the trees was a dog on a chain. He got to his feet when he saw them and stretched. Theron started pumping the air rifle. The dog came forward, wagging its tail, its chain paying out.

Theron steadied Aurel against the side of the house and leveled the air rifle at the dog's head. The dog sniffed at the muzzle, licking the tip of it, and tried to pass underneath. Theron pushed the barrel flush against the dog's forehead. Closing his eyes, he shot.

He heard the dog yelp. Opening his eyes, he found the dog's eye burst and bubbling, the dog staggering and revolving in a mutilated circle, its paws tangling in the chain. He pumped the rifle. The dog moaned, wavering its way back toward the tree.

He followed it, pumping the rifle. He put the barrel's end between the shoulder blades. As the dog turned and snapped, he jerked the trigger.

The dog stumbled to its belly and lay spread a moment, then heaved back up. Theron could see a small burr of blood rising where the pellet had gone in, the pale lump of it resting just under the skin.

"This dog doesn't want to die," Theron called.

"Leave it alone," said Aurel.

Theron pumped the rifle and got around by the dog where it was spread under the tree and on its side, palsied. He reached his bare foot out and put it against the dog's jaw, pushing the head down, exposing the throat.

"I want to go home," said Aurel.

Theron pointed the gun and fired, shooting the dog through the throat, the pellet lodging somewhere within the breathpipe. The dog whimpered, the fur of its throat slowly darkening with blood. Theron pushed his foot down harder and lined the gun again, pumping. Wriggling beneath him, the dog shook its jaw free and bit him.

He cried out and began to jab at the dog's snout with the

barrel, the dog chacking its jaws tighter. Reversing the rifle, he brought the gunstock down hard across the dog's skull, feeling in the blow the dog's teeth shear deep through his flesh. The dog shuddered, let go.

Theron limped back a little distance and dropped to examine the wound, blood pushing up in the teethmarks and running in streaks down the side of the foot. The dog tried to get to its feet but could not and just stayed pawing the ground in front of it until it could not do that either, and curled its legs underneath and died.

He looked up for Aurel and found Aurel gone. Leaving the dog and the gun beside it, he hobbled around to the front of the house. Aurel he found on the porch clawing at a window.

"What is it?" asked Theron.

"I need air," said Aurel. "Let me out."

"Come off of there," said Theron, taking him by the hair and dragging him down. "This is not even our house."

Limping, he pulled Aurel back to the dog and let go. He unchained the dog and took it by the hind legs and began to drag it away.

"Come on, Aurel," said Theron. "Time to go home."

Aurel stayed put, watching him. "I don't want to go," he said.

"Jesus Christ," said Theron. "First you don't want to leave, then you don't want to go back. What's the matter with you?"

"Don't say that name, Theron," said Aurel. "You want to go to hell?"

"Are you walking or do I have to drag you?" asked Theron.

Aurel remained a moment standing and then sat down. Theron let go of the dog's legs and came over to hit Aurel in the face. He picked his brother up under the arms and found him light and cold to the touch. When Theron lifted and carried him, Aurel did not seem to notice, but lay in his arms without regard for anything.

Theron stumbled past the dead dog and a few meters later set

Aurel down on the ground. He went down stiffly. Theron went back for the dog, dragged it alongside his brother. Crouching down, he stared at first one then the other until Aurel's eyes opened.

"Can you walk?" he asked Aurel.

"I won't," said Aurel.

He alternated between lugging Aurel and the dog's carcass until he reached the main road, and then gave it up to carry the one while dragging the other. He tried to drag the dog and carry Aurel, but kept dropping his brother. He found it easier to drag Aurel by the feet, the boy's head jouncing across the asphalt while he slung the dog over his shoulders.

He could hardly walk for the pain in his foot. People slowed as they passed in cars, at times even pointed, shouted. He cursed them thoroughly and kept on.

The dog grew heavy around his neck, his chest and shoulders spattering with blood and foam. Behind, Aurel seemed to have fallen asleep though his eyes were still open. Theron kept turning around and asking, *Hey, you dead? Hey, you dead? Hey, you dead?* After a while, Theron stopped asking.

IV

THE HOLY WORD

The foot festered, and soon he could not walk on it. He left the carcass in the hall, slitting the skin and fur off of it with an old kitchen knife, cutting raw hunks for himself and Aurel until it was too difficult to pick out the maggots. He pulled himself back a few yards, watching the flesh vanish and the bones push through, the structure collapsing into a mere arthritic pile, flies turning circles on the walls and clinging to his face. Maggots struck blindly across the floor out from the carcass and only

Aurel had stomach enough to believe they were creatures of God and to eat them.

Soon both dog and maggots seemed to have vanished, though Theron discovered in himself no inclination to leave the hall or stand. Aurel, on the contrary, seemed to have regained his strength. He had risen suddenly to his feet, and was now rarely found in the hall. He seemed to have acquired color in his cheeks, and his eyes were less inclined to delirium. He roamed the upper levels of the house, though unlike Theron he never returned with anything. He would vanish for days, and then Theron would awaken to find Aurel crouched and peering over him. And then Aurel would vanish again.

The maggots returned, this time pushing their way out of Theron's injured foot. Aurel scraped them from the wound and swallowed them, but they originated deeper within the foot than Theron would permit him to scrape, and kept returning. The smaller, individual wounds became a single wound, the wound growing purple and deep, the flesh sloughing away almost painlessly at a touch.

Theron faded in and out of consciousness, Aurel seeming to grow immense. He could hear his brother's feet creak upon the ceiling above, the structure of the house swaying beneath his weight. He took to not seeing things, then to not hearing them. He kept his eyes closed and pulled himself, over the days, to a damp corner and leaned into it. His nerves dried out and his skin ceased to feel. His thoughts ran on for a while in all directions and then seemed to establish an equilibrium of sorts, and then fell silent.

He felt himself shaken. After some time, he brought himself to open his eyes. Before him was Aurel.

He tried to turn his head. He swallowed, coughed forth a web of phlegm, spread it onto the wall.

"What did you do with Daddy Norton's eyes?" asked Aurel.

"His eyes?"

"You removed them," said Aurel. "Where are they?"

Theron fumbled his hand into the corner behind him and seemed to fall asleep. Aurel nudged him and he brought his hand forth and opened his palm out, an irregular mass within.

Aurel took the eye from Theron's hand and examined it, the surface withered and collapsed, the lens sunken in and grown opaque.

"It might be Daddy's," said Theron. "It might be the dog's."

"Where's the other eye?" Aurel asked.

Theron swallowed, looked into his wound. "This is the one that has been watching me," he said.

Aurel sniffed the eye. He lifted it, held it against first one of his eyes then the other, then stretched it toward Theron. Theron let it come close then closed his eyes.

"Look," said Aurel. "Please look."

He brought the eye toward Theron slowly and Theron let him do it. He brought the eye near to Theron's living eye.

"What do you see?" he said.

"Nothing," said Theron. "Not a goddamn thing."

Upstairs, Aurel broke down Daddy Norton's door by simply leaning into it, the cheap hinges bursting apart. The room inside was dark and damp, reeking of Daddy Norton's pomade. He left the door open and felt around beside the door for a light mechanism, but did not find one. He took a few steps in and stood there, waiting for the dark to acquire depth and texture. He took a few more steps, then a few more. He stood still until he began to see.

One side of the room was lined with religious tokens of all sects and creeds, strung along the wall. There were, as well, holy books, many of them still in wrapping and apparently never opened, scattered over the floor.

The other side of the room was nearly empty—a stiff austere

bed, a low basin, a lectern which supported Daddy Norton's Holy Word.

He went to the Holy Word and opened it up. He began to read.

Those who strike against God's True and Everlasting Covenant as revealed by Him to Daddy Norton shall be numbered among the damned and cast into the outer dark.

Those who have known God's Own Truth, as revealed to Daddy Norton and written by his hand, guided by God's hand, in this holy book, and who turn against it, shall be numbered most visibly among the damned and cast into the outer dark.

To afflict Daddy Norton is to afflict God himself. Those who, knowingly or unknowingly, within faith or outside of it, challenge Daddy Norton on his sacred path toward Truth, will be damned with the damnation that sticks and cast well beyond the outer dark.

He took the book downstairs and shook Theron alive and read the verses to him.

"It's a good thing the bastard's dead," said Theron.

"Be quiet," said Aurel. "Do you want to be cast into the outer dark?"

"As long as Daddy Norton isn't there awaiting me."

Aurel shook his head. In closing the book, his eye passed across a line, and he opened the book again and began to read the verse in its full body.

He who converses with my enemies, though he claim loyalty to me and every whit of doctrine, is my enemy, for the law must be fulfilled. Brother shall turn against brother for my sake, and father against child.

He studied the words out and pondered them in his mind and wondered upon its application until the hall had fallen dark.

"Theron," he said. "Let me read this to you."

Theron did not answer yea or nay. Aurel read the passage slowly, haltingly, in his own voice, then looked up to see what his brother would say. Theron did not say anything, just stayed pressed up into the corner, pale and silent.

"I'm sorry, brother," said Aurel.

He closed the book. He stood and looked down at Theron. He prodded the festered leg with his own foot, his toes sinking into the flesh. He stood and left the hall.

He traveled through the upper rooms, the air hardly breathable, at one time stumbling into an attic filled with dead swallows, their heads screwed off and heaped in a corner. He lived for some time on the armload of swallows he carried out, stripping them free of their larger feathers and choking them down whole as he wandered on.

He could feel the house creak and sway beneath him, the wood groaning as if the rooms were never meant to be walked in. Many of the rooms were dark, and he found in these his eyes could not gather sufficient light to glean wisdom from the Holy Word, so he began to avoid them. Others rippled with heat, and these he came to avoid as well. He kept instead to the most narrow and rickety rooms nearest the top, chinks in their walls and ceilings, their floors as well, rooms which howled with wind and in which he had to hold the pages of the Holy Word pressed flat so they could not go adrift.

He read the book from cover to cover, a little in each room, and by the end came to believe in the divinity of the book and in the divine election of Daddy Norton, alive or dead, and in his own divine election as Daddy Norton's disciple, called of God in this, God's only true church. And then he read the book a second time and found himself no longer certain. It did not seem to him the same book the second time, for it began to reveal to him faces that he had not wanted to see before. He saw that his faith would fall in jeopardy were he to continue reading, and so, to preserve his faith, he abandoned the book in one of the upper rooms and never saw it again.

He lived on what scraps he could find, when these were gone peeling off the wallpaper and eating the paste underneath. He began to find other books in the rooms. These at first he left where they were, passing them clinging close to the wall and moving into other rooms beyond. But when he began to find them more often, he took to picking them up and hiding them beneath beds and tables, so as not to see them again. Still, the books appeared everywhere, in each new room he entered as well as in rooms he thought he had entered before, as if someone were moving them.

He stopped trying to hide the books and left them where they were. He tried to find his way downstairs but had no inkling of the way. He came into a room with a split-board floor where he thought the stairs should be. Light shone up hard through the floorcracks, the walls musted and blotched with mold. Kicking a hole through a wall, he crawled out into a narrow room, a globed glass fixture hanging from the ceiling and aglow. Lying on the floor, he watched the light and listened to fleas ping inside the globe, and fell asleep.

He awoke to find fleas strung up and down his veins and grown fat upon him. He began to crush them with stiff thumbs, leaving smears of blood. Getting to his feet he saw a book on a table, and this he took up and opened and read from silently without avail or feeling though like every other book it was most likely some god or other's sacred word. He read on blankly for many pages, until was given to him:

He that loveth his brother abideth in light, and there is none occasion of stumbling in him.

He put the book down as if struck and then as quickly scooped it up again. He took Daddy Norton's dessicated eye out of his underwear and held it toward the words, then put the eye away. Putting the book under his arm, he went out of the room through a door and from there through chambers with irregular floors and from there fell down a ramshackle staircase face first. He found himself in a room that seemed familiar to him, though he could place nothing about it. He made his way out through a door broken from its hinges and through a hall and down a staircase missing its treads. He entered what seemed at one time to have been a kitchen but which now seemed a repository for refuse of all kinds.

Wading across the room, he opened a door and came out into a long hall, a door at one end of it, a window at the other. In the corner, beneath the window, was a figure, vaguely human. The smell of it was hard to breathe at first, and then became sweet and made his head dance with light.

He could feel God watching. He approached the figure and sat beside it, pulling it over to lean against him. What he touched was soggy in his hands, as if impregnated with water, and it left portions of itself adhered to the wall even as it came away.

He read the verse aloud, but his brother did not respond. He pulled him closer and felt him come apart in his hands.

He gathered what he could and pushed it back into the corner. He took off the briefs he wore, the eye falling out and dropping away. He shaped the pile in the corner like a pillow and lay his head onto it.

"Brothers always," he said. And closed his eyes.

Afterword

I

The stories in *Altmann's Tongue* were written over a period of eight years, in a number of different locales, under a number of conditions. Several of the earliest stories were written in France, where I served in the mid-eighties as a Mormon missionary. Early on, living in Marseilles, I realized that I had almost no interest in the sort of proselytizing I was expected to do; I wasn't interested in being the religious equivalent of a door-to-door salesman. I took to contacting people in other ways, spending as much time as possible in libraries. I read Samuel Beckett's work in French, wrote, went to plays. I made friends with several lycée instructors, one of whom introduced me to Antonin Artaud's troubling *L'ombilic des limbes*. Eventually I took several unauthorized trips, including one to Paris, which led to my being sent home early under the Mormon equivalent of a dishonorable discharge.

After leaving France I spent a few weeks at home in Utah, where I allowed myself to be convinced by relatives, religious leaders, and a somewhat zealous girlfriend to continue my mission. Instead of sending me back to France, the Church packed me off to Wisconsin in the middle of winter. There I quickly encountered the same difficulties and Mormon narrow-mindedness that had been the basis for my objections to serving as a missionary in France. After six months I left of my own

volition, packing all my clothing in the middle of the night and
carrying my bags several miles to meet a friend who had a car.
Though I was quickly tracked down and threatened by the ap-
paratus of the Mormon Church, I refused to go back.

I spent the following year finishing my undergraduate degree
at Mormon-run Brigham Young University. I had as minimal a
relation to my religion as was possible, though it became difficult because soon after I re-enrolled at Brigham Young they began to instigate worthiness policies (documents that religious
leaders were expected to fill out and turn in to assure BYU's
administration that students were living worthily). The policies
required one to attend Church regularly. I lived in a Spanish
language house, spent part of a term in Mexico, and found church
a little more bearable in a language with whose clichés I was not
yet familiar. Just after graduation I married a relatively liberal
Mormon whom I'd met in a French class and started grudgingly
attending church on a regular basis. We moved to Seattle where
we both pursued advanced degrees. I again teetered on the edge
of abandoning Mormonism and might well have left had I not
been soon called to be a bishopric counselor, one of three religious
leaders in charge of a congregation having more than seven hundred people on the rolls. Surprised by the invitation, I didn't know
I would accept until I heard my voice say yes. I could, I felt, do some
good. I was under the (as it turned out mistaken) impression that
the Church was loosening up, that things were happening to suggest
that I could stand to live within the Church after all.

During all this time I had been writing stories, some of which
were later published in revised form in *Altmann's Tongue* or in
one of my two other books of stories, *The Din of Celestial Birds*
and *Contagion*. Strangely, it was during the three years that I was
a religious leader—very active and very committed to the religion and my role in it—that more than two thirds of the trans-
gressive stories in *Altmann's Tongue* were written. My wife and I
had children during that same three years. I also attended gradu-

ate school, specializing in twentieth-century Continental theory, eventually receiving a joint interdepartmental Ph.D. in critical theory and English. My life felt satisfying spiritually, intellectually, and familially. I was insanely busy, sleeping hardly at all, but happy. I often spent as many as ten hours on Sunday as well as an additional five to fifteen hours during the week handling Church business but somehow still found time to do schoolwork and write fiction. At school I was studying Deleuze, Lacan, Hegel, Derrida, Kojève, and Heidegger. I had grown interested in twentieth-century notions of subjectivity and epistemology. I was taking classes in comparative literature and French, and reviewing contemporary French and Hispanic literature for *World Literature Today*. On my own I was reading Thomas Bernhard, Ben Okri, Gabriel García Márquez, Vladimir Nabokov, Jorge Luis Borges. I took a course concerning the Marquis de Sade's influence on twentieth-century French theory, something that would have shocked members of my congregation had they known about it. To me, however, it seemed as if my life was able to stretch enough to take in everything.

During my time in Seattle I sometimes acted as a transient bishop. I would receive calls in the middle of the night and would have to go, as a representative of the Mormon Church, to meet travelers who had gotten stranded, homeless people who wanted money or support, or marginalized people who had been left derelict by themselves or by others. I picked them up at the bus station or on street corners in downtown Seattle. I drove around conversing with them, trying to determine what their needs really were, how I could best serve them. I listened to their stories while driving around at two or three in the morning, trying not to judge them or to react too strongly to what they told me, just listening, maintaining a neutral voice. I met a vast range of people: some had fallen on hard times and needed very little to get back on track, others were deceptive or befuddled or confused or simply entirely apathetic; some had HIV and had been

shunned by their families; some struggled with addictions; a few
were schizophrenic. I remember once sitting in the car with a
member of the Spokane tribe, a man nearly a head taller and at
least fifty pounds heavier than I (though I'm not small), someone whom I had never met before and who had been sitting on
a heating vent waiting for me to come get him. We drove around
in silence for fifteen minutes, with me looking at his hands (which
were large enough to crush my head) until, at last, he began to
speak.

Early Mormon leader Brigham Young suggested that everything in heaven, everything in hell, and everything in between is
worthy of our attention. I came to feel, driving around in the car
with these anonymous people whom I had never seen before
and who I was likely never to see again, that my task was not
only or not even primarily to decide whether to help them
materially; my task was to allow them to vocalize what they
needed to say about themselves. In school I was reading about
the sacred and the profane in George Bataille's *Erotisme*. I was
reformulating my way of thinking about my role as a religious
leader, particularly as a religious counselor, in terms of Lacan's
ideas of the relation of analyst to analysand. I saw myself (partly
in response to Lacan, partly for other reasons) as a reflector, a
surface to allow the people I counseled formally and informally
to see themselves more clearly or, in many cases, to help them
begin the process of constructing a self to see. When I was there
in the car I was there less as a self than as an absence of self. As a
mirror.

Altmann's Tongue took form around these ideas and my experiences. Characteristic of one strand of writing that I had been
doing both in France and after coming back to America was a
neutrality of voice, an absence of authorial commentary, an attempt to present difficult situations without judgment. In France
and in Wisconsin and in Utah, where I felt constantly under
surveillance by my religion, that absence had been, as I see it

now, a representation of a basic and very personal desire to live an unobserved life, to stop existing in the eyes of the institution. In Seattle, however, where I no longer felt threatened by religion, it had annealed into something else: an unblinking eye that operated from a point of personal stability. All observed experience, I was convinced, was useful; difficult experiences, if they were fully apprehended, could smelt forth something significant from the dross of life. I was interested in giving readers an experience devoid of conventional mediation, and I saw the story as a catalyst whose effect and whose success would be determined by the reader's ability to interact with it.

I became particularly interested in breaking through the clichés that are most frequently applied to violence, masks that make it palatable to movie or television viewers. I wanted instead to depict murder, violence, and absence of human response in a way that allowed readers, if they were willing to keep their eyes open, to perceive violence not as symbolic, not as meaningful, but as a basic and irrecoverable act—using violence that overflows the boundaries of expectation, violence as a kind of deterritorialization that floods society and leaves it drowning underwater. Violence as insignificant in that it doesn't signify anything. Not violence as glitzily evil and *chic*, but as neutral and blank and indifferent.

At the same time I was deeply interested in style and form. I saw—and continue to see—the story as a conscious manipulation of sound and rhythm, as a means of arranging language, as artifice. The problem facing me in assembling the stories of *Altmann's Tongue* was how I might use style to allow readers to feel that they were entering into a relatively unmediated experience. I was not interested in the portrayal of violence as banal, the likes of which can be found in Evan S. Connell's *The Diary of a Rapist* or Camilo José Cela's *La Familia de Pascal Duarte*. Indeed, ultimately I was less interested in *depicting* violence than I was in wanting readers to *apprehend a sensation*, to engage in a path along a certain emotional vector of their own. Traditional mimetic representation has a certain safety to it—one has a sense of frame, as if standing at a distance from an object. I was interested in offering up an affective artistic object that used sound, rhythm, and other subcomponents of language as a means of rupturing that frame. I wanted to move the reader away from seeing something mimetically depicted, toward feeling (and perhaps sometimes resenting) that they are being drawn into the artistic object, into the transgressions therein. I could tell about driving around Seattle with a stranger I'd just picked up holding a gun to my head, waiting to see if he was going to kill me or rob me or simply put the gun away. But I wanted to draw the reader into the sensation of having the gun snouting against his or her own fragile temple, to draw the reader into a situation in which sensation outweighs mimesis.

So violence is depicted but then superseded by style operating as a kind of violence toward the reader: the two working sometimes concertedly, sometimes in tension, to create a world that feels at once stark and yet stylized, in slant relation to the actual world.

II

Altmann's Tongue is meant to be a challenging book, is postulated as a challenge to the reader. The stories in it are meant to function beyond their initial reading, in the way readers choose over time to process the reading experience and supply their own moral response to the absence of response within the text proper. A sort of virus, as it were.

At their worst, if read in naive terms the stories and the demands they put on readers seem to provoke intense hatred of their author. When *Altmann's Tongue* first appeared I had been teaching for about eight months at Brigham Young University. Someone sent an anonymous letter to an upper echelon member of the Mormon Church, accusing me of promoting incest and cannibalism, of corrupting the youth, of writing the sort of book that was precisely the opposite of what a Mormon should write. I know about this letter because that Mormon Church leader passed it along to the university and eventually it filtered its way through all the major members of the administration down to me. My department chairman asked me to write a response to the anonymous letter. I was told my response would make its way up the chain of command to all the people who had seen the anonymous letter on its way down. After sitting on my response for six weeks the chairman passed it up the line, including with it a note from himself which he claimed spoke out strongly against anonymous letters, declaring that they would not be tolerated. This letter also included a sentence reading "The bottom line is that [Brian] knows that this book is unacceptable coming from a BYU faculty member and that further publications like it will bring repercussions."

What does this sentence mean? I asked my chair. I didn't believe that *Altmann's Tongue* was unacceptable. I was operating from an aesthetic position I felt was justified. My chair, I suspected, had been assigned the task of convincing me that the book was inappropriate and that I needed to stop writing such books. Furthermore, he seemed to think he had done so. I told him I stood behind my book, which I had made amply clear in the pages of my response to the anonymous letter. I had seen my response as a defense, something to show to the authorities who had seen and validated the anonymous letter, something to inform them of what I thought I was doing with my work. Was what he said true? I asked. Would further publications bring repercussions? My understanding had been that I would be protected by the university's policies on academic freedom and that I was writing something that fell within the purview of those protections. Was that not the case?

The following several months produced administrative hemming and hawing, various noncommittal utterances with vaguely apocalyptic and threatening subtexts, the leak of the situation to the press, television and newspaper coverage, strange anonymous threats by phone and by mail, public and private writing by faculty and students both for and against the book, and a brown bag luncheon discussion of the book by the German department (which turned out to be much more supportive and open than the English department, and whose members read the book in the context of European literature). The book was widely reviewed, often to high praise, and became a regional bestseller. Yet that acclaim seemed little consolation for the intricacies of the bureaucratic maze which seemed to grow increasingly complex and consumed more and more of my time. As I met with one administrator after another it became clear that my response to the anonymous letter didn't matter. I was expected neither to think nor to defend my project but rather to fall in line, stop publishing, be a good boy. I was reminded of what I had hated so thoroughly about my experience as a Mormon missionary and about my time as a student at BYU: obedience was the rule that superseded all other rules. My local Church leaders declared themselves "concerned" and demanded an explanation of my fiction. My explanations puzzled my bishop, a graphic designer by trade, but he was willing, after a certain amount of exhortation, to give me the benefit of the doubt.

Finally I met with a panel of administrators—the president, the provost, the dean, the department chair—who promised to clarify BYU's academic freedom policy. It was the institution's (rather than the individual's) academic freedom that was at stake, the provost told me. I was being put "on notice." He stated that BYU faculty members "had a responsibility to members of the Church to do work that will not offend them." If I cared to stay at Brigham Young University—where, I was told, faculty were granted "continuing status" rather than tenure (a very different thing, he insisted)—it would be looked upon as a show of good faith and very much in my favor if I stopped writing.

How does one respond to such requests? I was twenty-eight, it was my first job out of graduate school, I had just bought my first house. I was trying to support a wife and two small children on a substandard BYU salary. There were all sorts of practical reasons to buckle under. I was advised by certain faculty members that I should lay low for a while, save any other work I had, prove myself a good citizen and then, once I had tenure and pressure loosened up, publish. Some of the faculty had been "laying low," I realized, for several decades; other faculty advised me to get out soon, leave while I still could.

University of Utah fiction writer Francois Camoin, while taking my picture for a newspaper article, mentioned that he knew of a one-year position open at Oklahoma State University. I applied, received the job. I drove the twenty hours from Utah to Oklahoma with my daughter, Valerie, who was five at the time, in a car with no air conditioning and an AM radio that seemed to pick up nothing but Rush Limbaugh. We played twenty hours of games like "What's the Name of This Town?" and "Brown Cow." Stillwater proved to be flat, muggy, and hot. I accepted the job, then rented a house that later proved to have a skunk living in its crawlspace and buckets of broken glass in the backyard. Three months into the one-year contract I was offered a tenure-track position. Shortly after that I officially severed my connections with BYU. Over the next six years I gradually severed my connections with the Mormon Church, and in 2000 initiated action to have my name stricken from Church records. Now, as of 2001, I have been excommunicated by my own choice. I am no longer a member of the Mormon Church, have separated from my still-Mormon wife over tensions involving my relationship to religion and writing, and am trying to figure out how to make sense of my life.

III

Despite the negative aspects of my experience with Mormonism, one thing the religion and my conflict with it has given me is a sense that what I am writing matters. I know that my work is scrutinized, that I will be held responsible for what I write. This has caused me to measure each word carefully. It has made me attentive both to the style and the content of what I write, has made writing a serious task to me, and has helped me realize that my commitment to writing, for good or ill, is greater than most of my other commitments in life.

Yet Mormonism is not the only important, or even the most important, influence on my work. *Altmann's Tongue* exists in a kind of cross-pollination of cultural influences. The writers I most admire are those who seem capable of sliding back and forth between influences and nationalities. I believe, along with Dambudzo Marechera, that the first and primary country of writers is writing itself.

The stories of *Altmann's Tongue* present an odd relationship to place. And, while a certain narrative blankness, a certain kind of absence of response, is characteristic of these stories, this relationship to place remains stylized. When I came back from France I was confronted with an America that had grown unfamiliar, largely because by living away I myself had grown unfamiliar. The America that appears in some of these stories strikes me as that America: stylized and rarefied, with people and actions defined in terms of a limited range of objects and the structure of their modes of dwelling. In "The Father, Unblinking," one enters into a space that is recognizable as the American West, though time period and exact locale remain rather vague. It is a West defined by a few items, a few gestures: shovels, a barn, a way of standing at a cutting board, an appraisal of the way a board has been cut. "Objects of the highest danger," the narrator of one story calls his dead wife's dishes, "objects I would have to approach with the most terminal ruthlessness." Any object has the potential to resonate, and most objects in these stories function synecdochically to stand in for a larger, yet largely absent, world.

It is not just the American West that is stylized here; Europe is treated in the same way. Nazi Germany in "The Auschwitz Barber" is condensed into the image of a pair of shears. "The Sanza Affair" takes place in a country that is never identified but is a combination of several European countries, a sort of EEC community whose outlines are defined by scattered phrases intruding from different cultures, stilted moments of character speech, and objects that seem to have wandered in from outside. It is a world that operates according to its own peculiar logic, a logic that remains beyond the grasp of Lund, the story's protagonist, who appears to lack vital "moments" of the cultural code. Indeed, if the collection begins with a story in which knowledge is withheld, it ends with a story that suggests that the world might finally be unknowable.

Place, too, is not so much the sense of a particular region (though there is that), but rather is known in a more basic sense: how one occupies a house, how people, like dogs, carve tracks from one house to another, how people try to link one place symbolically with another. I am obsessed with the "thereness" of characters, the way they inscribe their paths on the world. I am interested in the way characters establish a pattern of physical movement and the way that mode of movement both reflects and defines the nature of a mode of living, of an ethics. Indeed, while these stories are a critique of violence they are at the same time an exploration of human movement. I have chosen in *Altmann's Tongue* to observe simple interactions, movements that are at once the basis for and manifestation of more advanced thought.

IV

It is perhaps a mistake to speak of my own work (not to mention my life), and I want to stop before I reify the reader's understanding of either. Talking about one's stories is a little too much like nailing a dog to the floor—you can get it to stay put that way but it doesn't do much for the dog. Many paths transect *Altmann's Tongue*; like most literary books it is a rhizome, sprouting in different directions, the stories connecting with one another in different ways. Violence, movement, ontology, and epistemology deflect off one another and off other ideas and notions in a way that I hope will continue to shimmer and shift after the experience of reading the book is over.

V

A final word: You have been driving in the car, a man pointing a gun at your head, and now he has left the car and you are free. Everything around you has gone strange. You are no longer in the same world you were in before the gun bruised your temple. You have the suspicion that you are no longer yourself.

Now, now that you are free (if it really *is* you), the question is, How do you make sense of your life?

BRIAN EVENSON
222 East Vassar Ave.
Denver, CO 80210